NORTH OF FIFTY-THREE

NORTH OF FIFTY-THREE

BERTRAND W. SINCLAIR

Sagebrush
Large Print Westerns

First published in the United States by Little, Brown

First published in Great Britain by Allen

Published in Large Print 2004 by ISIS Publishing Ltd,
7 Centremead, Osney Mead, Oxford OX2 0ES,
United Kingdom
by arrangement with
Golden West Literary Agency

British Library Cataloguing in Publication Data
Sinclair, Bertrand W.
    North of fifty-three. – Large print ed. –
    (Sagebrush western series)
    1. Western stories
    2. Large type books
    I. Title
    813.5'2 [F]

ISBN 0–7531–7118–X (hb)

Printed and bound by Antony Rowe, Chippenham

Contents

CHAPTER ONE

A Lady and Two Gentlemen

Dressed in a plain white shirt waist and an equally plain black cloth skirt, Miss Hazel Weir, on week days, was merely a unit in the office force of Harrington & Bush, implement manufacturers. Neither in personality nor in garb would a casual glance have differentiated her from the other female units, occupied at various desks. A close observer might have noticed that she was a bit younger than the others, possessed of a clear skin and large eyes that seemed to hold all the shades between purple and gray — eyes, moreover, that had not yet begun to weaken from long application to clerical work. A business office is no place for a woman to parade her personal charms. The measure of her worth there is simply the measure of her efficiency at her machine or ledgers. So that if any member of the firm had been asked what sort of a girl Miss Hazel Weir might be, he would probably have replied — and with utmost truth — that Miss Weir was a capable stenographer.

But when Saturday evening released Miss Hazel Weir from the plain brick office building, she became, until

1

she donned her working clothes at seven A. M. Monday morning, quite a different sort of a person. In other words, she chucked the plain shirt waist and the plain skirt into the discard, got into such a dress as a normal girl of twenty-two delights to put on, and devoted a half hour or so to "doing" her hair. Which naturally effected a more or less complete transformation, a transformation that was subjective as well as purely objective. For Miss Weir then became an entity at which few persons of either sex failed to take a second glance.

Upon a certain Saturday night Miss Weir came home from an informal little party escorted by a young man. They stopped at the front gate.

"I'll be here at ten sharp," said he. "And you get a good beauty sleep to-night, Hazel. That confounded office! I hate to think of you drudging away at it. I wish we were ready to —"

"Oh, bother the office!" she replied lightly. "I don't think of it out of office hours. Anyway, I don't mind. It doesn't tire me. I *will* be ready at ten *this* time. Good night, dear."

"Good night, Hazie," he whispered. "Here's a kiss to dream on."

Miss Weir broke away from him laughingly, ran along the path, and up the steps, kissed her finger-tips to the lingering figure by the gate, and went in.

"Bed," she soliloquized, "is the place for me right quickly if I'm going to be up and dressed and have that lunch ready by ten o'clock. I wish I weren't such a sleepyhead — or else that I weren't a 'pore wurrkin' gurl.'"

At which last conceit she laughed softly. Because, for a "pore wurrkin' gurl," Miss Weir was fairly well content with her lot. She had no one dependent on her — a state of affairs which, if it occasionally leads to loneliness, has its compensations. Her salary as a stenographer amply covered her living expenses, and even permitted her to put by a few dollars monthly. She had grown up in Granville. She had her own circle of friends. So that she was comfortable, even happy, in the present — and Jack Barrow proposed to settle the problem of her future; with youth's optimism, they two considered it already settled. Six months more, and there was to be a wedding, a three-weeks' honeymoon, and a final settling down in a little cottage on the West Side; everybody in Granville who amounted to anything lived on the West Side. Then she would have nothing to do but make the home nest cozy, while Jack kept pace with a real-estate business that was growing beyond his most sanguine expectations.

She threw her light wraps over the back of a chair, and, standing before her dresser, took the multitude of pins out of her hair and tumbled it, a cloudy black mass, about her shoulders. Occupying the center of the dresser, in a leaning silver frame, stood a picture of Jack Barrow. She stood looking at it a minute, smiling absently. It was spring, and her landlady's daughter had set a bunch of wild flowers in a jar beside the picture. Hazel picked out a daisy and plucked away the petals one by one.

"He loves me — he loves me not — he loves me —" Her lips formed the words inaudibly, as countless lips

3

have formed them in love's history, and the last petal fluttered away at "not."

She smiled.

"I wonder if that's an omen?" she murmured "Pshaw! What a silly idea! I'm going to bed. Good night, Johnny boy."

She kissed her finger-tips to him again across the rooftops all grimed with a winter's soot, and within fifteen minutes Miss Weir was sound asleep.

She gave the lie, for once, to the saying that a woman is never ready at the appointed time by being on the steps a full ten minutes before Jack Barrow appeared. They walked to the corner and caught a car, and in the span of half an hour got off at Granville Park.

The city fathers, hampered in days gone by with lack of municipal funds, had left the two-hundred-acre square of the park pretty much as nature made it; that is to say, there was no ornate parking, no attempt at landscape gardening. Ancient maples spread their crooked arms untrimmed, standing in haphazard groves. Wherever the greensward flourished, there grew pink-tipped daisies and kindred flowers of the wild. It was gutted in the middle with a ravine, the lower end of which, dammed by an earth embankment, formed a lake with the inevitable swans and other water-fowl. But, barring the lake and a wide drive that looped and twined through the timber, Granville Park was a bit of the old Ontario woodland, and as such afforded a pleasant place to loaf in the summer months. It was full of secluded nooks, dear to the hearts of young couples.

And upon a Sunday the carriages of the wealthy affected the smooth drive.

When Jack Barrow and Hazel had finished their lunch under the trees, in company with a little group of their acquaintances, Hazel gathered scraps of bread and cake into a paper bag.

Barrow whispered to her: "Let's go down and feed the swans. I'd just as soon be away from the crowd."

She nodded assent, and they departed hastily lest some of the others should volunteer their company. It took but a short time to reach the pond. They found a log close to the water's edge, and, taking a seat there, tossed morsels to the birds and chattered to each other.

"Look," said Barrow suddenly; "that's us ten years from now."

A carriage passed slowly, a solemn, liveried coachman on the box, a handsome, smooth-shaven man of thirty-five and a richly gowned woman leaning back and looking out over the pond with bored eyes. And that last, the half-cynical, half-contemptuous expression on the two faces, impressed Hazel Weir far more than the showy equipage, the outward manifestation of wealth.

"I hope not," she returned impulsively.

"Hope not!" Barrow echoed. "Those people are worth a barrel of money. Wouldn't you like your own carriage, and servants, and income enough to have everything you wanted?"

"Of course," Hazel answered. "But they don't look as if they really enjoyed it."

"Fiddlesticks!" Barrow smilingly retorted. "Everybody enjoys luxury."

"Well, one should," Hazel admitted. But she still held to the impression that the couple passing got no such pleasure out of their material possessions as Jack seemed to think. It was merely an intuitive divination. She could not have found any basis from which to argue the point. But she was very sure that she would not have changed places with the woman in the carriage, and her hand stole out and gave his a shy little squeeze.

"Look," she murmured; "here's another of the plutocrats. One of my esteemed employers, if you please. You'll notice that he's walking and looking at things just like us ordinary, everyday mortals."

Barrow glanced past her, and saw a rather tall, middle-aged man, his hair tinged with gray, a fine-looking man, dressed with exceeding nicety, even to a flower in his coat lapel, walking slowly along the path that bordered the pond. He stopped a few yards beyond them, and stood idly glancing over the smooth stretch of water, his gloved hands resting on the knob of a silver-mounted cane.

Presently his gaze wandered to them, and the cool, well-bred stare gradually gave way to a slightly puzzled expression. He moved a step or two and seated himself on a bench. Miss Weir became aware that he was looking at her most of the time as she sat casting the bits of bread to the swans and ducks. It made her self-conscious. She did not know why she should be of any particular interest.

6

"Let's walk around a little," she suggested. The last of the crumbs were gone.

"All right," Barrow assented. "Let's go up the ravine."

They left the log. Their course up the ravine took them directly past the gentleman on the bench. And when they came abreast of him, he rose and lifted his hat at the very slight inclination of Miss Weir's head.

"How do you do, Miss Weir?" said he. "Quite a pleasant afternoon."

To the best of Hazel's knowledge, Mr. Andrew Bush was little given to friendly recognition of his employees, particularly in public. But he seemed inclined to be talkative; and, as she caught a slightly inquiring glance at her escort, she made the necessary introduction. So for a minute or two the three of them stood there exchanging polite banalities. Then Mr. Bush bowed and passed on.

"He's one of the biggest guns in Granville, they say," Jack observed. "I wouldn't mind having some of his business to handle. He started with nothing, too, according to all accounts. Now, that's what I call success."

"Oh, yes, in a business way he's a success," Hazel responded. "But he's awfully curt most of the time around the office. I wonder what made him thaw out so to-day?"

And that question recurred to her mind again in the evening, when Jack had gone home and she was sitting in her own room. She wheeled her chair around and took a steady look at herself in the mirror. A woman may never admit extreme plainness of feature, and she may deprecate her own fairness, if she be possessed of fairness, but she seldom has any illusions about one or the other. She knows. Hazel Weir knew that she was far above the average in point of looks. If she had never taken stock of herself before, the reflection facing her now was sufficient to leave no room for doubt on the score of beauty. Her skin was smooth, delicate in texture, and as delicately tinted. The tan pongee dress she wore set off her dark hair and expressive, bluish-gray eyes.

She was smiling at herself just as she had been smiling at Jack Barrow while they sat on the log and fed the swans. And she made an amiable grin at the reflection in the glass. But even though Miss Weir was twenty-two and far from unsophisticated, it did not strike her that the transition of herself from a demure, business-like office person in sober black and white to a radiant creature with the potent influences of love and spring brightening her eyes and lending a veiled caress to her every supple movement, satisfactorily accounted for the sudden friendliness of Mr. Andrew Bush.

CHAPTER TWO

Heart, Hand — and Pocketbook

Miss Weir was unprepared for what subsequently transpired as a result of that casual encounter with the managing partner of the firm. By the time she went to work on Monday morning she had almost forgotten the meeting in Granville Park. And she was only reminded of it when, at nine o'clock, Mr. Andrew Bush walked through the office, greeting the force with his usual curt nod and inclusive "good morning" before he disappeared behind the ground-glass door lettered "Private." With the weekday he had apparently resumed his business manner.

Hazel's work consisted largely of dictation from the shipping manager, letters relating to outgoing consignments of implements. She was rapid and efficient, and, having reached the zenith of salary paid for such work, she expected to continue in the same routine until she left Harrington & Bush for good.

It was, therefore, something of a surprise to be called into the office of the managing partner on Tuesday afternoon. Bush's private stenographer sat at her machine in one corner.

Mr. Bush turned from his desk at Hazel's entrance.

"Miss Weir," he said, "I wish you to take some letters."

Hazel went back for her notebook, wondering mildly why she should be called upon to shoulder a part of Nelly Morrison's work, and a trifle dubious at the prospect of facing the rapid-fire dictation Mr. Bush was said to inflict upon his stenographer now and then. She had the confidence of long practice, however, and knew that she was equal to anything in reason that he might give her.

When she was seated, Bush took up a sheaf of letters, and dictated replies. Though rapid, his enunciation was perfectly clear, and Hazel found herself getting his words with greater ease than she had expected.

"That's all, Miss Weir," he said, when he reached the last letter. "Bring those in for verification and signature as soon as you can get them done."

In the course of time she completed the letters and took them back. Bush glanced over each, and appended his signature.

"That's all, Miss Weir," he said politely. "Thank you."

And Hazel went back to her machine, wondering why she had been requested to do those letters when Nelly Morrison had nothing better to do than sit picking at her type faces with a toothpick.

She learned the significance of it the next morning, however, when the office boy told her that she was wanted by Mr. Bush. This time when she entered Nelly Morrison's place was vacant. Bush was going through his mail. He waved her to a chair.

"Just a minute," he said.

Presently he wheeled from the desk and regarded her with disconcerting frankness — as if he were appraising her, point by point, so to speak.

"My — ah — dictation to you yesterday was in the nature of a try-out, Miss Weir," he finally volunteered. "Miss Morrison has asked to be transferred to our Midland branch. Mr. Allan recommended you. You are a native of Granville, I understand?"

"Yes," Hazel answered, wondering what that had to do with the position Nelly Morrison had vacated.

"In that case you will not likely be desirous of leaving suddenly," he went on. "The work will not be hard, but I must have someone dependable and discreet, and careful to avoid errors. I think you will manage it very nicely if you — ah — have no objection to giving up the more general work of the office for this. The salary will be considerably more."

"If you consider that my work will be satisfactory," Miss Weir began.

"I don't think there's any doubt on that score. You have a good record in the office," he interrupted smilingly, and Hazel observed that he could be a very agreeable and pleasant-speaking gentleman when he chose — a manner not altogether in keeping with her former knowledge of him — and she had been with the firm nearly two years. "Now, let us get to work and clean up this correspondence."

Thus her new duties began. There was an air of quiet in the private office, a greater luxury of appointment, which suited Miss Hazel Weir to a nicety. The work was no more difficult than she had been accustomed to doing — a trifle less in volume, and more exacting in attention to detail, and necessarily more confidential, for Mr. Andrew Bush had his finger-tips on the pulsing heart of a big business.

Hazel met Nelly Morrison the next day while on her way home to lunch.

"Well, how goes the new job?" quoth Miss Morrison.

"All right so far," Hazel smiled. "Mr. Bush said you were going to Midland."

"Leaving for there in the morning," said Nelly. "I've been wanting to go for a month, but Mr. Bush objected to breaking in a new girl — until just the other day. I'm sort of sorry to go, too, and I don't suppose I'll have nearly so good a place. For one thing, I'll not get so much salary as I had with Mr. Bush. But mamma's living in Midland, and two of my brothers work there. I'd much rather live at home than room and live in a trunk. I can have a better time even on less a week."

"Well, I hope you get along nicely," Hazel proffered.

"Oh, I will. Leave that to me," Miss Morrison laughed. "By the way, what do you think of Mr. Bush, anyway? But of course you haven't had much to do with him yet. You'll find him awfully nice and polite, but, my, he can be cutting when he gets irritated! I've known him to do some awfully mean things in a business way. I wouldn't want to get him down on me. I think he'd hold a grudge forever."

They walked together until Hazel turned into the street which led to her boarding place. Nelly Morrison chattered principally of Mr. Bush. No matter what subject she opened up, she came back to discussion of her employer. Hazel gathered that she had found him rather exacting, and also that she was inclined to resent his curt manner. Withal, Hazel knew Nelly Morrison to be a first-class stenographer, and found herself wondering how long it would take the managing partner to find occasion for raking *her* over the coals.

As the days passed, she began to wonder whether Miss Morrison had been quite correct in her summing up of Mr. Andrew Bush. She was not a great deal in his company, for unless attending to the details of business Mr. Bush kept himself in a smaller office opening out of the one where she worked. Occasionally the odor of cigar smoke escaped therefrom, and in that inner sanctum he received his most important callers. Whenever he was in Miss Weir's presence, however, he manifested none of the disagreeable characteristics that Nelly Morrison had ascribed to him.

The size of the check which Hazel received in her weekly envelope was increased far beyond her expectations. Nelly Morrison had drawn twenty dollars a week. Miss Hazel Weir drew twenty-five — a substantial increase over what she had received in the shipping department. And while she wondered a trifle at the voluntary raising of her salary, it served to make her anxious to competently fill the new position, so long as she worked for wages. With that extra money there were plenty of little things she could get for the home she and Jack Barrow had planned.

Things moved along in routine channels for two months or more before Hazel became actively aware that a subtle change was growing manifest in the ordinary manner of Mr. Andrew Bush. She shrugged her shoulders at the idea at first. But she was a woman; moreover, a woman of intelligence, her perceptive faculties naturally keen.

The first symptom was flowers, dainty bouquets of which began to appear on his desk. Coincident with this, Mr. Bush evinced an inclination to drift into talk on subjects nowise related to business. Hazel accepted the tribute to her sex reluctantly, giving him no encouragement to overstep the normal bounds of cordiality. She was absolutely sure of herself and of her love for Jack Barrow. Furthermore, Mr. Andrew Bush, though well preserved, was drawing close to fifty — and she was twenty-two. That in itself reassured her. If he had been thirty, Miss Weir might have felt herself upon dubious ground. He admired her as a woman. She began to realize that. And no woman ever blames a man for paying her that compliment, no matter what she may say to the contrary. Particularly when he does not seek to annoy her by his admiration.

So long as Mr. Bush confined himself to affable conversation, to sundry gifts of hothouse flowers, and only allowed his feelings outlet in certain telltale glances when he thought she could not see, Hazel felt disinclined to fly from what was at worst a possibility.

Thus the third month of her tenure drifted by, and beyond the telltale glances aforesaid, Mr. Bush remained tentatively friendly and nothing more. Hazel spent her Sundays as she had spent them for a year past — with Jack Barrow; sometimes rambling afoot in the country or in the park, sometimes indulging in the luxury of a hired buggy for a drive. Usually they went alone; occasionally with a party of young people like themselves.

But Mr. Bush took her breath away at a time and in a manner totally unexpected. He finished dictating a batch of letters one afternoon, and sat tapping on his desk with a pencil. Hazel waited a second or two, expecting him to continue, her eyes on her notes, and at the unbroken silence she looked up, to find him staring fixedly at her. There was no mistaking the expression on his face. Hazel flushed and shrank back involuntarily. She had hoped to avoid that. It could not be anything but unpleasant.

She had small chance to indulge in reflection, for at her first self-conscious move he reached swiftly and caught her hand.

"Hazel," he said bluntly, "will you marry me?"

Miss Weir gasped. Coming without warning, it dumfounded her. And while her first natural impulse was to answer a blunt "No," she was flustered, and so took refuge behind a show of dignity.

"Mr. Bush!" she protested, and tried to release her hand.

But Mr. Bush had no intention of allowing her to do that.

"I'm in deadly earnest," he said. "I've loved you ever since that Sunday I saw you in the park feeding the swans. I want you to be my wife. Will you?"

"I'm awfully sorry," Hazel stammered. She was just the least bit frightened. The man who stared at her with burning eyes and spoke to her in a voice that quivered with emotion was so different from the calm, repressed individual she had known as her employer. "Why, you're —" The thing that was uppermost in her mind, and what she came near saying, was: "You're old enough to be my father." And beside him there instantly flashed a vision of Jack Barrow. Of course it was absurd — even though she appreciated the honor. But she did not finish the sentence that way. "I don't — oh, it's simply impossible. I couldn't think of such a thing."

"Why not?" he asked. "I love you. You know that — you can see it, can't you?" He leaned a little nearer, and forced her to meet his gaze. "I can make you happy; I can make you love me. I can give you all that a woman could ask."

"Yes, but —"

He interrupted her quickly. "Perhaps I've surprised and confused you by my impulsiveness," he continued. "But I've had no chance to meet you socially. Sitting here in the office, seeing you day after day, I've had to hold myself in check. And a man only does that so long, and no longer. Perhaps right now you don't feel as I do, but I can teach you to feel that way. I can give you everything — money, social position, everything

16

that's worth having — and love. I'm not an empty-headed boy. I can make you love me."

"You couldn't," Hazel answered flatly. There was a note of dominance in that last statement that jarred on her. Mr. Bush was too sure of his powers. "And I have no desire to experiment with my feelings as you suggest — not for all the wealth and social position in the world. I would have to love a man to think of marrying him — and I do. But you aren't the man. I appreciate the compliment of your offer, and I'm sorry to hurt you, but I can't marry you."

He released her hand. Miss Weir found herself suddenly shaky. Not that she was afraid, or had any cause for fear, but the nervous tension somehow relaxed when she finished speaking so frankly.

His face clouded. "You are engaged?"

"Yes."

He got up and stood over her. "To some self-centered cub — some puny egotist in his twenties, who'll make you a slave to his needs and whims, and discard you for another woman when you've worn out your youth and beauty," he cried. "But you won't marry him. I won't let you!"

Miss Weir rose. "I think I shall go home," she said steadily.

"You shall do nothing of the sort! There is no sense in your running away from me and giving rise to gossip — which will hurt yourself only."

"I am not running away, but I can't stay here and listen to such things from you. It's impossible, under the circumstances, for me to continue working here, so I may as well go now."

Bush stepped past her and snapped the latch on the office door. "I shan't permit it," he said passionately. "Girl, you don't seem to realize what this means to me. I want you — and I'm going to have you!"

"Please don't be melodramatic, Mr. Bush."

"Melodramatic! If it is melodrama for a man to show a little genuine feeling, I'm guilty. But I was never more in earnest in my life. I want a chance to win you. I value you above any woman I have ever met. Most women that —"

"Most women would jump at the chance," Hazel interrupted. "Well, I'm not most women. I don't consider myself as a marketable commodity, nor my looks as an aid to driving a good bargain in a matrimonial way. I simply don't care for you as you would want me to — and I'm very sure I never would. And, seeing that you do feel that way, it's better that we shouldn't be thrown together as we are here. That's why I'm going."

"That is to say, you'll resign because I've told you I care for you and proposed marriage?" he remarked.

"Exactly. It's the only thing to do under the circumstances."

"Give me a chance to show you that I can make you happy," he pleaded. "Don't leave. Stay here where I can at least see you and speak to you. I won't annoy you. And you can't tell. After you get over this surprise you might find yourself liking me better."

"That's just the trouble," Hazel pointed out. "If I were here you would be bringing this subject up in spite of yourself. And that can only cause pain. I can't stay."

"I think you had better reconsider that," he said; and a peculiar — an ugly — light crept into his eyes, "unless you desire to lay yourself open to being the most-talked-of young woman in this town, where you were born, where all your friends live. Many disagreeable things might result."

"That sounds like a threat, Mr. Bush. What do you mean?"

"I mean just what I say. I will admit that mine is, perhaps, a selfish passion. If you insist on making me suffer, I shall do as much for you. I believe in paying all debts in full, even with high interest. There are two characteristics of mine which may not have come to your attention: I never stop struggling for what I want. And I never forgive or forget an injury or an insult."

"Well?" Hazel was beginning to see a side of Mr. Andrew Bush hitherto unsuspected.

"Well?" he repeated. "If you drive me to it, you will find yourself drawing the finger of gossip. Also, you will find yourself unable to secure a position in Granville. Also, you may find yourself losing the — er — regard of this — ah — fortunate individual upon whom you have bestowed your affections; but you'll never lose mine," he burst out wildly. "When you get done butting your head against the wall that will mysteriously rise in your way, I'll be waiting for you. That's how I love. I've never failed in anything I ever undertook, and I don't care how I fight, fair or foul, so that I win."

"This isn't the fifteenth century," Hazel let her indignation flare, "and I'm not at all afraid of any of the things you mention. Even if you could possibly bring these things about, it would only make me despise you, which I'm in a fair way to do now. Even if I weren't engaged, I'd never think of marrying a man old enough to be my father — a man whose years haven't given him a sense of either dignity or decency. Wealth and social position don't modify gray hairs and advancing age. Your threats are an insult. This isn't the stone age. Even if it were," she concluded cuttingly, "you'd stand a poor chance of winning a woman against a man like — well —" She shrugged her shoulders, but she was thinking of Jack Barrow's broad shoulders, and the easy way he went up a flight of stairs, three steps at a time. "Well, any *young* man."

With that thrust, Miss Hazel Weir turned to the rack where hung her hat and coat. She was thoroughly angry, and her employment in that office ended then and there so far as she was concerned.

Bush caught her by the shoulders before she took a second step.

"Gray hairs and advancing age!" he said. "So I strike you as approaching senility, do I? I'll show you whether I'm the worn-out specimen you seem to think I am. Do you think I'll give you up just because I've made you angry? Why, I love you the more for it; it only makes me the more determined to win you."

"You can't. I dislike you more every second. Take your hands off me, please. Be a gentleman — if you can."

20

For answer he caught her up close to him, and there was no sign of decadent force in the grip of his arms. He kissed her; and Hazel, in blind rage, freed one arm, and struck at him man fashion, her hand doubled into a small fist. By the grace of chance, the blow landed on his nose. There was force enough behind it to draw blood. He stood back and fumbled for his handkerchief. Something that sounded like an oath escaped him.

Hazel stared, aghast, astounded. She was not at all sorry; she was perhaps a trifle ashamed. It seemed unwomanly to strike. But the humor of the thing appealed to her most strongly of all. In spite of herself, she smiled as she reached once more for her hat. And this time Mr. Bush did not attempt to restrain her.

She breathed a sigh of relief when she had gained the street, and she did not in the least care if her departure during business hours excited any curosity in the main office. Moreover, she was doubly glad to be away from Bush. The expression on his face as he drew back and stanched his bleeding nose had momentarily chilled her.

"He looked perfectly devilish," she told herself. "My, I loathe that man! He *is* dangerous. Marry him? The idea!"

She knew that she must have cut him deeply in a man's tenderest spot — his self-esteem. But just how well she had gauged the look and possibilities of Mr. Andrew Bush, Hazel scarcely realized.

"I won't tell Jack," she reflected. "He'd probably want to thrash him. And that *would* stir up a lot of horrid talk. Dear me, that's one experience I don't want

21

repeated. I wonder if he made court to his first wife in that high-handed, love-me-or-I'll-beat-you-to-death fashion?"

She laughed when she caught herself scrubbing vigorously with her handkerchief at the place where his lips had touched her cheek. She was primitive enough in her instincts to feel a trifle glad of having retaliated in what her training compelled her to consider a "perfectly hoydenish" manner. But she could not deny that it had proved wonderfully effective.

CHAPTER
THREE

"I Do Give and Bequeath"

When Jack Barrow called again, which happened to be that very evening, Hazel told him simply that she had left Harrington & Bush, without entering into any explanation except the general one that she had found it impossible to get on with Mr. Bush in her new position. And Jack, being more concerned with her than with her work, gave the matter scant consideration.

This was on a Friday. The next forenoon Hazel went downtown. When she returned, a little before eleven, the maid of all work was putting the last touches to her room. The girl pointed to an oblong package on a chair.

"That came for you a little while ago, Miss Weir," she said. "Mr. Bush's carriage brought it."

"Mr. Bush's carriage!" Hazel echoed.

"Yes'm. Regular swell turnout, with a footman in brown livery. My, you could see the girls peeking all along the square when it stopped at our door. It quite flustered the missus."

The girl lingered a second, curiosity writ large on her countenance. Plainly she wished to discover what Miss

Hazel Weir would be getting in a package that was delivered in so aristocratic a manner. But Hazel was in no mood to gratify any one's curiosity. She was angry at the presumption of Mr. Andrew Bush. It was an excellent way of subjecting her to remark. And it did not soothe her to recollect that he had threatened that very thing.

She drew off her gloves, and, laying aside her hat, picked up a newspaper, and began to read. The girl, with no excuse for lingering, reluctantly gathered up her broom and dustpan, and departed. When she was gone, and not till then, Miss Weir investigated the parcel.

Roses — two dozen long-stemmed La Frances — filled the room with their delicate odor when she removed the pasteboard cover. And set edgewise among the stems she found his card. Miss Weir turned up her small nose.

"I wonder if he sends these as a sort of peace offering?" she snorted. "I wonder if a few hours of reflection has made him realize just how exceedingly caddish he acted? Well, Mr. Bush, I'll return your unwelcome gift — though they are beautiful flowers."

And she did forthwith, squandering forty cents on a messenger boy to deliver them to Mr. Bush at his office. She wished him to labor under no misapprehension as to her attitude.

The next day — Sunday — she spent with Jack Barrow on a visit to his cousin in a near-by town. They parted, as was their custom, at the door. It was still early in the evening — eight-thirty, or thereabout —

and Hazel went into the parlor on the first floor. Mrs. Stout and one of her boarders sat there chatting, and at Hazel's entrance the landlady greeted her with a startling bit of news:

"Evenin', Miss Weir. 'Ave you 'eard about Mr. Bush, pore gentleman?" Mrs. Stout was very English.

"Mr. Bush? No. What about him?" Hazel resented Mr. Bush, his name, and his affairs being brought to her attention at every turn. She desired nothing so much since that scene in the office as to ignore his existence.

"'E was 'urt shockin' bad this awft'noon," Mrs. Stout related. "Out 'orseback ridin', and 'is 'orse ran away with 'im, and fell on 'im. Fell all of a 'eap, they say. Terrible — terrible! The pore man isn't expected to live. 'Is back's broke, they say. W'at a pity! Shockin' accident, indeed."

Miss Weir voiced perfunctory sympathy, as was expected of her, seeing that she was an employee of the firm — or had been lately. But close upon that she escaped to her own room. She did not relish sitting there discussing Mr. Andrew Bush. Hazel lacked nothing of womanly sympathy, but he had forfeited that from her.

Nevertheless she kept thinking of him long after she went to bed. She was not at all vindictive, and his misfortune, the fact — if the report were true — that he was facing his end, stirred her pity. She could guess that he would suffer more than some men; he would rebel bitterly against anything savoring of extinction. And she reflected that his love for her was very likely gone by the board now that he was elected to go the way of all flesh.

The report of his injury was verified in the morning papers. By evening it had pretty well passed out of Hazel's mind. She had more pleasant concerns. Jack Barrow dropped in about six-thirty to ask if she wanted to go with him to a concert during the week. They were sitting in the parlor, by a front window, chattering to each other, but not so engrossed that they failed to notice a carriage drawn by two splendid grays pull up at the front gate. The footman, in brown livery, got down and came to the door. Hazel knew the carriage. She had seen Mr. Andrew Bush abroad in it many a time. She wondered if there was some further annoyance in store for her, and frowned at the prospect.

She heard Mrs. Stout answer the bell in person. There was a low mumble of voices. Then the landlady appeared in the parlor doorway, the footman behind her.

"This is the lady." Mrs. Stout indicated Hazel. "A message for you, Miss Weir."

The liveried person bowed and extended an envelope. "I was instructed to deliver this to you personally," he said, and lingered as if he looked for further instructions.

Hazel looked at the envelope. She could not understand why, under the circumstances, any message should come to her through such a medium. But there was her name inscribed. She glanced up. Mrs. Stout gazed past the footman with an air of frank anticipation. Jack also was looking. But the landlady caught Hazel's glance and backed out the door, and Hazel opened the letter.

The note was brief and to the point:

MISS WEIR: Mr. Bush, being seriously injured and unable to write, bids me say that he is very anxious to see you. He sends his carriage to convey you here. His physicians fear that he will not survive the night, hence he begs of you to come. Very truly,

ETHEL B. WATSON, Nurse in Waiting.

"The idea! Of course I won't! I wouldn't think of such a thing!" Hazel exclaimed.

"Just a second," she said to the footman.

Over on the parlor mantel lay some sheets of paper and envelopes. She borrowed a pencil from Barrow and scribbled a brief refusal. The footman departed with her answer. Hazel turned to find Jack staring his puzzlement.

"What did he want?" Barrow asked bluntly. "That was the Bush turnout, wasn't it?"

"You heard about Mr. Bush getting hurt, didn't you?" she inquired.

"Saw it in the paper. Why?"

"Nothing, except that he is supposed to be dying — and he wanted to see me. At least — well, read the note," Hazel answered.

Barrow glanced over the missive and frowned.

"What do you suppose he wanted to see you for?" he asked.

"How should I know?" Hazel evaded.

She felt a reluctance to enter into any explanations. That would necessitate telling the whole story, and she felt some delicacy about relating it when the man involved lay near to death. Furthermore, Jack might misunderstand, might blame her. He was inclined to jealousy on slight grounds, she had discovered before now. Perhaps that, the natural desire to avoid anything disagreeable coming up between them, helped constrain her to silence.

"Seems funny," he remarked slowly.

"Oh, let's forget it." Hazel came and sat down on the couch by him. "I don't know of any reason why he should want to see me. I wouldn't go merely out of curiosity to find out. It was certainly a peculiar request for him to make. But that's no reason why we should let it bother us. If he's really so badly hurt, the chances are he's out of his head. Don't scowl at that bit of paper so, Johnnie-boy."

Barrow laughed and kissed her, and the subject was dropped forthwith. Later they went out for a short walk. In an hour or so Barrow left for home, promising to have the concert tickets for Thursday night.

Hazel took the note out of her belt and read it again when she reached her room. Why should he want to see her? She wondered at the man's persistence. He had insulted her, according to her view of it — doubly insulted her with threats and an enforced caress. Perhaps he merely wanted to beg her pardon; she had heard of men doing such things in their last moments. But she could not conceive of Mr. Andrew Bush being sorry for anything he did. Her estimate of him was that his only regret would be over failure to achieve his own ends. He struck her as being an individual whose own personal desires were paramount. She had heard vague stories of his tenacity of purpose, his disregard of anything and everybody but himself. The gossip she had heard and half forgotten had been recalled and confirmed by her own recent experience with him.

Nevertheless, she considered that particular episode closed. She believed that she had convinced him of that. And so she could not grasp the reason for that eleventh-hour summons. But she could see that a repetition of such incidents might put her in a queer light. Other folk might begin to wonder and inquire why Mr. Andrew Bush took such an "interest" in her — a mere stenographer. Well, she told herself, she did not care — so long as Jack Barrow's ears were not assailed by talk. She smiled at that, for she could picture the reception any scandal peddler would get from *him*.

The next day's papers contained the obituary of Mr. Andrew Bush. He had died shortly after midnight. And despite the fact that she held no grudge, Hazel felt a sense of relief. He was powerless to annoy or persecute her, and she could not escape the conviction that he would have attempted both had he lived.

She had now been idle a matter of days. Nearly three months were yet to elapse before her wedding. She and Barrow had compromised on that after a deal of discussion. Manlike, he had wished to be married as soon as she accepted him, and she had held out for a date that would permit her to accumulate a trousseau according to her means.

"A girl only gets married once, Johnnie-boy," she had declared. "I don't want to get married so — so offhand, like going out and buying a pair of gloves or something. Even if I do love you ever so much."

She had gained her point after a lot of argument. There had been no thought then of her leaving Harrington & Bush so abruptly. Jack had wanted to get the license as soon as he learned that she had thrown up her job. But she refused to reset the date. They had made plans for October. There was so sense in altering those plans.

It seemed scarcely worthwhile to look for another position. She had enough money saved to do everything she wanted to do. It was not so much lack of money, the need to earn, as the monotony of idleness that irked her. She had acquired the habit of work, and that is a thing not lightly shaken off. But during that day she gathered together the different Granville papers, and went carefully over the "want" columns. Knowing the town as she did, she was enabled to eliminate the unlikely, undesirable places. Thus by evening she was armed with a list of firms and individuals requiring a stenographer. And in the morning she sallied forth.

Her quest ended with the first place she sought. The fact of two years' service with the biggest firm in Granville was ample recommendation; in addition to which the office manager, it developed in their conversation, had known her father in years gone by. So before ten o'clock Miss Hazel Weir was entered on the pay-roll of a furniture-manufacturing house. It was not a permanent position; one of their girls had been taken ill and was likely to take up her duties again in six weeks or two months. But that suited Hazel all the better. She could put in the time usefully, and have a breathing spell before her wedding.

At noon she telephoned Jack Barrow that she was at work again, and she went straight from lunch to the office grind.

Three days went by. Hazel attended the concert with Jack the evening of the day Mr. Andrew Bush received ostentatious burial. At ten the next morning the telephone girl called her.

"Some one wants you on the phone, Miss Weir," she said.

Hazel took up the dangling receiver.

"Hello!"

"That you, Hazel?"

She recognized the voice, half guessing it would be he, since no one but Jack Barrow would be likely to ring her up.

"Surely. Doesn't it sound like me?"

"Have you seen the morning papers?"

"No. What —"

"Look 'em over. Particularly the *Gazette*."

The harsh rattle of a receiver slammed back on its hook without even a "good-by" from him struck her like a slap in the face. She hung up slowly, and went back to her work. Never since their first meeting, and they had not been exempt from lovers' quarrels, had Jack Barrow ever spoken to her like that. Even through

31

the telephone the resentful note in his voice grated on her and mystified her.

Something in the papers lay at the bottom of it, but she could comprehend nothing, absolutely nothing, she told herself hotly, that should make Jack snarl at her like that. His very manner of conveying the message was maddening, put her up in arms.

She was chained to her work — which, despite her agitation, she managed to wade through without any radical errors — until noon. The twelve-to-one intermission gave her opportunity to hurry up the street and buy a *Gazette*. Then, instead of going home to her luncheon, she entered the nearest restaurant. She wanted a chance to read, more than food. She did not unfold the paper until she was seated.

A column heading on the front page caught her eye. The caption ran: "Andrew Bush Leaves Money to Stenographer." And under it the subhead: "Wealthy Manufacturer Makes Peculiar Bequest to Miss Hazel Weir."

The story ran a full column, and had to do with the contents of the will, made public following his interment. There was a great deal of matter anent the principal beneficiaries. But that which formed the basis of the heading was a codicil appended to the will a few hours before his death, in which he did "give and bequeath to Hazel Weir, until lately in my employ, the sum of five thousand dollars in reparation for any wrong I may have done her."

The *Gazette* had copied that portion verbatim, and used it as a peg upon which to hang some adroitly worded speculation as to what manner of wrong Mr. Andrew Bush could have done Miss Hazel Weir. Mr. Bush was a widower of ten years' standing. He had no children. There was plenty of room in his life for romance. And wealthy business men who wrong pretty stenographers are not such an unfamiliar type. The *Gazette* inclined to the yellow side of journalism, and it overlooked nothing that promised a sensation.

Hazel stared at the sheet, and her face burned. She could understand now why Jack Barrow had hung up his receiver with a slam. She could picture him reading that suggestive article and gritting his teeth. Her hands clenched till the knuckles stood white under the smooth skin, and then quite abruptly she got up and left the restaurant even while a waiter hurried to take her order. If she had been a man, and versed in profanity, she could have cursed Andrew Bush till his soul shuddered on its journey through infinite space. Being a woman, she wished only a quiet place to cry.

CHAPTER
FOUR

An Explanation
Demanded

Hazel's pride came to her rescue before she was
halfway home. Instinctively she had turned to that
refuge, where she could lock herself in her own room
and cry her protest against it all. But she had done no
wrong, nothing of which to be ashamed, and when the
first shock of the news article wore off, she threw up
her head and refused to consider what the world at
large might think. So she went back to the office at one
o'clock and took up her work. Long before evening she
sensed that others had read the *Gazette*. Not that any
one mentioned it, but sundry curious glances made her
painfully aware of the fact.

Mrs. Stout evidently was on the watch, for she
appeared in the hall almost as the front door closed
behind Hazel.

"How de do, Miss Weir?" she greeted. "My, but you
fell into quite a bit of a fortune, ain't you?"

"I only know what the papers say," Hazel returned
coldly.

34

"Just fancy! You didn't know nothing about it?" Mrs. Stout regarded her with frank curiosity. "There's been two or three gentlemen from the papers 'ere to-day awskin' for you. Such terrible fellows to quiz one, they are."

"Well?" Hazel filled in the pause.

"Oh, I just thought I'd tell you," Mrs. Stout observed, "that they got precious little out o' *me*. I ain't the talkin' kind. I told 'em nothink whatever, you may be sure."

"They're perfectly welcome to learn all that can be learned about me," Hazel returned quietly. "I don't like newspaper notoriety, but I can't muzzle the papers, and it's easy for them to get my whole history if they want it."

She was on the stairs when she finished speaking. She had just reached the first landing when she heard the telephone bell, and a second or two later the landlady called:

"Oh, Miss Weir! Telephone."

Barrow's voice hailed her over the line.

"I'll be out by seven," said he. "We had better take a walk. We can't talk in the parlor; there'll probably be a lot of old tabbies there out of sheer curiosity."

"All right," Hazel agreed, and hung up. There were one or two questions she would have liked to ask, but she knew that eager ears were close by, taking in every word. Anyway, it was better to wait until she saw him.

She dressed herself. Unconsciously the truly feminine asserted its dominance — the woman anxious to please and propitiate her lover. She put on a dainty

35

summer dress, rearranged her hair, powdered away all trace of the tears that insisted on coming as soon as she reached the sanctuary of her own room. And then she watched for Jack from a window that commanded the street. She had eaten nothing since morning, and the dinner bell rang unheeded. It did not occur to her that she was hungry; her brain was engrossed with other matters more important by far than food.

Barrow appeared at last. She went down to meet him before he rang the bell. Just behind him came a tall man in a gray suit. This individual turned in at the gate, bestowing a nod upon Barrow and a keen glance at her as he passed.

"That's Grinell, from the *Times*," Barrow muttered sourly. "Come on; let's get away from here. I suppose he's after you for an interview. Everybody in Granville's talking about that legacy, it seems to me."

Hazel turned in beside him silently. Right at the start she found herself resenting Barrow's tone, his manner. She had done nothing to warrant suspicion from him. But she loved him, and she hoped she could convince him that it was no more than a passing unpleasantness, for which she was nowise to blame.

"Hang it!" Barrow growled, before they had traversed the first block. "Here comes Grinell! I suppose that old cat of a landlady pointed us out. No dodging him now."

"There's no earthly reason why I should dodge him, as you put it," Hazel replied stiffly. "I'm not an escaped criminal."

Barrow shrugged his shoulders in a way that made Hazel bring her teeth together and want to shake him.

Grinell by then was hurrying up with long strides. Hat in hand, he bowed to her. "Miss Hazel Weir, I believe?" he interrogated.

"Yes," she confirmed.

"I'm on the *Times*, Miss Weir," Grinell went straight to the business in hand. "You are aware, I presume, that Mr. Andrew Bush willed you a sum of money under rather peculiar conditions — that is, the bequest was worded in a peculiar way. Probably you have seen a reference to it in the papers. It has caused a great deal of interest. The *Times* would be pleased to have a statement from you which will tend to set at rest the curiosity of the public. Some of the other papers have indulged in unpleasant innuendo. We would be pleased to publish your side of the matter. It would be an excellent way for you to quiet the nasty rumors that are going the rounds."

"I have no statement to make," Hazel said coolly. "I am not in the least concerned with what the papers print or what the people say. I absolutely refuse to discuss the matter."

Grinell continued to point out — with the persistence and persuasive logic of a good newspaper man bent on learning what his paper wants to know — the desirability of her giving forth a statement. And in the midst of his argument Hazel bade him a curt "good evening" and walked on. Barrow kept step with her. Grinell gave it up for a bad job evidently, for he turned back.

They walked five blocks without a word. Hazel glanced at Barrow now and then, and observed with an uncomfortable sinking of her heart that he was sullen, openly resentful, suspicious.

"Johnnie-boy," she said suddenly, "don't look so cross. Surely you don't blame me because Mr. Bush wills me a sum of money in a way that makes people wonder?"

"I can't understand it at all," he said slowly. "It's very peculiar — and deucedly unpleasant. Why should he leave you money at all? And why should he word the will as he did? What wrong did he ever do you?"

"None," Hazel answered shortly. His tone wounded her, cut her deep, so eloquent was it of distrust. "The only wrong he has done me lies in willing me that money as he did."

"But there's an explanation for that," Barrow declared moodily. "There's a key to the mystery, and if anybody has it you have. What is it?"

"Jack," Hazel pleaded, "don't take that tone with me. I can't stand it — I won't. I'm not a little child to be scolded and browbeaten. This morning when you telephoned you were almost insulting, and it hurt me dreadfully. You're angry now, and suspicious. You seem to think I must have done some dreadful thing. I know what you're thinking. The *Gazette* hinted at some 'affair' between me and Mr. Bush; that possibly that was a sort of left-handed reparation for ruining me. If that didn't make me angry, it would amuse me — it's so absurd. Haven't you any faith in me at all? I haven't done anything to be ashamed of. I've got nothing to conceal."

"Don't conceal it, then," Barrow muttered sulkily. "I've got a right to know whatever there is to know if I'm going to marry you. You don't seem to have any idea what this sort of talk that's going around means to a man."

Hazel stopped short and faced him. Her heart pounded sickeningly, and hurt pride and rising anger choked her for an instant. But she managed to speak calmly, perhaps with added calmness by reason of the struggle she was compelled to make for self-control.

"If you are going to marry me," she repeated, "you have got a right to know all there is to know. Have I refused to explain? I haven't had much chance to explain yet. Have I refused to tell you anything? If you ever thought of anybody beside yourself, you might be asking yourself how all this talk would affect a girl like me. And, besides, I think from your manner that you've already condemned me — for what? Would any reasonable explanation make an impression on you in your present frame of mind? I don't want to marry you if you can't trust me. Why, I couldn't — I *wouldn't* — marry you any time, or any place, under those conditions, no matter how much I may foolishly care for you."

"There's just one thing, Hazel," Barrow persisted stubbornly. "There must have been something between you and Bush. He sent flowers to you, and I myself saw when he was hurt he sent his carriage to bring you to his house. And then he leaves you this money. There

39

was something between you, and I want to know what it was. You're not helping yourself by getting on your dignity and talking about my not trusting you instead of explaining these things."

"A short time ago," Hazel told him quietly, "Mr. Bush asked me to marry him. I refused, of course. He —"

"You refused!" Barrow interrupted cynically. "Most girls would have jumped at the chance."

"Jack!" she protested.

"Well," Barrow defended, "he was almost a millionaire, and I've got nothing but my hands and my brain. But suppose you did refuse him. How does that account for the five thousand dollars?"

"I think," Hazel flung back passionately, "I'll let you find that out for yourself. You've said enough now to make me hate you almost. Your very manner's an insult."

"If you don't like my manner —" Barrow retorted stormily. Then he cut his sentence in two, and glared at her. Her eyes glistened with slow-welling tears, and she bit nervously at her under lip. Barrow shrugged his shoulders. The twin devils of jealousy and distrust were riding him hard, and it flashed over Hazel that in his mind she was prejudged, and that her explanation, if she made it, would only add fuel to the flame. Moreover, she stood in open rebellion at being, so to speak, put on the rack.

She turned abruptly and left him. What did it matter, anyway? She was too proud to plead, and it was worse than useless to explain.

Even so, womanlike, she listened, expecting to hear Jack's step hurrying up behind. She could not imagine him letting her go like that. But he did not come, and when, at a distance of two blocks, she stole a backward glance, he had disappeared.

She returned to the boarding-house. The parlor door stood wide, and the curious, quickly averted glance of a girl she knew sent her quivering up to her room. Safe in that refuge, she sat down by the window, with her chin on her palms, struggling with the impulse to cry, protesting with all her young strength against the bitterness that had come to her through no fault of her own. There was only one cheerful gleam. She loved Jack Barrow. She believed that he loved her, and she could not believe — she could not conceive — him capable of keeping aloof, obdurate and unforgiving, once he got out of the black mood he was in. Then she could snuggle up close to him and tell him how and why Mr. Andrew Bush had struck at her from his death-bed.

She was still sitting by the window, watching the yellow crimson of the sunset, when some one rapped at her door. A uniformed messenger boy greeted her when she opened it:

"Package for Miss Hazel Weir."

She signed his delivery sheet. The address on the package was in Jack's handwriting. A box of chocolates, or some little peace offering, maybe. That was like Jack when he was sorry for anything. They had quarreled before — over trifles, too.

She opened it hastily. A swift heart sinking followed. In the small cardboard box rested a folded scarf, and thrust in it a small gold stickpin — the only thing she had ever given Jack Barrow. There was no message. She needed none to understand.

The sparkle of the small diamond on her finger drew her gaze. She worked his ring over the knuckle, and dropped it on the dresser, where the face in the silver frame smiled up at her. She stared at the picture for one long minute fixedly, with unchanging expression, and suddenly she swept it from the dresser with a savage sweep of her hand, dashed it on the floor, and stamped it shapeless with her slippered heel.

"Oh, oh!" she gasped. "I hate you — I hate you! I despise you!"

And then she flung herself across the bed and sobbed hysterically into a pillow.

CHAPTER
FIVE

The Way of the World at Large

Through the night Hazel dozed fitfully, waking out of uneasy sleep to lie staring, wide-eyed, into the dark, every nerve in her body taut, her mind abnormally active. She tried to accept things philosophically, but her philosophy failed. There was a hurt, the pain of which she could not ease by any mental process. Grief and anger by turns mastered her, and at daybreak she rose, heavy-lidded and physically weary.

The first thing upon which her gaze alighted was the crumpled photo in its shattered frame; and, sitting on the side of her bed, she laughed at the sudden fury in which she had destroyed it; but there was no mirth in her laughter.

" 'Would we not shatter it to little bits — and then,' " she murmured. "No, Mr. John Barrow, I don't believe I'd want to mold you nearer to my heart's desire. Not after yesterday evening. There's such a thing as being hurt so badly that one finally gets numb; and one always shrinks from anything that can deliver such a

43

hurt. Well, it's another day. And there'll be lots of other days, I suppose."

She gathered up the bits of broken glass and the bent frame, and put them in a drawer, dressed herself, and went down to breakfast. She was too deeply engrossed in her own troubles to notice or care whether any subtle change was becoming manifest in the attitude of her fellow boarders. The worst, she felt sure, had already overtaken her. In reaction to the sensitive, shrinking mood of the previous day, a spirit of defiance had taken possession of her. Figuratively she declared that the world could go to the devil, and squared her shoulders with the declaration.

She had a little time to spare, and that time she devoted to making up a package of Barrow's ring and a few other trinkets which he had given her. This she addressed to his office and posted while on her way to work.

She got through the day somehow, struggling against thoughts that would persist in creeping into her mind and stirring up emotions that she was determined to hold in check. Work, she knew, was her only salvation. If she sat idle, thinking, the tears would come in spite of her, and a horrible, choky feeling in her throat. She set her teeth and thumped away at her machine, grimly vowing that Jack Barrow nor any other man should make her heart ache for long.

And so she got through the week. Saturday evening came, and she went home, dreading Sunday's idleness, with its memories. The people at Mrs. Stout's establishment, she plainly saw, were growing a trifle shy of her. She had never been on terms of intimacy with any of them during her stay there, hence their attitude troubled little after the first supersensitiveness wore off. But her own friends, girls with whom she had played in the pinafore-and-pigtail stages of her youth, young men who had paid court to her until Jack Barrow monopolized her — she did not know how they stood. She had seen none of them since Bush launched his last bolt. Barrow she had passed on the street just once, and when he lifted his hat distantly, she looked straight ahead, and ignored him. Whether she hurt him as much as she did herself by the cut direct would be hard to say.

On Saturday evenings and Sunday afternoons ordinarily from two to a dozen girl friends called her up at the boarding-house, or dropped in by ones and twos to chat a while, tease her about Jack, or plan some mild frivolity. Hazel went home, wondering if they, too, would stand aloof.

When Sunday noon arrived, and the phone had failed to call her once, and not one of all her friends had dropped in, Hazel twisted her chair so that she could stare at the image of herself in the mirror.

"You're in a fair way to become a pariah, it seems," she said bitterly. "What have you done, I wonder, that you've lost your lover, and that Alice and May and Hortense and all the rest of them keep away from you? Nothing — not a thing — except that your looks attracted a man, and the man threw stones when he couldn't have his way. Oh, well, what's the difference?

You've got two good hands, and you're not afraid of work."

She walked out to Granville Park after luncheon, and found a seat on a shaded bench beside the lake. People passed and repassed — couples, youngsters, old people, children. It made her lonely beyond measure. She had never been isolated among her own kind before. She could not remember a time when she had gone to Granville Park by herself. But she was learning fast to stand on her own feet.

A group of young people came sauntering along the path. Hazel looked up as they neared her, chattering to each other. Maud Steele and Bud Wells, and — why, she knew every one of the party. They were swinging an empty picnic basket, and laughing at everything and nothing. Hazel caught her breath as they came abreast, not over ten feet away. The three young men raised their hats self-consciously.

"Hello, Hazel!" the girl said.

But they passed on. It seemed to Hazel that they quickened their pace a trifle. It made her grit her teeth in resentful anger. Ten minutes later she left the park and caught a car home. Once in her room she broke down.

"Oh, I'll go mad if I stay here and this sort of thing goes on!" she cried forlornly.

A sudden thought struck her.

"Why *should* I stay here?" she said aloud. "Why? What's to keep me here? I can make my living anywhere."

"But, no," she asserted passionately, "I won't run away. That would be running away, and I haven't anything to be ashamed of. I will *not* run."

Still the idea kept recurring to her. It promised relief from the hurt of averted faces and coolness where she had a right to expect sympathy and friendship. She had never been more than two hundred miles from Granville in her life. But she knew that a vast, rich land spread south and west. She was human and thoroughly feminine; loneliness appalled her, and she had never suffered as Granville at large was making her suffer.

The legal notice of the bequest was mailed to her. She tore up the letter and threw it in the fire as if it were some poisonous thing. The idea of accepting his money stirred her to a perfect frenzy. That was piling it up.

All during the next week she worked at her machine in the office of the furniture company, keeping strictly to herself, doing her work impassively, efficiently, betraying no sign of the feelings that sometimes rose up, the despairing protest and angry rebellion against the dubious position she was in through no fault of her own. She swore she would not leave Granville, and it galled her to stay. It was a losing fight, and she knew it even if she did not admit the fact. If she could have poured the whole miserable tale into some sympathetic ear she would have felt better, and each day would have seemed less hard. But there was no such ear. Her friends kept away.

Saturday of the second week her pay envelope contained a brief notice that the firm no longer required her services. There was no explanation, only perfunctory regrets; and, truth to tell, Hazel cared little to know the real cause. Any one of a number of reasons might have been sufficient. But she realized how those who knew her would take it, what cause they would ascribe. It did not matter, though. The very worst, she reasoned, could not be so bad as what had already happened — could be no more disagreeable than the things she had endured in the past two weeks. Losing a position was a trifle. But it set her thinking again.

"It doesn't seem to be a case of flight," she reflected on her way home, "so much as a case of being frozen out, compelled to go. I can't stay here and be idle. I have to work in order to live. Well, I'm not gone yet."

She stopped at a news stand and bought the evening papers. Up in the top rack of the stand the big heads of an assorted lot of Western papers caught her eye. She bought two or three on the impulse of the moment, without any definite purpose except to look them over out of mere curiosity. With these tucked under her arm, she turned into the boarding-house gate, ran up the steps, and, upon opening the door, her ears were gladdened by the first friendly voice she had heard — it seemed to her — in ages, a voice withal that she had least expected to hear. A short, plump woman rushed out of the parlor, and precipitated herself bodily upon Hazel.

"Kitty Ryan! Where in the wide, wide world did you come from?" Hazel cried.

48

"From the United States and everywhere," Miss Ryan replied. "Take me up to your room, dear, where we can talk our heads off.

"And, furthermore, Hazie, I'll be pleased to have you address me as Mrs. Brooks, my dear young woman," the plump lady laughed, as she settled herself in a chair in Hazel's room.

"So you're married?" Hazel said.

"I am that," Mrs. Kitty responded emphatically, "to the best boy that ever drew breath. And so should you be, dear girl. I don't see how you've escaped so long — a good-looking girl like you. The boys were always crazy after you. There's nothing like having a good man to take care of you, dear."

"Heaven save me from them!" Hazel answered bitterly. "If you've got a good one, you're lucky. I can't see them as anything but self-centered, arrogant, treacherous brutes."

"Lord bless us — it's worse than I thought!" Kitty jumped up and threw her arms around Hazel. "There, there — don't waste a tear on them. I know all about it. I came over to see you just as soon as some of the girls — nasty little cats they are; a woman's always meaner than a man, dear — just as soon as they gave me an inkling of how things were going with you. Pshaw! The world's full of good, decent fellows — and you've got one coming."

"I hope not," Hazel protested.

"Oh, yes, you have," Mrs. Brooks smilingly assured her. "A woman without a man is only half a human being, anyway, you know — and vice versa. I know. We can cuss the men all we want to, my dear, and some of us unfortunately have a nasty experience with one now and then. But we can't get away from the fundamental laws of being."

"If you'd had my experience of the last two weeks you'd sing a different tune," Hazel vehemently declared. "I hate — I —"

And then she gave way, and indulged in the luxury of turning herself loose on Kitty's shoulder. Presently she was able to wipe her eyes and relate the whole story from the Sunday Mr. Bush stopped and spoke to her in the park down to that evening.

Kitty nodded understandingly. "But the girls have handed it to you worse than the men, Hazel," she observed sagely. "Jack Barrow was just plain crazy jealous, and a man like that can't help acting as he did. You're really fortunate, I think, because you'd not be really happy with a man like that. But the girls that you and I grew up with — they should have stood by you, knowing you as they did; yet you see they were ready to think the worst of you. They nearly always do when there's a man in the case. That's a weakness of our sex, dear. My, what a vindictive old Turk that Bush must have been! Well, you aren't working. Come and stay with me. Hubby's got a two-year contract with the World Advertising Company. We'll be located here that long at least. Come and stay with us. We'll show these little-minded folk a thing or two. Leave it to us."

"Oh, no, I couldn't think of that, Kitty!" Hazel faltered. "You know I'd love to, and it's awfully good of you, but I think I'm just about ready to go away from Granville."

"Well, come and stop with us till you do go," Kitty insisted. "We are going to take a furnished cottage for a while. Though, between you and me, dear, knowing people as I do, I can't blame you for wanting to be where their nasty tongues can't wound you."

But Hazel was obdurate. She would not inflict herself on the one friend she had left. And Kitty, after a short talk, berated her affectionately for her independence, and rose to go.

"For," said she, "I didn't get hold of this thing till Addie Horton called at the hotel this afternoon, and I didn't stop to think that it was near teatime, but came straight here. Jimmie'll think I've eloped. So ta-ta. I'll come out to-morrow about two. I have to confab with a house agent in the forenoon. By-by."

Hazel sat down and actually smiled when Kitty was gone. Somehow a grievous burden had fallen off her mind. Likewise, by some psychological quirk, the idea of leaving Granville and making her home elsewhere no longer struck her as running away under fire. She did not wish to subject Kitty Brooks to the difficulties, the embarrassment that might arise from having her as a guest; but the mere fact that Kitty stood stanchly by her made the world seem less harsh and dreary, made it seem as if she had, in a measure, justified herself. She felt that she could adventure forth among strangers in a strange country with a better heart, knowing that Kitty Brooks would put a swift quietus on any gossip that came her way.

So that Hazel went down to the dining-room light-heartedly, and when the meal was finished came back and fell to reading her papers. The first of the Western papers was a Vancouver *World*. In a real-estate man's half-page she found a diminutive sketch plan of the city on the shores of Burrard Inlet, Canada's principal outpost on the far Pacific.

"It's quite a big place," she murmured absently. "One would be far enough away there, goodness knows."

Then she turned to the "Help Wanted" advertisements. The thing which impressed her quickly and most vividly was the dearth of demand for clerks and stenographers, and the repeated calls for domestic help and such. Domestic service she shrank from except as a last resort. And down near the bottom of the column she happened on an inquiry for a school-teacher, female preferred, in an out-of-the-way district in the interior of the province.

"Now, that —" Hazel thought.

She had a second-class certificate tucked away among her belongings. Originally it had been her intention to teach, and she had done so one term in a backwoods school when she was eighteen. With the ending of the term she had returned to Granville, studied that winter, and got her second certificate; but at the same time she had taken a business-college course, and the following June found her clacking a typewriter at nine dollars a week. And her teacher's diploma had remained in the bottom of her trunk ever since.

"I could teach, I suppose, by rubbing up a little on one or two subjects as I went along," she reflected. "I wonder now —"

What she wondered was how much salary she could expect, and she took up the paper again, and looked carefully for other advertisements calling for teachers. In the *World* and in a Winnipeg paper she found one or two vacancies to fill out the fall term, and gathered that Western schools paid from fifty to sixty dollars a month for "schoolma'ams" with certificates such as she held.

"Why not?" she asked herself. "I've got two resources. If I can't get office work I can teach. I can do *anything* if I have to. And it's far enough away, in all conscience — all of twenty-five hundred miles."

Unaccountably, since Kitty Brooks' visit, she found herself itching to turn her back on Granville and its unpleasant associations. She did not attempt to analyze the feeling. Strange lands, and most of all the West, held alluring promise. She sat in her rocker, and could not help but dream of places where people were a little broader gauge, a little less prone to narrow, conventional judgments. Other people had done as she proposed doing — cut loose from their established environment, and made a fresh start in countries where none knew or cared whence they came or who they were. Why not she? One thing was certain: Granville, for all she had been born there, and grown to womanhood there, was now no place for her. The very people who knew her best would make her suffer most.

She spent that evening going thoroughly over the papers and writing letters to various school boards, taking a chance at one or two she found in the Manitoba paper, but centering her hopes on the country west of the Rockies. Her letters finished, she took stock of her resources — verified them, rather, for she had not so much money that she did not know almost where she stood. Her savings in the bank amounted to three hundred odd dollars, and cash in hand brought the sum to a total of three hundred and sixty-five. At any rate, she had sufficient to insure her living for quite a long time. And she went to bed feeling better than she had felt for two weeks.

Kitty Brooks came again the next afternoon, and, being a young woman of wide experience and good sense, made no further attempt to influence Hazel one way or the other.

"I hate to see you go, though," she remarked truthfully. "But you'll like the West — if it happens that you go there. You'll like it better than the East; there's a different sort of spirit among the people. I've traveled over some of it, and if Jimmie's business permitted we'd both like to live there. And — getting down to strictly practical things — a girl can make a much better living there. Wages are high. And — who knows? — you might capture a cattle king."

Hazel shrugged her shoulders, and Mrs. Kitty forbore teasing. After that they gossiped and compared notes covering the two years since they had met until it was time for Kitty to go home.

Very shortly thereafter — almost, it seemed, by return mail — Hazel got replies to her letters of inquiry.

The fact that each and every one seemed bent on securing her services astonished her.

"Schoolma'ams must certainly be scarce out there," she told herself. "This is an embarrassment of riches. I'm going somewhere, but which place shall it be?"

But the reply from Cariboo Meadows, B. C., the first place she had thought of, decided her. The member of the school board who replied held forth the natural beauty of the country as much as he did the advantages of the position. The thing that perhaps made the strongest appeal to Hazel was a little kodak print inclosed in the letter, showing the schoolhouse.

The building itself was primitive enough, of logs, with a pole-and-sod roof. But it was the huge background, the timbered mountains rising to snow-clad heights against a cloudless sky, that attracted her. She had never seen a greater height of land than the rolling hills of Ontario. Here was a frontier, big and new and raw, holding out to her as she stared at the print a promise — of what? She did not know. Adventure? If she desired adventure, it was purely a subconscious desire. But she had lived in a rut a long time without realizing it more than vaguely, and there was something in her nature that responded instantly when she contemplated journeying alone into a far country. She found herself hungering for change, for a measure of freedom from petty restraints, for elbow-room in the wide spaces, where one's neighbor might be ten or forty miles away. She knew nothing whatever of such a life, but she could feel a certain envy of those who led it.

She sat for a long time looking at the picture, thinking. Here was the concrete, visible presentment of something that drew her strongly. She found an atlas, and looked up Cariboo Meadows on the map. It was not to be found, and Hazel judged it to be a purely local name. But the letter told her that she would have to stage it a hundred and sixty-five miles north from Ashcroft, B. C., where the writer would meet her and drive her to the Meadows. She located the stage-line terminal on the map, and ran her forefinger over the route. Mountain and lake and stream lined and dotted and criss-crossed the province from end to end of its seven-hundred-mile length. Back of where Cariboo Meadows should be three or four mining camps snuggled high in the mountains.

"What a country!" she whispered. "It's wild; really, truly wild; and everything I've ever seen has been tamed and smoothed down, and made eminently respectable and conventional long ago. That's the place. That's where I'm going, and I'm going it blind. I'm not going to tell any one — not even Kitty — until, like a bear, I've gone over the mountain to see what I can see."

Within an hour of that Miss Hazel Weir had written to accept the terms offered by the Cariboo Meadows school district, and was busily packing her trunk.

CHAPTER
SIX

Cariboo Meadows

A tall man, sunburned, slow-speaking, met Hazel at Soda Creek, the end of her stage journey, introducing himself as Jim Briggs.

"Pretty tiresome trip, ain't it?" he observed. "You'll have a chance to rest decent to-night, and I got a team uh bays that'll yank yuh to the Meadows in four hours 'n' a half. My wife'll be plumb tickled to have yuh. They ain't much more'n half a dozen white women in ten miles uh the Meadows. We keep a boardin'-house. Hope you'll like the country."

That was a lengthy speech for Jim Briggs, as Hazel discovered when she rolled out of Soda Creek behind the "team uh bays." His conversation was decidedly monosyllabic. But he could drive, if he was no talker, and his team could travel. The road, albeit rough in spots, a mere track through timber and little gems of open where the yellowing grass waved knee-high, and over hills which sloped to deep cañons lined with pine and spruce, seemed short enough. And so by eleven o'clock Hazel found herself at Cariboo Meadows.

"Schoolhouse's over yonder." Briggs pointed out the place — an unnecessary guidance, for Hazel had already marked the building set off by itself and fortified with a tall flagpole. "And here's where we live. Kinda out uh the world, but blame good place to live."

Hazel did like the place. Her first impression was thankfulness that her lot had been cast in such a spot. But it was largely because of the surroundings, essentially primitive, the clean air, guiltless of smoke taint, the aromatic odors from the forest that ranged for unending miles on every hand. For the first time in her life, she was beyond hearing of the clang of street cars, the roar of traffic, the dirt and smells of a city. It seemed good. She had no regrets, no longing to be back. There was a pain sometimes, when in spite of herself she would fall to thinking of Jack Barrow. But that she looked upon as a closed chapter. He had hurt her where a woman can be most deeply wounded — in her pride and her affections — and the hurt was dulled by the smoldering resentment that thinking of him always fanned to a flame. Miss Hazel Weir was neither meek nor mild, even if her environment had bred in her a repression that had become second nature.

So with the charm of the wild land fresh upon her, she took kindly to Cariboo Meadows. The immediate, disagreeable past bade fair to become as remote in reality as the distance made it seem. Surely no ghosts would walk here to make people look askance at her.

Her first afternoon she spent loafing on the porch of the Briggs domicile, within which Mrs. Briggs, a fat, good-natured person of forty, toiled at her cooking for the "boarders," and kept a brood of five tumultuous youngsters in order — the combined tasks leaving her scant time to entertain her newly arrived guest. From the vantage ground of the porch Hazel got her first glimpse of the turns life occasionally takes when there is no policeman just around the corner.

Cariboo Meadows, as a town, was simply a double row of buildings facing each other across a wagon road. Two stores, a blacksmith shop, a feed stable, certain other nondescript buildings, and a few dwellings, mostly of logs, was all. Probably not more than a total of fifty souls made permanent residence there. But the teams of ranchers stood in the street, and a few saddled cow ponies whose listlessness was mostly assumed. Before one of the general stores a prospector fussed with a string of pack horses. Directly opposite Briggs' boarding-house stood a building labeled "Regent Hotel." Hazel could envisage it all with a half turn of her head.

From this hotel there presently issued a young man dressed in the ordinary costume of the country — wide hat, flannel shirt, overalls, boots. He sat down on a box close by the hotel entrance. In a few minutes another came forth. He walked past the first a few steps, stopped, and said something. Hazel could not hear the words. The first man was filling a pipe. Apparently he made no reply; at least, he did not trouble to look up. But she saw his shoulders lift in a shrug. Then he who had passed turned square about and spoke again, this time lifting his voice a trifle. The young fellow sitting on the box instantly became galvanized into action. He flung out an oath that carried across the street and made Hazel's ears burn. At the same time he leaped from his seat straight at the other man.

Hazel saw it quite distinctly, saw him who jumped dodge a vicious blow and close with the other; and saw, moreover, something which amazed her. For the young fellow swayed with his adversary a second or two, then lifted him bodily off his feet almost to the level of his head, and slammed him against the hotel wall with a sudden twist. She heard the thump of the body on the logs. For an instant she thought him about to jump with his booted feet on the prostrate form, and involuntarily she held her breath. But he stepped back, and when the other scrambled up, he side-stepped the first rush, and knocked the man down again with a blow of his fist. This time he stayed down. Then other men — three or four of them — came out of the hotel, stood uncertainly a few seconds, and Hazel heard the young fellow say:

"Better take that fool in and bring him to. If he's still hungry for trouble, I'll be right handy. I wonder how many more of you fellers I'll have to lick before you'll get wise enough not to start things you can't stop?"

They supported the unconscious man through the doorway; the young fellow resumed his seat on the box, also his pipe filling.

"Roarin' Bill's goin' to get himself killed one uh these days."

Hazel started, but it was only Jim Briggs in the doorway beside her.

"I guess you ain't much used to seein' that sort of exhibition where you come from, Miss Weir," Briggs'

wife put in over his shoulder. "My land, it's disgustin'
— men fightin' in the street where everybody can see
'em. Thank goodness, it don't happen very often.
'Specially when Bill Wagstaff ain't around. You ain't
shocked, are you, honey?"

"Why, I didn't have time to be shocked," Hazel
laughed. "It was done so quickly."

"If them fellers would leave Bill alone," Briggs
remarked, "there wouldn't be no fight. But he goes off
like a hair-trigger gun, and he'd scrap a dozen quick as
one. I'm lookin' to see his finish one uh these days."

"What a name!" Hazel observed, caught by the
appellation Briggs had first used. "Is that Roaring Bill
over there?"

"That's him — Roarin' Bill Wagstaff," Briggs
answered. "If he takes a few drinks, you'll find out
to-night how he got the name. Sings — just like a bull
moose — hear him all over town. Probably whip two or
three men before mornin'."

His spouse calling him at that moment, Briggs
detailed no more information about Roaring Bill. And
Hazel sat looking across the way with considerable
interest at the specimen of a type which hitherto she
had encountered in the pages of fiction — a fighting
man, what the West called a "bad actor." She had,
however, no wish for closer study of that particular
type. The men of her world had been altogether
different, and the few frontier specimens she had met at
the Briggs' dinner table had not impressed her with
anything except their shyness and manifest awkward-
ness in her presence. The West itself appealed to her, its

61

bigness, its nearness to the absolutely primeval, but not the people she had so far met. They were not wrapped in a glamor of romance; she was altogether too keen to idealize them. They were not her kind, and while she granted their worth, they were more picturesque about their own affairs than when she came in close contact with them. Those were her first impressions. And so she looked at Roaring Bill Wagstaff, over the way, with a quite impersonal interest.

He came into Briggs' place for supper. Mrs. Briggs was her own waitress. Briggs himself sat beside Hazel. She heard him grunt, and saw a mild look of surprise flit over his countenance when Roaring Bill walked in and coolly took a seat. But not until Hazel glanced at the newcomer did she recognize him as the man who had fought in the street. He was looking straight at her when she did glance up, and the mingled astonishment and frank admiration in his clear gray eyes made Hazel drop hers quickly to her plate. Since Mr. Andrew Bush, she was beginning to hate men who looked at her that way. And she could not help seeing that many did so look.

Roaring Bill ate his supper in silence. No one spoke to him, and he addressed no one except to ask that certain dishes be passed. Among the others conversation was general. Hazel noticed that, and wondered why — wondered if Roaring Bill was taboo. She had sensed enough of the Western point of view to know that the West held nothing against a man who was quick to blows — rather admired such a one, in fact. And her conclusions were not complimentary to Mr.

Bill Wagstaff. If people avoided him in that country, he must be a very hard citizen indeed. And Hazel no more than formulated this opinion than she was ashamed of it, having her own recent experience in mind. Whereupon she dismissed Bill Wagstaff from her thoughts altogether when she left the table.

Exactly three days later Hazel came into the dining-room at noon, and there received her first lesson in the truth that this world is a very small place, after all. A nattily dressed gentleman seated to one side of her place at table rose with the most polite bows and extended hand. Hazel recognized him at a glance as Mr. Howard Perkins, traveling salesman for Harrington & Bush. She had met him several times in the company offices. She was anything save joyful at the meeting, but after the first unwelcome surprise she reflected that it was scarcely strange that a link in her past life should turn up here, for she knew that in the very nature of things a firm manufacturing agricultural implements would have its men drumming up trade on the very edge of the frontier.

Mr. Perkins was tolerably young, good looking, talkative, apparently glad to meet someone from home. He joined her on the porch for a minute when the meal was over. And he succeeded in putting Hazel unqualifiedly at her ease so far as he was concerned. If he had heard any Granville gossip, if he knew why she had left Granville, it evidently cut no figure with him. As a consequence, while she was simply polite and negatively friendly, deep in her heart Hazel felt a pleasant reaction from the disagreeable things for which Granville stood; and, though she nursed both resentment and distrust against men in general, it did not seem to apply to Mr. Perkins. Anyway, he was here to-day, and on the morrow he would be gone.

Being a healthy, normal young person, Hazel enjoyed his company without being fully aware of the fact. So much for natural gregariousness. Furthermore, Mr. Perkins in his business had been pretty much everywhere on the North American continent, and he knew how to set forth his various experiences. Most women would have found him interesting, particularly in a community as isolated as Cariboo Meadows, where tailored clothes and starched collars seemed unknown, and every man was his own barber — at infrequent intervals.

So Hazel found it quite natural to be chatting with him on the Briggs' porch when her school work ended at three-thirty in the afternoon. It transpired that Mr. Perkins, like herself, had an appreciation of the scenic beauties, and also the picturesque phases of life as it ran in the Cariboo country. They talked of many things, discussed life in a city as compared with existence in the wild, and were agreed that both had desirable features — and drawbacks. Finally Mr. Perkins proposed a walk up on a three-hundred-foot knoll that sloped from the back door, so to speak, of Cariboo Meadows. Hazel got her hat, and they set out. She had climbed that hill by herself, and she knew that it commanded a great sweep of the rolling land to the west.

They reached the top in a few minutes, and found a seat on a dead tree trunk. Mr. Perkins was properly impressed with the outlook. But before very long he seemed to suffer a relaxation of his interest in the view and a corresponding increase of attention to his companion. Hazel recognized the symptoms. At first it amused, then it irritated her. The playful familiarity of Mr. Perkins suddenly got on her nerves.

"I think I shall go down," she said abruptly.

"Oh, I say, now, there's no hurry," Perkins responded smilingly.

But she was already rising from her seat, and Mr. Perkins, very likely gauging his action according to his experience in other such situations, did an utterly foolish thing. He caught her as she rose, and laughingly tried to kiss her. Whereupon he discovered that he had caught a tartar, for Hazel slapped him with all the force she could muster — which was considerable, judging by the flaming red spot which the *smack* of her palm left on his smooth-shaven cheek. But he did not seem to mind that. Probably he had been slapped before, and regarded it as part of the game. He attempted to draw her closer.

"Why, you're a regular scrapper," he smiled. "Now, I'm sure you didn't cuff Bush that way."

Hazel jerked loose from his grip in a perfect fury, using at the same time the weapons nature gave her according to her strength, whereby Mr. Perkins suffered sundry small bruises, which were as nothing to the bruises his conceit suffered. For, being free of him, Hazel stood her ground long enough to tell him that he was a cad, a coward, an ill-bred nincompoop, and other epithets grievous to masculine vanity. With that she fled incontinently down the hill, furious, shamed almost to tears, and wishing fervently that she had the muscle of a man to requite the insult as it deserved. To cap the climax, Mrs. Briggs, who had seen the two depart, observed her return alone, and, with a curious look, asked jokingly:

"Did you lose the young man in the timber?"

And Hazel, being keyed to a fearful pitch, unwisely snapped back:

"I hope so."

Which caused Mrs. Briggs' gaze to follow her wonderingly as she went hastily to her own room.

Like other mean souls of similar pattern, it suited Mr. Perkins to seek revenge in the only way possible — by confidentially relating to divers individuals during that evening the Granville episode in the new teacher's career. At least, Hazel guessed he must have told the tale of that ambiguously worded bequest and the subsequent gossip, for as early as the next day she caught certain of Jim Briggs' boarders looking at her with an interest they had not heretofore displayed — or, rather, it should be said, with a *different* sort of interest. They were discussing her. She could not know it positively, but she felt it.

The feeling grew to certainty after Perkins' departure that day. There was a different atmosphere. Probably, she reflected, he had thrown in a few embellishments of his own for good measure. She felt a tigerish impulse to choke him. But she was proud, and she carried her head in the air, and, in effect, told Cariboo Meadows to believe as it pleased and act as it pleased. They could do no more than cut her and cause her to lose her school. She managed to keep up an air of cool indifference that gave no hint of the despairing protest that surged close to the surface. Individually and collectively, she reiterated to herself, she despised men. Her resentment had not yet extended to the women of Cariboo Meadows. They were mostly too busy with their work to be much in the foreground. She did observe, or thought she observed, a certain coolness in Mrs. Briggs' manner — a sort of suspended judgment.

In the meantime, she labored diligently at her appointed task of drilling knowledge into the heads of a dozen youngsters. From nine until three-thirty she had that to occupy her mind to the exclusion of more troublesome things. When school work for the day ended, she went to her room, or sat on the porch, or took solitary rambles in the immediate vicinity, avoiding the male contingent as she would have avoided contagious disease. Never, never, she vowed, would she trust another man as far as she could throw him.

The first Saturday after the Perkins incident, Hazel went for a tramp in the afternoon. She avoided the little hill close at hand. It left a bad taste in her mouth to look at the spot. This was foolish, and she realized that it was foolish, but she could not help the feeling — the insult was still too fresh in her mind. So she skirted its base and ranged farther afield. The few walks she had taken had lulled all sense of uneasiness in venturing into the infolding forest. She felt that those shadowy woods were less sinister than man. And since she had always kept her sense of direction and come straight to the Meadows whenever she went abroad, she had no fear or thought of losing her way.

A mile or so distant a bare spot high on a wooded ridge struck her as a likely place to get an unobstructed view. To reach some height and sit in peace, staring out over far-spreading vistas, contented her. She could put away the unpleasantness of the immediate past, discount the possible sordidness of the future, and lose herself in dreams.

To reach her objective point, she crossed a long stretch of rolling land, well timbered, dense in parts with thickets of berry bushes. Midway in this she came upon a little brook, purring a monotone as it crawled over pebbled reaches and bathed the tangled roots of trees along its brink. By this she sat a while. Then she idled along, coming after considerable difficulty to abruptly rising ground. Though in the midst of timber the sun failed to penetrate, she could always see it through the branches and so gauge her line of travel. On the hillside it was easier, for the forest thinned out. Eventually she gained a considerable height, and while she failed to reach the opening seen from the Meadows, she found another that served as well. The sun warmed it, and the sun rays were pleasant to bask in, for autumn drew close, and there was a coolness in the shade even at noon. She could not see the town, but she could mark the low hills behind it. At any rate, she knew where it lay, and the way back.

So she thought. But the short afternoon fled, and, warned by the low dip of the sun, she left her nook on the hillside to make her way home. Though it was near sundown, she felt no particular concern. The long northern twilight gave her ample time to cover the distance.

But once down on the rolling land, among the close-ranked trees, she began to experience a difficulty that had not hitherto troubled her. With the sun hanging low, she lost her absolute certainty of east and west, north and south. The forest seemed suddenly to grow confusingly dim and gloomier, almost menacing in its uncanny evening silence. The birds were hushed, and the wind.

She blundered on, not admitting to herself the possibility of being unable to find Cariboo Meadows. As best she could, and to the best of her belief, she held in a straight line for the town. But she walked far enough to have overrun it, and was yet upon unfamiliar ground. The twilight deepened. The sky above showed turquoise blue between the tall tree-tops, but the woods themselves grew blurred, dusky at a little distance ahead. Even to a seasoned woodsman, twilight in a timbered country that he does not know brings confusion; uncertainty leads him far wide of his mark. Hazel, all unused to woods travel, hurried the more, uneasy with the growing conviction that she had gone astray.

The shadows deepened until she tripped over roots and stones, and snagged her hair and clothing on branches she could not see in time to fend off. As a last resort, she turned straight for the light patch still showing in the northwest, hoping thus to cross the wagon road that ran from Soda Creek to the Meadows — it lay west, and she had gone northeast from town. And as she hurried, a fear began to tug at her that she had passed the Meadows unknowingly. If she could only cross a trail — trails always led somewhere, and she was going it blind. The immensity of the unpeopled areas she had been looking out over for a week appalled her.

Presently it was dark, and darkness in the woods is the darkness of the pit itself. She found a fallen tree, and climbed on it to rest and think. Night in gloomy places brings an eerie feeling sometimes to the bravest — dormant sense impressions, running back to the cave age and beyond, become active, harry the mind with subtle, unreasoning qualms — and she was a girl, brave enough, but out of the only environment she knew how to grapple with. All the fearsome tales of forest beasts she had ever heard rose up to harass her. She had not lifted up her voice while it was light because she was not the timid soul that cries in the face of a threatened danger. Also because she would not then admit the possibility of getting lost. And now she was afraid to call. She huddled on the log, shuddering with the growing chill of the night air, partly with dread of the long, black night itself that walled her in. She had no matches to light a fire.

After what seemed an age, she fancied she saw a gleam far distant in the timber. She watched the spot fixedly, and thought she saw the faint reflection of a light. That heartened her. She advanced toward it, hoping that it might be the gleam of a ranch window. Her progress was slow. She blundered over the litter of a forest floor, tripping over unseen obstacles. But ten minutes established beyond peradventure the fact that it was indeed a light. Whether a house light or the reflection of a camp fire she was not woodwise enough to tell. But a fire must mean human beings of one sort or another, and thereby a means to reach home.

She kept on. The wavering gleam came from behind a thicket — an open fire, she saw at length. Beyond the fire she heard a horse sneeze. Within a few yards of the thicket through which wavered the yellow gleam she halted, smitten with a sudden panic. This endured but a few seconds. All that she knew or had been told of frontier men reassured her. She had found them to a man courteous, awkwardly considerate. And she could not wander about all night.

She moved cautiously, however, to the edge of the thicket, to a point where she could see the fire. A man sat humped over the glowing embers, whereon sizzled a piece of meat. His head was bent forward, as if he were listening. Suddenly he looked up, and she gasped — for the firelight showed the features of Roaring Bill Wagstaff.

She was afraid of him. Why she did not know nor stop to reason. But her fear of him was greater than her fear of the pitch-black night and the unknown dangers of the forest. She turned to retreat. In the same instant Roaring Bill reached to his rifle and stood up.

"Hold on there!" he said coolly. "You've had a look at me — I want a look at you, old feller, whoever you are. Come on — show yourself."

He stepped sidewise out of the light as he spoke. Hazel started to run. The crack of a branch under foot betrayed her, and he closed in before she took three steps. He caught her rudely by the arm, and yanked her bodily into the firelight.

"Well — for the — love of — Mike!"

Wagstaff drawled the exclamation out in a rising crescendo of astonishment. Then he laid his gun down across a roll of bedding, and stood looking at her in speechless wonder.

CHAPTER
SEVEN

A Different Sort of Man

"For the love of Mike!" Roaring Bill said again. "What are *you* doing wandering around in the woods at night? Good Lord! Your teeth are chattering. Sit down here and get warm. It is sort of chilly."

Even in her fear, born of the night, the circumstances, and partly of the man, Hazel noticed that his speech was of a different order from that to which she had been listening the past ten days. His enunciation was perfect. He dropped no word endings, nor slurred his syllables. And cast in so odd a mold is the mind of civilized woman that the small matter of a little refinement of speech put Hazel Weir more at her ease than a volume of explanation or protest on his part would have done. She had pictured him a ruffian in thought, speech, and deed. His language cleared him on one count, and she observed that almost his first thought was for her comfort, albeit he made no sort of apology for handling her so roughly in the gloom beyond the fire.

"I got lost," she explained, growing suddenly calm. "I was out walking, and lost my way."

"Easy thing to do when you don't know timber," Bill remarked. "And in consequence you haven't had any supper; you've been scared almost to death — and probably all of Cariboo Meadows is out looking for you. Well, you've had an adventure. That's worth something. Better eat a bite, and you'll feel better."

He turned over the piece of meat on the coals while he spoke. Hazel saw that it lay on two green sticks, like a steak on a gridiron. It was quite simple, but she would never have thought of that. The meat exhaled savory odors. Also, the warmth of the fire seemed good. But —

"I'd rather be home," she confessed.

"Sure! I guess you would — naturally. I'll see that you get there, though it won't be easy. It's no snap to travel these woods in the dark. You couldn't have been so far from the Meadows. How did it come you didn't yell once in a while?"

"I didn't think it was necessary," Hazel admitted, "until it began to get dark. And then I didn't like to."

"You got afraid," Roaring Bill supplied. "Well, it does sound creepy to holler in the timber after night. I know how that goes. I've made noises after night that scared myself."

He dug some utensils out of his pack layout — two plates, knife, fork, and spoons, and laid them by the fire. Opposite the meat a pot of water bubbled. Roaring Bill produced a small tin bucket, black with the smoke of many an open fire, and a package, and made coffee.

74

Then he spread a canvas sheet, and laid on that bread, butter, salt, a jar of preserved fruit.

"How far is it to Cariboo Meadows?" Hazel asked.

Bill looked up from his supper preparations.

"You've got me," he returned carelessly. "Probably four or five miles. I'm not positive; I've been running in circles myself this afternoon."

"Good heavens!" Hazel exclaimed. "But you know the way?"

"Like a book — in the daytime," he replied. "But night in the timber is another story, as you've just been finding out for yourself."

"I thought men accustomed to the wilderness could always find their way about, day or night," Hazel observed tartly.

"They can — in stories," Bill answered dryly.

He resumed his arranging of the food while she digested this. Presently he sat down beside the fire, and while he turned the meat with a forked stick, came back to the subject again.

"You see, I'm away off any trail here," he said, "and it's all woods, with only a little patch of open here and there. It's pure accident I happen to be here at all; accident which comes of unadulterated cussedness on the part of one of my horses. I left the Meadows at noon, and Nigger — that's this confounded cayuse of mine — he had to get scared and take to the brush. He got plumb away from me, and I had to track him. I didn't come up with him till dusk, and then the first good place I struck, which was here, I made camp. I was all for catching that horse, so I didn't pay much attention to where I was going. Didn't need to, because I know the country well enough to get anywhere in daylight, and I'm fixed to camp wherever night overtakes me. So I'm not dead sure of my ground. But you don't need to worry on that account. I'll get you home all right. Only it'll be mean traveling — and slow — unless we happen to bump into some of those fellows out looking for you. They'd surely start out when you didn't come home at dusk; they know it isn't any joke for a girl to get lost in these woods. I've known men to get badly turned round right in this same country. Well, sit up and eat a bite."

She had to be satisfied with his assurance that he would see her to Cariboo Meadows. And, accepting the situation with what philosophy she could command, Hazel proceeded to fall to — and soon discovered herself relishing the food more than any meal she had eaten for a long time. Hunger is the king of appetizers, and food cooked in the open has a flavor of its own which no aproned chef can duplicate. Roaring Bill put half the piece of meat on her plate, sliced bread for her, and set the butter handy. Also, he poured her a cup of coffee. He had a small sack of sugar, and his pack boxes yielded condensed milk.

"Maybe you'd rather have tea," he said. "I didn't think to ask you. Most Canadians don't drink anything else."

"No, thanks. I like coffee," Hazel replied.

"You're not a true-blue Canuck, then," Bill observed.

"Indeed, I am," she declared. "Aren't you a Canadian?"

"Well, I don't know that the mere accident of birth in some particular locality makes any difference," he answered. "But I'm a lot shy of being a Canadian, though I've been in this country a long time. I was born in Chicago, the smokiest, windiest old burg in the United States."

"It's a big place, isn't it?" Hazel kept the conversation going. "I don't know any of the American cities, but I have a girl friend working in a Chicago office."

"Yes, it's big — big and noisy and dirty, and full of wrecks — human derelicts in an industrial Sargasso Sea — like all big cities the world over. I don't like 'em."

Wagstaff spoke casually, as much to himself as to her, and he did not pursue the subject, but began his meal.

"What sort of meat is this?" Hazel asked after a few minutes of silence. It was fine-grained and of a rich flavor strange to her mouth. She liked it, but it was neither beef, pork, nor mutton, nor any meat she knew.

"Venison. Didn't you ever eat any before?" he smiled.

"Never tasted it," she answered. "Isn't it nice? No, I've read of hunters cooking venison over an open fire, but this is my first taste. Indeed, I've never seen a real camp fire before."

"Lord — what a lot you've missed!" There was real pity in his tone. "I killed that deer to-day. In fact, the little circus I had with Mr. Buck was what started Nigger off into the brush. Have some more coffee."

He refilled her tin cup, and devoted himself to his food. Before long they had satisfied their hunger. Bill laid a few dry sticks on the fire. The flames laid hold of them and shot up in bright, wavering tongues. It seemed to Hazel that she had stepped utterly out of her world. Cariboo Meadows, the schoolhouse, and her classes seemed remote. She found herself wishing she were a man, so that she could fare into the wilds with horses and a gun in this capable man fashion, where routine went by the board and the unexpected hovered always close at hand. She looked up suddenly, to find him regarding her with a whimsical smile.

"In a few minutes," said he, "I'll pack up and try to deliver you as per contract. Meantime, I'm going to smoke."

He did not ask her permission, but filled his pipe and lighted it with a coal. And for the succeeding fifteen minutes Roaring Bill Wagstaff sat staring into the dancing blaze. Once or twice he glanced at her, and when he did the same whimsical smile would flit across his face. Hazel watched him uneasily after a time. He seemed to have forgotten her. His pipe died, and he sat holding it in his hand. She was uneasy, but not afraid. There was nothing about him or his actions to make her fear. On the contrary, Roaring Bill at close quarters inspired confidence. Why she could not and did not attempt to determine, psychological analysis being rather out of her line.

Physically, however, Roaring Bill measured up to a high standard. He was young, probably twenty-seven or thereabouts. There was power — plenty of it — in the wide shoulders and deep chest of him, with arms in proportion. His hands, while smooth on the backs and well cared for, showed when he exposed the palms the callouses of ax handling. And his face was likable, she decided, full of character, intensely masculine. In her heart every woman despises any hint of the effeminate in man. Even though she may decry what she is pleased to term the brute in man, whenever he discards the dominant, overmastering characteristics of the male she will have none of him. Miss Hazel Weir was no exception to her sex.

Consciously or otherwise she took stock of Bill Wagstaff. She knew him to be in bad odor with Cariboo Meadows for some unknown reason. She had seen him fight in the street, knock a man unconscious with his fists. According to her conceptions of behavior that was brutal and vulgar. Drinking came under the same head, and she had Jim Briggs' word that Bill Wagstaff not only got drunk, but was a "holy terror" when in that condition. Yet she could not quite associate the twin traits of brutality and vulgarity with the man sitting close by with that thoughtful look on his face. His speech stamped him as a man of education; every line of him showed breeding in all that the word implies.

Nevertheless, he was "tough." And she had gathered enough of the West's wide liberality of view in regard to personal conduct to know that Roaring Bill Wagstaff must be a hard citizen indeed to be practically ostracized in a place like Cariboo Meadows. She wondered what Cariboo Meadows would say if it could see her sitting by Bill Wagstaff's fire at nine in the evening in the heart of the woods. What would they say when he piloted her home?

In the midst of her reflections Roaring Bill got up.

"Well, we'll make a move," he said, and disappeared abruptly into the dark.

She heard him moving around at some distance. Presently he was back, leading three horses. One he saddled. The other two he rigged with his pack outfit, storing his varied belongings in two pair of kyaks, and loading kyaks and bedding on the horses with a deft speed that bespoke long practice. He was too busy to talk, and Hazel sat beside the fire, watching in silence. When he had tucked up the last rope end, he turned to her.

"There," he said; "we're ready to hit the trail. Can you ride?"

"I don't know," Hazel answered dubiously. "I never have ridden a horse."

"My, my!" he smiled. "Your education has been sadly neglected — and you a schoolma'am, too!"

"My walking education hasn't been neglected," Hazel retorted. "I don't need to ride, thank you."

"Yes, and stub your toe and fall down every ten feet," Bill observed. "No, Miss Weir, your first lesson in horsemanship is now due — if you aren't afraid of horses."

"I'm not afraid of horses at all," Hazel declared. "But I don't think it's a very good place to take riding lessons. I can just as well walk, for I'm not in the least afraid." And then she added as an afterthought: "How do you happen to know my name?"

"In the same way that you know mine," Bill replied, "even if you haven't mentioned it yet. Lord bless you, do you suppose Cariboo Meadows could import a lady school-teacher from the civilized East without everybody in fifty miles knowing who she was, and where she came from, and what she looked like? You furnished them a subject for conversation and speculation — the same as I do when I drop in there and whoop it up for a while. I guess you don't realize what old granny gossips we wild Westerners are. Especially where girls are concerned."

Hazel stiffened a trifle. She did not like the idea of Cariboo Meadows discussing her with such freedom. She was becoming sensitive on that subject — since the coming and going of Mr. Howard Perkins, for she felt that they were considering her from an angle that she did not relish. She wondered also if Roaring Bill Wagstaff had heard that gossip. And if he had — At any rate, she could not accuse him of being impertinent or curious in so far as she was concerned. After the first look and exclamation of amazement he had taken her as a matter of course. If anything, his personal attitude was tinctured with indifference.

"Well," said he, "we won't argue the point."

He disappeared into the dark again. This time he came back with the crown of his hat full of water, which he sprinkled over the dwindling fire. As the red glow of the embers faded in a sputter of steam and ashes, Hazel realized more profoundly the blackness of a cloudy night in the woods. Until her eyes accustomed themselves to the transition from firelight to the gloom, she could see nothing but vague shapes that she knew to be the horses, and another dim, moving object that was Bill Wagstaff. Beyond that the inky canopy above and the forest surrounding seemed a solid wall.

"It's going to be nasty traveling, Miss Weir," Roaring Bill spoke at her elbow. "I'll walk and lead the packs. You ride Silk. He's gentle. All you have to do is sit still, and he'll stay right behind the packs. I'll help you mount."

If Hazel had still been inclined to insist on walking, she had no chance to debate the question. Bill took her by the arm and led her up beside the horse. It was a unique experience for her, this being compelled to do things. No man had ever issued ultimatums to her. Even Jack Barrow, with all an accepted lover's privileges, had never calmly told her that she must do thus and so, and acted on the supposition that his word was final. But here was Roaring Bill Wagstaff telling her how to put her foot in the stirrup, putting her for the first time in her life astride a horse, warning her to duck low branches. In his mind there seemed to be no question as whether or not she would ride. He had settled that.

Unused to mounting, she blundered at the first attempt, and flushed in the dark at Bill's amused chuckle. The next instant he caught her under the arms, and, with the leverage of her one foot in the stirrup, set her gently in the seat of the saddle.

"You're such a little person," he said, "these stirrups are a mile too long. Put your feet in the leather above — so. Now play follow your leader. Give Silk his head."

He moved away. The blurred shapes of the pack horses forged ahead, rustling in the dry grass, dry twigs snapping under foot. Obedient to Bill's command, she let the reins dangle, and Silk followed close behind his mates. Hazel lurched unsteadily at first, but presently she caught the swinging motion and could maintain her balance without holding stiffly to the saddle horn.

They crossed the small meadow and plunged into thick woods again. For the greater part of the way Hazel could see nothing; she could tell that Wagstaff and the pack horses moved before her by the sounds of their progress, and that was all. Now and then low-hanging limbs reached suddenly out of the dark, and touched her with unseen fingers, or swept rudely across her face and hair.

The night seemed endless as the wilderness itself. Unused to riding, she became sore, and then the sore muscles stiffened. The chill of the night air intensified. She grew cold, her fingers numb. She did not know where she was going, and she was assailed with doubts of Roaring Bill's ability to find Cariboo Meadows.

For what seemed to her an interminable length of time they bore slowly on through timber, crossed openings where the murk of the night thinned a little, enabling her to see the dim form of Wagstaff plodding in the lead. Again they dipped down steep slopes and ascended others as steep, where Silk was forced to scramble, and Hazel kept a precarious seat. She began to feel, with an odd heart sinking, that sufficient time had elapsed for them to reach the Meadows, even by a roundabout way. Then, as they crossed a tiny, gurgling stream, and came upon a level place beyond, Silk bumped into the other horses and stopped. Hazel hesitated a second. There was no sound of movement.

"Mr. Wagstaff!" she called.

"Yours truly," his voice hailed back, away to one side. "I'll be there in a minute."

In less time he appeared beside her.

"Will you fall off, or be lifted off?" he said cheerfully.

"Where are we?" she demanded.

"Ask me something easy," he returned. "I've been going it blind for an hour, trying to hit the Soda Creek Trail, or any old trail that would show me where I am. It's no use. Too dark. A man couldn't find his way over country that he knew to-night if he had a lantern and a compass."

"What on earth am I going to do?" Hazel cried desperately.

"Camp here till daylight," Roaring Bill answered evenly. "The only thing you can do. Good Lord!" His hand accidentally rested on hers. "You're like ice. I didn't think about you getting cold riding. I'm a mighty thoughtless escort, I'm afraid. Get down and put on a coat, and I'll have a fire in a minute."

"I suppose if I must, I must; but I can get off without any help, thank you," Hazel answered ungraciously.

Roaring Bill made no reply, but stood back, and when her feet touched solid earth he threw over her shoulders the coat he had worn himself. Then he turned away, and Hazel saw him stooping here and there, and heard the crack of dry sticks broken over his knee. In no time he was back to the horses with an armful of dry stuff, and had a small blaze licking up

84

through dry grass and twigs. As it grew he piled on larger sticks till the bright flame waved two feet high, lighting up the near-by woods and shedding a bright glow on the three horses standing patiently at hand. He paid no attention to Hazel until she came timidly up to the fire. Then he looked up at her with his whimsical smile.

"That's right," he said; "come on and get warm. No use worrying — or getting cross. I suppose from your civilized, conventional point of view it's a terrible thing to be out in the woods all night alone with a strange man. But I'm not a bear — I won't eat you."

"I'm sorry if I seemed rude," Hazel said penitently; Roaring Bill's statement was reassuring in its frankness. "I can't help thinking of the disagreeable side of it. People talk so. I suppose I'll be a nine days' wonder in Cariboo Meadows."

Bill laughed softly.

"Let them take it out in wondering," he advised. "Cariboo Meadows is a very small and insignificant portion of the world, anyway."

He went to one of the packs, and came back with a canvas cover, which he spread on the ground.

"Sit on that," he said. "The earth's always damp in the woods."

Then he stripped the horses of their burdens and tied them out of sight among the trees. That task finished, he took his ax and rustled a pile of wood, dragging dead poles up to the fire and chopping them into short lengths. When finally he laid aside his ax, he busied himself with gathering grass and leaves and pine needles until he had several armfuls collected and spread in an even pile to serve as a mattress. Upon this he laid his bedding, two thick quilts, two or three pairs of woolen blankets, a pillow, the whole inclosed with a long canvas sheet, the bed tarpaulin of the cattle ranges.

"There," he said; "you can turn in whenever you feel like it."

For himself he took the saddle blankets and laid them close by the fire within reaching distance of the woodpile, taking for cover a pack canvas. He stretched himself full length, filled his pipe, lit it, and fell to staring into the fire while he smoked.

Half an hour later he raised his head and looked across the fire at Hazel.

"Why don't you go to bed?" he asked.

"I'm not sleepy," she declared, which was a palpable falsehood, for her eyelids were even then drooping.

"Maybe not, but you need rest," Bill said quietly. "Quit thinking things. It'll be all the same a hundred years from now. Go on to bed. You'll be more comfortable."

Thus peremptorily commanded, Hazel found herself granting instant obedience. The bed, as Bill had remarked, was far more comfortable than sitting by the fire. She got into the blankets just as she stood, even to her shoes, and drew the canvas sheet up so that it hid her face — but did not prevent her from seeing.

In spite of herself, she slept fitfully. Now and then she would wake with a start to a half-frightened realization of her surroundings and plight, and whenever she did wake and look past the fire it was to see Roaring Bill Wagstaff stretched out in the red glow, his brown head pillowed on one folded arm. Once she saw him reach to the wood without moving his body and lay a stick on the fire.

Then all at once she wakened out of sound slumber with a violent start. Roaring Bill was shaking the tarpaulin over her and laughing.

"Arise, Miss Sleeping Beauty!" he said boyishly. "Breakfast's ready."

He went back to the fire. Hazel sat up, patting her tousled hair into some semblance of order. Off in the east a reddish streak spread skyward into somber gray. In the west, black night gave ground slowly.

"Well, it's another day," she whispered, as she had whispered to herself once before. "I wonder if there will ever be any more like it?"

CHAPTER
EIGHT

In Deep Water

The dawn thrust aside night's somber curtains while they ate, revealing a sky overcast with slaty clouds. What with her wanderings of the night before and the journey through the dark with Roaring Bill, she had absolutely no idea of either direction or locality. The infolding timber shut off the outlook. Forest-clad heights upreared here and there, but no landmark that she could place and use for a guide. She could not guess whether Cariboo Meadows was a mile distant, or ten, nor in what direction it might lie. If she had not done so before, she now understood how much she had to depend on Roaring Bill Wagstaff.

"Do you suppose I can get home in time to open school?" she inquired anxiously.

Roaring Bill smiled. "I don't know," he answered. "It all depends."

Upon what it depended he did not specify, but busied himself packing up. In half an hour or less they were ready to start. Bill spent a few minutes longer shortening the stirrups, then signified that she should mount. He seemed more thoughtful, less inclined to speech.

"You know where you are now, don't you?" she asked.

"Not exactly," he responded. "But I will before long — I hope."

The ambiguity of his answer did not escape her. She puzzled over it while Silk ambled sedately behind the other horses. She hoped that Bill Wagstaff knew where he was going. If he did not — but she refused to entertain the alternative. And she began to watch eagerly for some sign of familiar ground.

For two hours Roaring Bill tramped through aisles bordered with pine and spruce and fir, through thickets of berry bush, and across limited areas of grassy meadow. Not once did they cross a road or a trail. With the clouds hiding the sun, she could not tell north from south after they left camp. Eventually Bill halted at a small stream to get a drink. Hazel looked at her watch. It was half past eight.

"Aren't we ever going to get there?" she called impatiently.

"Pretty soon," he called back, and struck out briskly again.

Another hour passed. Ahead of her, leading one pack horse and letting the other follow untrammeled, Roaring Bill kept doggedly on, halting for nothing, never looking back. If he did not know where he was going, he showed no hesitation. And Hazel had no choice but to follow.

They crossed a ravine and slanted up a steep hill-side. Presently Hazel could look away over an area of woodland undulating like a heavy ground swell at sea. Here and there ridges stood forth boldly above the general roll, and distantly she could descry a white-capped mountain range. They turned the end of a thick patch of pine scrub, and Bill pulled up in a small opening. From a case swinging at his belt he took out a pair of field glasses, and leisurely surveyed the country.

"Well?" Hazel interrogated.

She herself had cast an anxious glance over the wide sweep below and beyond, seeing nothing but timber and hills, with the silver thread of a creek winding serpentwise through the green. But of habitation or trail there was never a sign. And it was after ten o'clock. They were over four hours from their camp ground.

"Nothing in sight, is there?" Bill said thoughtfully. "If the sun was out, now. Funny I can't spot that Soda Creek Trail."

"Don't you know this country at all?" she asked gloomily.

"I thought I did," he replied. "But I can't seem to get my bearings to work out correctly. I'm awfully sorry to keep you in such a pickle. But it can't be helped."

Thus he disarmed her for the time being. She could not find fault with a man who was doing his best to help her. If Roaring Bill were unable to bear straight for the Meadows, it was unfortunate for her, but no fault of his. At the same time, it troubled her more than she would admit.

"Well, we won't get anywhere standing on this hill," he remarked at length.

He took up the lead rope and moved on. They dropped over the ridge crest and once more into the woods. Roaring Bill made his next halt beside a spring, and fell to unlashing the packs.

"What are you going to do?" Hazel asked.

"Cook a bite, and let the horses graze," he told her. "Do you realize that we've been going since daylight? It's near noon. Horses have to eat and rest once in a while, just the same as human beings."

The logic of this Hazel could not well deny, since she herself was tired and ravenously hungry. By her watch it was just noon.

Bill hobbled out his horses on the grass below the spring, made a fire, and set to work cooking. For the first time the idea of haste seemed to have taken hold of him. He worked silently at the meal getting, fried steaks of venison, and boiled a pot of coffee. They ate. He filled his pipe, and smoked while he repacked. Altogether, he did not consume more than forty minutes at the noon halt. Hazel, now woefully saddle sore, would fain have rested longer, and, in default of resting, tried to walk and lead Silk. Roaring Bill offered no objection to that. But he hit a faster gait. She could not keep up, and he did not slacken pace when she began to fall behind. So she mounted awkwardly, and Silk jolted and shook her with his trotting until he caught up with his mates. Bill grinned over his shoulder.

"You're learning fast," he called back. "You'll be able to run a pack train by and by."

The afternoon wore on without bringing them any nearer Cariboo Meadows so far as Hazel could see. Traveling over a country swathed in timber and diversified in contour, she could not tell whether Roaring Bill swung in a circle or bore straight for some given point. She speculated futilely on the outcome of the strange plight she was in. It was a far cry from pounding a typewriter in a city office to jogging through the wilderness, lost beyond peradventure, her only company a stranger of unsavory reputation. Yet she was not frightened, for all the element of unreality. Under other circumstances she could have relished the adventure, taken pleasure in faring gypsy fashion over the wide reaches where man had left no mark. As it was —

She called a halt at four o'clock.

"Mr. Wagstaff!"

Bill stopped his horses and came back to her.

"Aren't we *ever* going to get anywhere?" she asked soberly.

"Sure! But we've got to keep going. Got to make the best of a bad job," he returned. "Getting pretty tired?"

"I am," she admitted. "I'm afraid I can't ride much longer. I could walk if you wouldn't go so fast. Aren't there any ranches in this country at all?"

He shook his head. "They're few and far between," he said. "Don't worry, though. It isn't a life-and-death matter. If we were out here without grub or horses it might be tough. You're in no danger from exposure or hunger."

"You don't seem to realize the position it puts me in," Hazel answered. A wave of despondency swept over her, and her eyes grew suddenly bright with the tears she strove to keep back. "If we wander around in the woods much longer, I'll simply be a sensation when I do get back to Cariboo Meadows. I won't have a shred of reputation left. It will probably result in my losing the school. You're a man, and it's different with you. You can't know what a girl has to contend with where no one knows her. I'm a stranger in this country, and what little they do know of me —"

She stopped short, on the point of saying that what Cariboo Meadows knew of her through the medium of Mr. Howard Perkins was not at all to her credit.

Roaring Bill looked up at her impassively. "I know," he said, as if he had read her thought. "Your friend Perkins talked a lot. But what's the difference? Cariboo Meadows is only a fleabite. If you're right, and you know you're right, you can look the world in the eye and tell it collectively to go to the devil. Besides, you've got a perverted idea. People aren't so ready to give you the bad eye on somebody else's say-so. It would take a lot more than a flash drummer's word to convince me that you're a naughty little girl. Pshaw — forget it!"

Hazel colored hotly at his mention of Perkins, but for the latter part of his speech she could have hugged him. Bill Wagstaff went a long way, in those brief sentences, toward demolishing her conviction that no man ever overlooked an opportunity of taking advantage of a woman. But Bill said nothing further. He stood a moment longer by her horse, resting one hand on Silk's mane, and scraping absently in the soft earth with the toe of his boot.

"Well, let's get somewhere," he said abruptly. "If you're too saddle sore to ride, walk a while. I'll go slower."

She walked, and the exercise relieved the cramping ache in her limbs. Roaring Bill's slower pace was fast enough at that. She followed till her strength began to fail. And when in spite of her determination she lagged behind, he stopped at the first water.

"We'll camp here," he said. "You're about all in, and we can't get anywhere to-night, I see plainly."

Hazel accepted this dictum as best she could. She sat down on a mossy rock while he stripped the horses of their gear and staked them out. Then Bill started a fire and fixed the roll of bedding by it for her to sit on. Dusk crept over the forest while he cooked supper, making a bannock in the frying pan to take the place of bread; and when they had finished eating and washed the few dishes, night shut down black as the pit.

They talked little. Hazel was in the grip of utter forlornness, moody, wishful to cry. Roaring Bill humped on his side of the fire, staring thoughtfully into the blaze. After a long period of abstraction he glanced at his watch, then arose and silently arranged her bed. After that he spread his saddle blankets and lay down.

Hazel crept into the covers and quietly sobbed her self to sleep. The huge and silent land appalled her. She had been chucked neck and crop into the primitive, and she had not yet been able to react to her environment. She was neither faint-hearted nor hysterical. The grind of fending for herself in a city had taught her the necessity of self-control. But she was worn out, unstrung, and there is a limit to a woman's endurance.

As on the previous night, she wakened often and glanced over to the fire. Roaring Bill kept his accustomed position, flat in the glow. She had no fear of him now. But he was something of an enigma. She had few illusions about men in general. She had encountered a good many of them in one way and another since reaching the age when she coiled her hair on top of her head. And she could not recall one — not even Jack Barrow — with whom she would have felt at ease in a similar situation. She knew that there was a something about her that drew men. If the presence of her had any such effect on Bill Wagstaff, he painstakingly concealed it.

And she was duly grateful for that. She had not believed it a characteristic of his type — the virile, intensely masculine type of man. But she had not once found him looking at her with the same expression in his eyes that she had seen once over Jim Briggs' dining table.

Night passed, and dawn ushered in a clearing sky. Ragged wisps of clouds chased each other across the blue when they set out again. Hazel walked the stiffness out of her muscles before she mounted. When she did get on Silk, Roaring Bill increased his pace. He was long-legged and light of foot, apparently tireless. She asked no questions. What was the use? He would eventually come out somewhere. She was resigned to wait.

After a time she began to puzzle, and the old uneasiness came back. The last trailing banner of cloud vanished, and the sun rode clear in an opal sky, smiling benignly down on the forested land. She was thus enabled to locate the cardinal points of the compass. Wherefore she took to gauging their course by the shadows. And the result was what set her thinking. Over level and ridge and swampy hollow, Roaring Bill drove straight north in an undeviating line. She recollected that the point from which she had lost her way had lain northeast of Cariboo Meadows. Even if they had swung in a circle, they could scarcely be pointing for the town in that direction. For another hour Bill held to the northern line as a needle holds to the pole. A swift rush of misgiving seized her.

"Mr. Wagstaff!" she called sharply.

Roaring Bill stopped, and she rode Silk up past the pack horses.

"Where are you taking me?" she demanded.

"Why, I'm taking you home — or trying to," he answered mildly.

"But you're going *north*," she declared. "You've been going north all morning. I was north of Cariboo Meadows when I got lost. How can we get back to Cariboo Meadows by going still farther north?"

"You're more of a woodsman than I imagined," Bill remarked gently. He smiled up at her, and drew out his pipe and tobacco pouch.

She looked at him for a minute. "Do you know where we are now?" she asked quietly.

He met her keen gaze calmly. "I do," he made laconic answer.

"Which way is Cariboo Meadows, then, and how far is it?" she demanded.

"General direction south," he replied slowly. "Fifty miles more or less. Rather more than less."

"And you've been leading me straight north!" she cried. "Oh, what am I going to do?"

"Keep right on going," Wagstaff answered.

"I won't — I won't!" she flashed. "I'll find my own way back. What devilish impulse prompted you to do such a thing?"

"You'll have a beautiful time of it," he said dryly, completely ignoring her last question. "Take you three days to walk there — if you knew every foot of the way. And you don't know the way. Traveling in timber is confusing, as you've discovered. You'll never see Cariboo Meadows, or any other place, if you tackle it single-handed, without grub or matches or bedding. It's fall, remember. A snowstorm is due any time. This is a whopping big country. A good many men have got lost in it — and other men have found their bones."

He let this sink in while she sat there on his horse choking back a wild desire to curse him by bell, book, and candle for what he had done, and holding in check the fear of what he might yet do. She knew him to be a different type of man from any she had ever encountered. She could not escape the conclusion that Roaring Bill Wagstaff was something of a law unto himself, capable of hewing to the line of his own desires at any cost. She realized her utter helplessness, and the realization left her without words. He had drawn a vivid picture, and the instinct of self-preservation asserted itself.

"You misled me." She found her voice at last. "Why?"

"Did I mislead you?" he parried. "Weren't you already lost when you came to my camp? And have I mistreated you in any manner? Have I refused you food, shelter, or help?"

"My home is in Cariboo Meadows," she persisted. "I asked you to take me there. You led me away from there deliberately, I believe now."

"My trail doesn't happen to lead to Cariboo Meadows, that's all," Roaring Bill coolly told her. "If you must go back there, I shan't restrain you in any way whatever. But I'm for home myself. And that," he came close, and smiled frankly up at her, "is a better place than Cariboo Meadows. I've got a little house back there in the woods. There's a big fireplace where the wind plays tag with the snowflakes in winter time. There's grub there, and meat in the forest, and fish in the streams. It's home for me. Why should I go back to Cariboo Meadows? Or you?"

"Why should *I* go with you?" she demanded scornfully.

"Because I want you to," he murmured.

They matched glances for a second, Wagstaff smiling, she half horrified.

"Are you clean mad?" she asked angrily. "I was beginning to think you a gentleman."

Bill threw back his head and laughed. Then on the instant he sobered. "Not a gentleman," he said. "I'm just plain man. And lonesome sometimes for a mate, as nature has ordained to be the way of flesh."

"Get a squaw, then," she sneered. "I've heard that such people as you do that."

"Not me," he returned, unruffled. "I want a woman of my own kind."

"Heaven save *me* from that classification!" she observed, with emphasis on the pronoun.

"Yes?" he drawled. "Well, there's no profit in arguing that point. Let's be getting on."

He reached for the lead rope of the nearest pack horse.

Hazel urged Silk up a step. "Mr. Wagstaff," she cried, "I *must* go back."

"You can't go back without me," he said. "And I'm not traveling that way, thank you."

"Please — oh, please!" she begged forlornly.

Roaring Bill's face hardened. "I will not," he said flatly. "I'm going to play the game my way. And I'll play fair. That's the only promise I will make."

She took a look at the encompassing woods, and her heart sank at facing those shadowy stretches alone and unguided. The truth of his statement that she would never reach Cariboo Meadows forced itself home. There was but the one way out, and her woman's wit would have to save her.

"Go on, then," she gritted, in a swift surge of anger. "I am afraid to face this country alone. I admit my helplessness. But so help me Heaven, I'll make you pay for this dirty trick! You're not a man! You're a cur — a miserable, contemptible scoundrel!"

"Whew!" Roaring Bill laughed. "Those are pretty names. Just the same, I admire your grit. Well, here we go!"

He took up the lead rope, and went on without even looking back to see if she followed. If he had made the slightest attempt to force her to come, if he had betrayed the least uncertainty as to whether she would come, Hazel would have swung down from the saddle and set her face stubbornly southward in sheer defiance of him. But such is the peculiar complexity of a woman that she took one longing glance backward, and then fell in behind the packs. She was weighted down with dread of the unknown, boiling over with rage at the man who swung light-footed in the lead; but nevertheless she followed him.

CHAPTER
NINE

The House that Jack Built

All the rest of that day they bore steadily northward. Hazel had no idea of Bill Wagstaff's destination. She was too bitter against him to ask, after admitting that she could not face the wilderness alone. Between going it alone and accompanying him, it seemed to be a case of choosing the lesser evil. Curiously she felt no fear of Bill Wagstaff in person, and she did have a dread vision of what might happen to her if she went wandering alone in the woods. There was one loophole left to comfort her. It seemed scarcely reasonable that they could fare on forever without encountering other frontier folk. Upon that possibility she based her hopes of getting back to civilization, not so much for love of civilization as to defeat Roaring Bill's object, to show him that a woman had to be courted rather than carried away against her will by any careless, strong-armed male. She knew nothing of the North, but she thought there must be some mode of communication or transportation. If she could once get in touch with other people — well, she would show

Roaring Bill. Of course, getting back to Cariboo Meadows meant a new start in the world, for she had no hope, nor any desire, to teach school there after this episode. She found herself facing that prospect unmoved, however. The important thing was getting out of her present predicament.

Roaring Bill made his camp that night as if no change in their attitude had taken place. To all his efforts at conversation she turned a deaf ear and a stony countenance. She proposed to eat his food and use his bedding, because that was necessary. But socially she would have none of him. Bill eventually gave over trying to talk. But he lost none of his cheerfulness. He lay on his own side of the fire, regarding her with the amused tolerance that one bestows upon the capricious temper of a spoiled child.

Thereafter, day by day, the miles unrolled behind them. Always Roaring Bill faced straight north. For a week he kept on tirelessly, and a consuming desire to know how far he intended to go began to take hold of her. But she would not ask, even when daily association dulled the edge of her resentment, and she found it hard to keep up her hostile attitude, to nurse bitterness against a man who remained serenely unperturbed, and who, for all his apparent lawlessness, treated her as a man might treat his sister.

To her unpracticed eye, the character of the country remained unchanged except for minor variations. Everywhere the timber stood in serried ranks, spotted with lakes and small meadows, and threaded here and there with little streams. But at last they dropped into a valley where the woods thinned out, and down the center of which flowed a sizable river. This they followed north a matter of three days. On the west the valley wall ran to a timbered ridge. Eastward the jagged peaks of a snow-capped mountain chain pierced the sky.

Two hours from their noon camp on the fourth day in the valley Hazel sighted some moving objects in the distance, angling up on the timber-patched hillside. She watched them, at first uncertain whether they were moose, which they had frequently encountered, or domestic animals. Accustomed by now to gauging direction at a glance toward the sun, she observed that these objects traveled south.

Presently, as the lines of their respective travel brought them nearer, she made them out to be men, mounted, and accompanied by packs. She counted the riders — five, and as many pack horses. One, she felt certain, was a woman — whether white or red she could not tell. But — there was safety in numbers. And they were going south.

Upon her first impulse she swung off Silk, and started for the hillside, at an angle calculated to intercept the pack train. There was a chance, and she was rapidly becoming inured to taking chances. At a distance of a hundred yards, she looked back, half fearful that Roaring Bill was at her heels. But he stood with his hands in his pockets, watching her. She did not look again until she was half a mile up the hill. Then he and his packs had vanished.

So, too, had the travelers that she was hurrying to meet. Off the valley floor, she no longer commanded the same sweeping outlook. The patches of timber intervened. As she kept on, she became more uncertain. But she bore up the slope until satisfied that she was parallel with where they should come out; then she stopped to rest. After a few minutes she climbed farther, endeavoring to reach a point whence she could see more of the slope. In so far had she absorbed woodcraft that she now began watching for tracks. There were enough of these, but they were the slender, triangle prints of the shy deer. Nothing resembling the hoofmark of a horse rewarded her searching. And before long, what with turning this way and that, she found herself on a plateau where the pine and spruce stood like bristles in a brush, and from whence she could see neither valley below nor hillside above.

She was growing tired. Her feet ached from climbing, and she was wet with perspiration. She rested again, and tried calling. But her voice sounded muffled in the timber, and she soon gave over that. The afternoon was on the wane, and she began to think of and dread the coming of night. Already the sun had dipped out of sight behind the western ridges; his last beams were gilding the blue-white pinnacles a hundred miles to the east. The shadows where she sat were thickening. She had given up hope of finding the pack train, and she had cut loose from Roaring Bill. It would be just like him to shrug his shoulders and keep on going, she thought resentfully.

As twilight fell a brief panic seized her, followed by frightened despair. The wilderness, in its evening hush, menaced her with huge emptinesses, utter loneliness. She worked her way to the edge of the wooded plateau. There was a lingering gleam of yellow and rose pink on the distant mountains, but the valley itself lay in a blur of shade, out of which rose the faint murmur of running water, a monotone in the silence. She sat down on a dead tree, and cried softly to herself.

"Well?"

She started, with an involuntary gasp of fear, it was so unexpected. Roaring Bill Wagstaff stood within five feet of her, resting one hand on the muzzle of his grounded rifle, smiling placidly.

"Well," he repeated, "this chasing up a pack train isn't so easy as it looks, eh?"

She did not answer. Her pride would not allow her to admit that she was glad to see him, relieved to be overtaken like a truant from school. And Bill did not seem to expect a reply. He slung his rifle into the crook of his arm.

"Come on, little woman," he said gently. "I knew you'd be tired, and I made camp down below. It isn't far."

Obediently she followed him, and as she tramped at his heels she saw why he had been able to come up on her so noiselessly. He had put on a pair of moccasins, and his tread gave forth no sound.

"How did you manage to find me?" she asked suddenly — the first voluntary speech from her in days.

Bill answered over his shoulder:

105

"Find you? Bless your soul, your little, high-heeled shoes left a trail a one-eyed man could follow. I've been within fifty yards of you for two hours.

"Just the same," he continued, after a minute's interval, "it's bad business for you to run off like that. Suppose you played hide and seek with me till a storm wiped out your track? You'd be in a deuce of a fix."

She made no reply. The lesson of the experience was not lost on her, but she was not going to tell him so.

In a short time they reached camp. Roaring Bill had tarried long enough to unpack. The horses grazed on picket. It was borne in upon her that short of actually meeting other people her only recourse lay in sticking to Bill Wagstaff, whether she liked it or not. To strike out alone was courting self-destruction. And she began to understand why Roaring Bill made no effort to watch or restrain her. He knew the grim power of the wilderness. It was his best ally in what he had set out to do.

Within forty-eight hours the stream they followed merged itself in another, both wide and deep, which flowed west through a level-bottomed valley three miles or more in width. Westward the land spread out in a continuous roll, marked here and there with jutting ridges and isolated peaks; but on the east a chain of rugged mountains marked the horizon as far as she could see.

Roaring Bill halted on the river brink and stripped his horses clean, though it was but two in the afternoon and their midday fire less than an hour extinguished.

She watched him curiously. When his packs were off he beckoned her.

"Hold them a minute," he said, and put the lead ropes in her hand.

Then he went up the bank into a thicket of saskatoons. Out of this he presently emerged, bearing on his shoulders a canoe, old and weather-beaten, but stanch, for it rode light as a feather on the stream. Bill seated himself in the canoe, holding to Silk's lead rope. The other two he left free.

"Now," he directed, "when I start across, you drive Nigger and Satin in if they show signs of hanging back. Bounce a rock or two off them if they lag."

Her task was an easy one, for Satin and Nigger followed Silk unhesitatingly. The river lapped along the sleek sides of them for fifty yards. Then they dropped suddenly into swimming water, and the current swept them downstream slantwise for the opposite shore, only their heads showing above the surface. Hazel wondered what river it might be. It was a good quarter of a mile wide, and swift.

Roaring Bill did not trouble to enlighten her as to the locality. When he got back he stowed the saddle and pack equipment in the canoe.

"All aboard for the north side," he said boyishly. And Hazel climbed obediently amidships.

On the farther side, Bill emptied the canoe, and stowed it out of sight in a convenient thicket, repacked his horses, and struck out again. They left the valley behind, and camped that evening on a great height of land that rolled up to the brink of the valley.

107

Thereafter the country underwent a gradual change as they progressed north, slanting a bit eastward. The heavy timber gave way to a sparser growth, and that in turn dwindled to scrubby thickets, covering great areas of comparative level. Long reaches of grassland opened before them, waving yellow in the autumn sun. They crossed other rivers of various degrees of depth and swiftness, swimming some and fording others. Hazel drew upon her knowledge of British Columbia geography, and decided that the big river where Bill hid his canoe must be the Fraser where it debouched from the mountains. And in that case she was far north, and in a wilderness indeed.

Her muscles gradually hardened to the saddle and to walking. Her appetite grew in proportion. The small supply of eatable dainties that Roaring Bill had brought from the Meadows dwindled and disappeared, until they were living on bannocks baked à la frontier in his frying pan, on beans and coffee, and venison killed by the way. Yet she relished the coarse fare even while she rebelled against the circumstances of its partaking. Occasionally Bill varied the meat diet with trout caught in the streams beside which they made their various camps. He offered to teach her the secrets of angling, but she shrugged her shoulders by way of showing her contempt for Roaring Bill and all his works.

"Do you realize," she broke out one evening over the fire, "that this is simply abduction?"

"Not at all," Bill answered promptly. "Abduction means to take away surreptitiously by force, to carry away wrongfully and by violence any human being, to

108

kidnap. Now, you can't by any stretch of the imagination accuse me of force, violence, or kidnaping — not by a long shot. You merely wandered into my camp, and it wasn't convenient for me to turn back. Therefore circumstances — not my act, remember — made it advisable for you to accompany me. Of course I'll admit that, according to custom and usage, you would expect me to do the polite thing and restore you to your own stamping ground. But there's no law making it mandatory for a fellow to pilot home a lady in distress. Isn't that right?

"Anyhow," he went on, when she remained silent, "I didn't. And you'll have to lay the blame on nature for making you a wonderfully attractive woman. I did honestly try to find the way to Cariboo Meadows that first night. It was only when I found myself thinking how fine it would be to pike through these old woods and mountains with a partner like you that I decided — as I did. I'm human — the woman, she tempted me. And aren't you better off? I could hazard a guess that you were running away from yourself — or something — when you struck Cariboo Meadows. And what's Cariboo Meadows but a little blot on the face of this fair earth, where you were tied to a deadly routine in order to earn your daily bread? You don't care two whoops about anybody there. Here you are free — free in every sense of the word. You have no responsibility except what you impose on yourself; no board bills to pay; nobody to please but your own little self. You've got the clean, wide land for a bedroom, and the sky for its ceiling, instead of a stuffy little ten-by-ten chamber.

Do you know that you look fifty per cent better for these few days of living in the open — the way every normal being likes to live? You're getting some color in your cheeks, and you're losing that worried, archangel look. Honest, if I were a physician, I'd have only one prescription: Get out into the wild country, and live off the country as your primitive forefathers did. Of course, you can't do that alone. I know because I've tried it. We humans don't differ so greatly from the other animals. We're made to hunt in couples or packs. There's a purpose, a law, you might say, behind that, too; only it's terribly obscured by a lot of other nonessentials in this day and age.

"Is there any comparison between this sort of life, for instance — if it appeals to one at all — and being a stenographer and bucking up against the things any good-looking, unprotected girl gets up against in a city? You know, if you'd be frank, that there isn't. Shucks! Herding in the mass, and struggling for a mere subsistence, like dogs over a bone, degenerates man physically, mentally, and morally — all our vaunted civilization and culture to the contrary notwithstanding. Eh?"

But she would not take up the cudgels against him, would not seem to countenance or condone his offense by discussing it from any angle whatsoever. And she was the more determined to allow no degree of friendliness, even in conversation, because she recognized the masterful quality of the man. She told herself that she could have liked Roaring Bill Wagstaff very well if he had not violated what she considered the rules of the game. And she had no mind to allow his personality to sweep her off her feet in the same determined manner that he had carried her into the wilderness. She was no longer afraid of him. She occasionally forgot, in spite of herself, that she had a deep-seated grievance against him. At such times the wild land, the changing vistas the journey opened up, charmed her into genuine enjoyment. She would find herself smiling at Bill's quaint tricks of speech. Then she would recollect that she was, to all intents and purposes, a prisoner, the captive of his bow and spear. That was maddening.

After a lapse of time they dropped into another valley, and faced westward to a mountain range which Bill told her was the Rockies. The next day a snowstorm struck them. At daybreak the clouds were massed overhead, lowering, and a dirty gray. An uncommon chill, a rawness of atmosphere foretold the change. And shortly after they broke camp the first snowflakes began to drift down, slowly at first, then more rapidly, until the grayness of the sky and the misty woods were enveloped in the white swirl of the storm. It was not particularly cold. Bill wrapped her in a heavy canvas coat, and plodded on. Noon passed, and he made no stop. If anything, he increased his pace.

Suddenly, late in the afternoon, they stepped out of the timber into a little clearing, in which the blurred outline of a cabin showed under the wide arms of a leafless tree.

The melting snow had soaked through the coat; her feet were wet with the clinging flakes, and the chill of a lowering temperature had set Hazel shivering.

111

Roaring Bill halted at the door and lifted her down from Silk's back without the formality of asking her leave. He pulled the latchstring, and led her in. Beside the rude stone fireplace wood and kindling were piled in readiness for use. Bill kicked the door shut, dropped on his knees, and started the fire. In five minutes a great blaze leaped and crackled into the wide throat of the chimney. Then he piled on more wood, and turned to her.

"This is the house that Jack built," he said, with a sober face and a twinkle in his gray eyes. "This is the man that lives in the house that Jack built. And this" — he pointed mischievously at her — "is the woman who's going to love the man that lives in the house that Jack built."

"That's a lie!" she flashed stormily through her chattering teeth.

"Well, we'll see," he answered cheerfully. "Get up here close to the fire and take off those wet things while I put away the horses."

And with that he went out, whistling.

CHAPTER
TEN

A Little Personal History

Hazel discarded the wet coat, and, drawing a chair up to the fire, took off her sopping footgear and toasted her bare feet at the blaze. Her clothing was also wet, and she wondered pettishly how in the world she was going to manage with only the garments on her back — and those dirty and torn from hacking through the brush for a matter of two weeks. According to her standards, that was roughing it with a vengeance. But presently she gave over thinking of her plight. The fire warmed her, and, with the chill gone from her body, she bestowed a curious glance on her surroundings.

Her experience of homes embraced only homes of two sorts — the middle-class, conventional sort to which she had been accustomed, and the few poorly furnished frontier dwellings she had entered since coming to the hinterlands of British Columbia. She had a vague impression that any dwelling occupied exclusively by a man must of necessity be dirty, disordered, and cheerless. But she had never seen a room such as the one she now found herself in. It conformed to none of her preconceived ideas.

There was furniture of a sort unknown to her, tables and chairs fashioned by hand with infinite labor and rude skill, massive in structure, upholstered with the skins of wild beasts common to the region. Upon the walls hung pictures, dainty black-and-white prints, and a water color or two. And between the pictures were nailed heads of mountain sheep and goat, the antlers of deer and caribou. Above the fire-place spread the huge shovel horns of a moose, bearing across the prongs a shotgun and fishing rods. The center of the floor — itself, as she could see, of hand-smoothed logs — was lightened with a great black and red and yellow rug of curious weave. Covering up the bare surface surrounding it were bearskins, black and brown. Her feet rested in the fur of a monster silvertip, fur thicker and softer than the pile of any carpet ever fabricated by man. All around the walls ran shelves filled with books. A guitar stood in one corner, a mandolin in another. The room was all of sixteen by twenty feet, and it was filled with trophies of the wild — and books.

Except for the dust that had gathered lightly in its owner's absence, the place was as neat and clean as if the housemaid had but gone over it. Hazel shrugged her shoulders. Roaring Bill Wagstaff became, if anything, more of an enigma than ever, in the light of his dwelling. She recollected that Cariboo Meadows had regarded him askance, and wondered why.

He came in while her gaze was still roving from one object to another, and threw his wet outer clothing, boy fashion, on the nearest chair.

"Well," he said, "we're here."

"Please don't forget, Mr. Wagstaff," she replied coldly, "that I would much prefer *not* to be here."

He stood a moment regarding her with his odd smile. Then he went into the adjoining room. Out of this he presently emerged, dragging a small steamer trunk. He opened it, got down on his knees, and pawed over the contents. Hazel, looking over her shoulder, saw that the trunk was filled with woman's garments, and sat amazed.

"Say, little person," Bill finally remarked, "it looks to me as if you could outfit yourself completely right here."

"I don't know that I care to deck myself in another woman's finery, thank you," she returned perversely.

"Now, see here," Roaring Bill turned reproachfully; "see here —"

He grinned to himself then, and went again into the other room, returning with a small, square mirror. He planted himself squarely in front of her, and held up the glass. Hazel took one look at her reflection, and she could have struck Roaring Bill for his audacity. She had not realized what an altogether disreputable appearance a normally good-looking young woman could acquire in two weeks on the trail, with no toilet accessories and only the clothes on her back. She tried to snatch the mirror from him, but Bill eluded her reach, and laid the glass on the table.

115

"You'll feel a whole better able to cope with the situation," he told her smilingly, "when you get some decent clothes on and your hair fixed. That's a woman. And you don't need to feel squeamish about these things. This trunk's got a history, let me tell you. A bunch of simon-pure tenderfeet strayed into the mountains west of here a couple of summers ago. There were two women in the bunch. The youngest one, who was about your age and size, must have had more than her share of vanity. I guess she figured on charming the bear and the moose, or the simple aborigines who dwell in this neck of the woods. Anyhow, she had all kinds of unnecessary fixings along, that trunkful of stuff in the lot. You can imagine what a nice time their guides had packing that on a horse, eh? They got into a deuce of a pickle finally, and had to abandon a lot of their stuff, among other things the steamer trunk. I lent them a hand, and they told me to help myself to the stuff. So I did after they were out of the country. That's how you come to have a wardrobe all ready to your hand. Now, you'd be awful foolish to act like a mean and stiff-necked female person. You're not going to, are you?" he wheedled. "Because I want to make you comfortable. What's the use of getting on your dignity over a little thing like clothes?"

"I don't intend to," Hazel suddenly changed front. "I'll make myself as comfortable as I can — particularly if it will put you to any trouble."

"You're bound to scrap, eh?" he grinned. "But it takes two to build a fight, and I positively refuse to fight with *you*."

116

He dragged the trunk back into the room, and came out carrying a great armful of masculine belongings. Two such trips he made, piling all his things onto a chair.

"There!" he said at last. "That end of the house belongs to you, little person. Now, get those wet things off before you catch a cold. Oh, wait a minute!"

He disappeared into the kitchen end of the house, and came back with a wash-basin and a pail of water.

"Your room is now ready, madam, an it please you." He bowed with mock dignity, and went back into the kitchen.

Hazel heard him rattling pots and dishes, whistling cheerfully the while. She closed the door, and busied herself with an inventory of the tenderfoot lady's trunk. In it she found everything needful for complete change, and a variety of garments to boot. Folded in the bottom of the trunk was a gray cloth skirt and a short blue silk kimono. There was a coat and skirt, too, of brown corduroy. But the feminine instinct asserted itself, and she laid out the gray skirt and the kimono.

For a dresser Roaring Bill had fashioned a wide shelf, and on it she found a toilet set complete — hand mirror, military brushes, and sundry articles, backed with silver and engraved with his initials. Perhaps with a spice of malice, she put on a few extra touches. There would be some small satisfaction in tantalizing Bill Wagstaff — even if she could not help feeling that it might be a dangerous game. And, thus arrayed in the weapons of her sex, she slipped on the kimono, and

117

went into the living-room to the cheerful glow of the fire.

Bill remained busy in the kitchen. Dusk fell. The gleam of a light showed through a crack in the door. In the big room only the fire gave battle to the shadows, throwing a ruddy glow into the far corners. Presently Bill came in with a pair of candles which he set on the mantel above the fireplace.

"By Jove!" he said, looking down at her. "You look good enough to eat! I'm not a cannibal, however," he continued hastily, when Hazel flushed. She was not used to such plain speaking. "And supper's ready. Come on!"

The table was set. Moreover, to her surprise — and yet not so greatly to her surprise, for she was beginning to expect almost anything from this paradoxical young man — it was spread with linen, and the cutlery was silver, the dishes china, in contradistinction to the tinware of his camp outfit.

As a cook Roaring Bill Wagstaff had no cause to be ashamed of himself, and Hazel enjoyed the meal, particularly since she had eaten nothing since six in the morning. After a time, when her appetite was partially satisfied, she took to glancing over his kitchen. There seemed to be some adjunct of a kitchen missing. A fire burned on a hearth similar to the one in the living room. Pots stood about the edge of the fire. But there was no sign of a stove.

Bill finished eating, and resorted to cigarette material instead of his pipe.

"Well, little person," he said at last, "what do you think of this joint of mine, anyway?"

"I've just been wondering," she replied. "I don't see any stove, yet you have food here that looks as if it were baked, and biscuits that must have been cooked in an oven."

"You see no stove for the good and sufficient reason," he returned, "that you can't pack a stove on a horse — and we're three hundred odd miles from the end of any wagon road. With a Dutch oven or two — that heavy, round iron thing you see there — I can guarantee to cook almost anything you can cook on a stove. Anybody can if they know how. Besides, I like things better this way. If I didn't, I suppose I'd have a stove — and maybe a hot-water supply, and modern plumbing. As it is, it affords me a sort of prideful satisfaction, which you may or may not be able to understand, that this cabin and everything in it is the work of my hands — of stuff I've packed in here with all sorts of effort from the outside. Maybe I'm a freak. But I'm proud of this place. Barring the inevitable lonesomeness that comes now and then, I can be happier here than any place I've ever struck yet. This country grows on one."

"Yes — on one's nerves," Hazel retorted.

Bill smiled, and, rising, began to clear away the dishes. Hazel resisted an impulse to help. She *would* not work; she would not lift her finger to any task, she reminded herself. He had put her in her present position, and he could wait on her. So she rested an

119

elbow on the table and watched him. In the midst of his work he stopped suddenly.

"There's oceans of time to do this," he observed. "I'm just a wee bit tired, if anybody should ask you. Let's camp in the other room. It's a heap more comfy."

He put more wood on the kitchen fire, and set a pot of water to heat. Out in the living-room Hazel drew her chair to one side of the hearth. Bill sprawled on the bearskin robe with another cigarette in his fingers.

"No," he began, after a long silence, "this country doesn't get on one's nerves — not if one is a normal human being. You'll find that. When I first came up here I thought so, too; it seemed so big and empty and forbidding. But the more I see of it the better it compares with the outer world, where the extremes of luxury and want are always in evidence. It began to seem like home to me when I first looked down into this little basin. I had a partner then. I said to him: 'Here's a dandy, fine place to winter.' So we wintered — in a log shack sixteen foot square that Silk and Satin and Nigger have for a stable now. When summer came my partner wanted to move on, so I stayed. Stayed and began to build for the next winter. And I've been working at it ever since, making little things like chairs and tables and shelves, and fixing up game heads whenever I got an extra good one. And maybe two or three times a year I'd go out. Get restless, you know. I'm not really a hermit by nature. Lord, the things I've packed in here from the outside! Books — I hired a whole pack train at Ashcroft once to bring in just books; they thought I was crazy, I guess. I've quit this place once or twice, but I always come back. It's got that home feel that I can't find anywhere else. Only it has always lacked one important home qualification," he finished softly. "Do you ever build air castles?"

"No," Hazel answered untruthfully, uneasy at the trend of his talk. She was learning that Bill Wagstaff, for all his gentleness and patience with her, was a persistent mortal.

"Well, I do," he continued, unperturbed. "Lots of 'em. But mostly around one thing — a woman — a dream woman — because I never saw one that seemed to fit in until I ran across you."

"Mr. Wagstaff," Hazel pleaded, "won't you please stop talking like that? It isn't — it isn't —"

"Isn't proper, I suppose," Bill supplied dryly. "Now, that's merely an error, and a fundamental error on your part, little person. Our emotion and instincts are perfectly proper when you get down to fundamentals. You've got an artificial standard to judge by, that's all. And I don't suppose you have the least idea how many lives are spoiled one way and another by the operation of those same artificial standards in this little old world. Now, I may seem to you a lawless, unprincipled individual indeed, because I've acted contrary to your idea of the accepted order of things. But here's my side of it: I'm in search of happiness. We all are. I have a few ideals — and very few illusions. I don't quite believe in this thing called love at first sight. That presupposes a volatility of emotion that people of any strength of character are not likely to indulge in. But — for instance, a man can have a very definite ideal of the

121

kind of woman he would like for a mate, the kind of woman he could be happy with and could make happy. And whenever he finds a woman who corresponds to that ideal he's apt to make a strenuous attempt to get her. That's pretty much how I felt about you."

"You had no right to kidnap me," Hazel cried.

"You had no business getting lost and making it possible for me to carry you off," Bill replied. "Isn't that logic?"

"I'll never forgive you," Hazel flashed. "It was treacherous and unmanly. There are other ways of winning a woman."

"There wasn't any other way open to me." Bill grew suddenly moody. "Not with you in Cariboo Meadows. I'm taboo there. You'd have got a history of me that would have made you cut me dead; you may have had the tale of my misdeeds for all I know. No, it was impossible for me to get acquainted with you in the conventional way. I knew that, and so I didn't make any effort. Why, I'd have been at your elbow when you left the supper table at Jim Briggs' that night if I hadn't known how it would be. I went there out of sheer curiosity to take a look at you — maybe out of a spirit of defiance, too, because I knew that I was certainly not welcome even if they were willing to take my money for a meal. And I came away all up in the air. There was something about you — the tone of your voice, the way your proud little head is set on your shoulders, your make-up in general — that sent me away with a large-sized grouch at myself, at Cariboo Meadows, and at you for coming in my way."

"Why?" she asked in wonder.

"Because you'd have believed what they told you, and Cariboo Meadows can't tell anything about me that isn't bad," he said quietly. "My record there makes me entirely unfit to associate with — that would have been your conclusion. And I wanted to be with you, to talk to you, to take you by storm and make you like me as I felt I could care for you. You can't have grown up, little person, without realizing that you do attract men very strongly. All women do, but some far more than others."

"Perhaps," she admitted coldly. "Men have annoyed me with their unwelcome attentions. But none of them ever dared go the length of carrying me away against my will. You can't explain or excuse that."

"I'm not attempting excuses," Bill made answer. "There are two things I never do — apologize or bully. I dare say that's one reason the Meadows gives me such a black eye. In the first place, the confounded, ignorant fools did me a very great injustice, and I've never taken the trouble to explain to them wherein they were wrong. I came into this country with a partner six years ago — a white man, if ever one lived — about the only real man friend I ever had. He was known to have over three thousand dollars on his person. He took sick and died the second year, at the head of the Peace, in midwinter. I buried him; couldn't take him out. Somehow the yarn got to going in the Meadows that I'd murdered him for his money. The gossip started there because we had an argument about outfitting while we were there, and roasted each other as only real

123

pals can. So they got it into their heads I killed him, and tried to have the provincial police investigate. It made me hot, and so I wouldn't explain to anybody the circumstances, nor what became of Dave's three thousand, which happened to be five thousand by that time, and which I sent to his mother and sister in New York, as he told me to do when he was dying. When they got to hinting things the next time I hit the Meadows, I started in to clean out the town. I think I whipped about a dozen men that time. And once or twice every season since I've been in the habit of dropping in there and raising the very devil out of sheer resentment. It's a wonder some fellow hasn't killed me, for it's a fact that I've thrashed every man in the blamed place except Jim Briggs — and some of them two or three times. And I make them line up at the bar and drink at my expense, and all that sort of foolishness.

"That may sound to you like real depravity," he concluded, "but it's a fact in nature that a man has to blow the steam off his chest about every so often. I have got drunk in Cariboo Meadows, and I have raised all manner of disturbances there, partly out of pure animal spirits, and mostly because I had a grudge against them. Consequently I really have given them reason to look askance at any one — particularly a nice girl from the East — who would have anything to do with me. If they weren't a good deal afraid of me, and always laying for a chance to do me up, they wouldn't let me stay in the town overnight. So you can see what a handicap I was under when it came to making your acquaintance and courting you in the orthodox manner."

"You've made a great mistake," she said bitterly, "if you think you've removed the handicap. I've suffered a great deal at the hands of men in the past six months. I'm beginning to believe that all men are brutes at heart."

Roaring Bill sat up and clasped his hands over his knees and stared fixedly into the fire.

"No," he said slowly, "all men are not brutes — any more than all women are angels. I'll convince you of that."

"Take me home, then," she cried forlornly. "That's the only way you can convince me or make amends."

"No," Bill murmured, "that isn't the way. Wait till you know me better. Besides, I couldn't take you out now if I wanted to without exposing you to greater hardships than you'll have to endure here. Do you realize that it's fall, and we're in the high latitudes? This snow may not go off at all. Even if it does it will storm again before a week. You couldn't wallow through snow to your waist in forty-below-zero weather."

"People will pass here, and I'll get word out," Hazel asserted desperately.

"What good would that do you? You've got too much conventional regard for what you term your reputation to send word to Cariboo Meadows that you're living back here with Roaring Bill Wagstaff, and won't some one please come and rescue you." He paused to let that sink in, then continued: "Besides, you won't see a white face before spring; then only by accident. No one in the

125

North, outside of a few Indians, has ever seen this cabin or knows where it stands."

She sat there, dumb, raging inwardly. For the minute she could have killed Roaring Bill. She who had been so sure in her independence carried, whether or no, into the heart of the wilderness at the whim of a man who stood a self-confessed rowdy, in ill repute among his own kind. There was a slumbering devil in Miss Hazel Weir, and it took little to wake her temper. She looked at Bill Wagstaff, and her breast heaved. He was responsible, and he could sit coolly talking about it. The resentment that had smoldered against Andrew Bush and Jack Barrow concentrated on Roaring Bill as the arch offender of them all. And lest she yield to a savage impulse to scream at him, she got up and ran into the bedroom, slammed the door shut behind her, and threw herself across the bed to muffle the sound of her crying in a pillow.

After a time she lifted her head. Outside, the wind whistled gustily around the cabin corners. In the hushed intervals she heard a steady pad, pad, sounding sometimes close by her door, again faintly at the far end of the room. A beam of light shone through the generous latchstring hole in the door. Stealing softly over, she peeped through this hole. From end to end of the big room and back again Roaring Bill paced slowly, looking straight ahead of him with a fixed, absent stare, his teeth closed on his nether lip. Hazel blinked wonderingly. Many an hour in the last three months she had walked the floor like that, biting her lip in mental agony. And then, while she was looking, Bill abruptly extinguished the candles. In the red gleam from the hearth she saw him go into the kitchen, closing the door softly. After that there was no sound but the swirl of the storm brushing at her window.

CHAPTER
ELEVEN

Winter — and a Truce

In line with Roaring Bill's forecast, the weather cleared for a brief span, and then winter shut down in earnest. Successive falls of snow overlaid the earth with a three-foot covering, loose and feathery in the depths of the forest, piled in hard, undulating windrows in the scattered openings. Daily the cold increased, till a half-inch layer of frost stood on the cabin panes. The cold, intense, unremitting, lorded it over a vast realm of wood and stream; lakes and rivers were locked fast under ice, and through the clear, still nights the aurora flaunted its shimmering banners across the northern sky.

But within the cabin they were snug and warm. Bill's ax kept the woodpile high. The two fireplaces shone red the twenty-four hours through. Of flour, tea, coffee, sugar, beans, and such stuff as could only be gotten from the outside he had a plentiful supply. Potatoes and certain vegetables that he had grown in a cultivated patch behind the cabin were stored in a deep cellar. He could always sally forth and get meat. And the ice was no bar to fishing, for he would cut a hole, sink a small net, and secure overnight a week's supply of trout and whitefish. Thus their material wants were provided for.

As time passed Hazel gradually shook off a measure of her depression, thrust her uneasiness and resentment into the background. As a matter of fact, she resigned herself to getting through the winter, since that was inevitable. She was out of the world, the only world she knew, and by reason of the distance and the snows there was scant chance of getting back to that world while winter gripped the North. The spring might bring salvation. But spring was far in the future, too far ahead to dwell upon. As much as possible, she refrained from thinking, wisely contenting herself with getting through one day after another.

And in so doing she fell into the way of doing little things about the house, finding speedily that time flew when she busied herself at some task in the intervals of delving in Roaring Bill's library.

She could cook — and she did. Her first meal came about by grace of Roaring Bill's absence. He was hunting, and supper time drew nigh. She grew hungry, and, on the impulse of the moment, turned herself loose in the kitchen — largely in a mood for experiment. She had watched Bill make all manner of things in his Dutch ovens, and observed how he prepared meat over the glowing coals often enough to get the hang of it. Wherefore, her first meal was a success. When Roaring Bill came in, an hour after dark, he found her with cheeks rosy from leaning over the fire, and a better meal than he could prepare all waiting for him. He washed and sat down. Hazel discarded her flour-sack apron and took her place opposite. Bill made no comment until he had finished and lighted a cigarette.

"You're certainly a jewel, little person," he drawled then. "How many more accomplishments have you got up your sleeve?"

"Do you consider ordinary cooking an accomplishment?" she returned lightly.

"I surely do," he replied, "when I remember what an awful mess I made of it on the start. I certainly did spoil a lot of good grub."

After that they divided the household duties, and Hazel forgot that she had vowed to make Bill Wagstaff wait on her hand and foot as the only penalty she could inflict for his misdeeds. It seemed petty when she considered the matter, and there was nothing petty about Hazel Weir. If the chance ever offered, she would make him suffer, but in the meantime there was no use in being childish.

She did not once experience the drear loneliness that had sat on her like a dead weight the last month before she turned her back on Granville and its unhappy associations. For one thing, Bill Wagstaff kept her intellectually on the jump. He was always precipitating an argument or discussion of some sort, in which she invariably came off second best. His scope of knowledge astonished her, as did his language. Bill mixed slang, the colloquialisms of the frontier, and the terminology of modern scientific thought with quaint impartiality. There were times when he talked clear over her head. And he was by turns serious and boyish, with always a saving sense of humor. So that she was eternally discovering new sides to him.

The other refuge for her was his store of books. Upon the shelves she found many a treasure-trove — books that she had promised herself to read some day when she could buy them and had leisure. Roaring Bill had collected bits of the world's best in poetry and fiction; and last, but by no means least, the books that stand for evolution and revolution, philosophy, economics, sociology, and the kindred sciences. Bill was not orderly. He could put his finger on any book he wanted, but on his shelves like as not she would find a volume of Haeckel and another of Bobbie Burns side by side, or a last year's novel snuggling up against a treatise on social psychology. She could not understand why a man — a young man — with the intellectual capacity to digest the stuff that Roaring Bill frequently became immersed in should choose to bury himself in the wilderness. And once, in an unguarded moment, she voiced that query. Bill closed a volume of Nietzsche, marking the place with his forefinger, and looked at her thoughtfully over the book.

"Well," he said, "there are one or two good and sufficient reasons, to which you, of course, may not agree. First, though, I'll venture to assert that your idea of the nature and purpose of life as we humans know and experience it is rather hazy. Have you ever seriously asked yourself why we exist as entities at all? And, seeing that we do find ourselves possessed of this existence, what constrains us to act along certain lines?"

Hazel shook her head. That was an abstraction which she had never considered. She had been too busy living to make a critical analysis of life. She had the average girl's conception of life, when she thought of it at all, as a state of being born, of growing up, of marrying, of trying to be happy, and ultimately — very remotely — of dying. And she had also the conventional idea that activity in the world, the world as she knew it, the doing of big things in a public or semipublic way, was the proper sphere for people of exceptional ability. But why this should be so, what law, natural or fabricated by man, made it so she had never asked herself. She had found it so, and taken it for granted. Roaring Bill Wagstaff was the first man to cross her path who viewed the struggle for wealth and fame and power as other than inevitable and desirable.

"You see, little person," he went on, "we have some very definite requirements which come of the will to live that dominates all life. We must eat, we must protect our bodies against the elements, and we need for comfort some sort of shelter. But in securing these essentials to self-preservation where is the difference, except in method, between the banker who manipulates millions and the post-hole digger on the farm? Not a darned bit, in reality. They're both after exactly the same thing — security against want. If the post-hole digger's wants are satisfied by two dollars a day he is getting the same result as the banker, whose standard of living crowds his big income. Having secured the essentials, then, what is the next urge of life?

Happiness. That, however, brings us to a more abstract question.

"In the main, though, that's my answer to your question. Here I can secure myself a good living — as a matter of fact, I can easily get the wherewithal to purchase any luxuries that I desire — and it is gotten without a petty-larceny struggle with my fellow men. Here I exploit only natural resources, take only what the earth has prodigally provided. Why should I live in the smoke and sordid clutter of a town when I love the clean outdoors? The best citizen is the man with a sound mind and a strong, healthy body; and the only obligation any of us has to society is not to be a burden on society. So I live in the wilds the greater part of the year, I keep my muscles in trim, and I have always food for myself and for any chance wayfarer — and I can look everybody in the eye and tell them to go to the fiery regions if I happen to feel that way. What business would I have running a grocery store, or a bank, or a real-estate office, when all my instincts rebel against it? What normal being wants to be chained to a desk between four walls eight or ten hours a day fifty weeks in the year? I'll bet a nickel there was many a time when you were clacking a typewriter for a living that you'd have given anything to get out in the green fields for a while. Isn't that so?"

Hazel admitted it.

"You see," Bill concluded, "this civilization of ours, with its peculiar business ethics, and its funny little air of importance, is a comparatively recent thing — a product of the last two or three thousand years, to give

133

it its full historic value. And mankind has been a great many millions of years in the making, all of which has been spent under primitive conditions. So that we are as yet barbarians, savages even, with just a little veneer. Why, man, as such, is only beginning to get a glimmering of his relation to the universe. Pshaw, though! I didn't set out to deliver a lecture on evolution. But, believe me, little person, if I thought that any great good or happiness would result from my being elsewhere, from scrapping with my fellows in the world crush, I'd be there with both feet. Do you think you'd be more apt to care for me if I were to get out and try to set the world afire with great deeds?"

"That wasn't the question," she returned distantly, trying, as she always did, to keep him off the personal note.

"But it is the question with me," he declared. "I don't know why I let you go on flouting me." He reached over and caught her arm with a grip that made her wince. The sudden leap of passion into his eyes quickened the beat of her heart. "I could break you in two with my hands without half trying — tame you as the cave men tamed their women, by main strength. But I don't — by reason of the same peculiar feeling that would keep me from kicking a man when he was down, I suppose. Little person, why can't you like me better?"

"Because you tricked me," she retorted hotly. "Because I trusted you, and you used that trust to lead me farther astray. Any woman would hate a man for that. What do you suppose — you, with your knowledge

134

of life — the world will think of me when I get out of here?"

But Roaring Bill had collected himself, and sat smiling, and made no reply. He looked at her thoughtfully for a few seconds, then resumed his reading of the Mad Philosopher, out of whose essays he seemed to extract a great deal of quiet amusement.

A day or two after that Hazel came into the kitchen and found Bill piling towels, napkins, and a great quantity of other soiled articles on an outspread tablecloth.

"Well," she inquired, "what are you going to do with those?"

"Take 'em to the laundry," he laughed. "Collect your dirty duds, and bring them forth."

"Laundry!" Hazel echoed. It seemed rather a farfetched joke.

"Sure! You don't suppose we can get along forever without having things washed, do you?" he replied. "I don't mind housework, but I do draw the line at a laundry job when I don't *have* to do it. Go on — get your clothes."

So she brought out her accumulation of garments, and laid them on the pile. Bill tied up the four corners of the tablecloth.

"Now," said he, "let's see if we can't fit you out for a more or less extended walk. You stay in the house altogether too much these days. That's bad business. Nothing like exercise in the fresh air."

Thus in a few minutes Hazel fared forth, wrapped in Bill's fur coat, a flap-eared cap on her head, and on her feet several pairs of stockings inside moccasins that Bill had procured from some mysterious source a day or two before.

The day was sunny, albeit the air was hazy with multitudes of floating frost particles, and the tramp through the forest speedily brought the roses back to her cheeks. Bill carried the bundle of linen on his back, and trudged steadily through the woods. But the riddle of his destination was soon read to her, for a two-mile walk brought them out on the shore of a fair-sized lake, on the farther side of which loomed the conical lodges of an Indian camp.

"You sabe now?" said he as they crossed the ice. "This bunch generally comes in here about this time, and stays till spring. I get the squaws to wash for me. Ever see Mr. Indian on his native heath?"

Hazel never had, and she was duly interested, even if a trifle shy of the red brother who stared so fixedly. She entered a lodge with Bill, and listened to him make laundry arrangements in broken English with a withered old beldame whose features resembled a ham that had hung overlong in the smokehouse. Two or three blanketed bucks squatted by the fire that sent its blue smoke streaming out the apex of the lodge.

"Heap fine squaw!" one suddenly addressed Bill. "Where you ketchum?"

Bill laughed at Hazel's confusion. "Away off." He gestured southward, and the Indian grunted some unintelligible remark in his own tongue — at which Roaring Bill laughed again.

136

Before they started home Bill succeeded in purchasing, after much talk, a pair of moccasins that Hazel conceded to be a work of art, what with the dainty pattern of beads and the ornamentation of colored porcupine quills. Her feminine soul could not cavil when Bill thrust them in the pocket of her coat, even if her mind was set against accepting any peace tokens at his hands.

And so in the nearing sunset they went home through the frost-bitten woods, where the snow crunched and squeaked under their feet, and the branches broke off with a pistol-like snap when they were bent aside.

A hundred yards from the cabin Bill challenged her to a race. She refused to run, and he picked her up bodily, and ran with her to the very door. He held her a second before he set her down, and Hazel's face whitened. She could feel his breath on her cheek, and she could feel his arms quiver, and the rapid beat of his heart. For an instant she thought Roaring Bill Wagstaff was about to make the colossal mistake of trying to kiss her.

But he set her gently on her feet and opened the door. And by the time he had his heavy outer clothes off and the fires started up he was talking whimsically about their Indian neighbors, and Hazel breathed more freely. The clearest impression that she had, aside from her brief panic, was of his strength. He had run with her as easily as if she had been a child.

After that they went out many times together. Bill took her hunting, initiated her into the mysteries of rifle

137

shooting, and the manipulation of a six-shooter. He taught her to walk on snowshoes, lightly over the surface of the crusted snow, through which otherwise she floundered. A sort of truce arose between them, and the days drifted by without untoward incident. Bill tended to his horses, chopped wood, carried water. She took upon herself the care of the house. And through the long evenings, in default of conversation, they would sit with a book on either side of the fireplace that roared defiance to the storm gods without.

And sometimes Hazel would find herself wondering why Roaring Bill Wagstaff could not have come into her life in a different manner. As it was — she never, *never* would forgive him.

CHAPTER
TWELVE

The Fires of Spring

There came a day when the metallic brilliancy went out of the sky, and it became softly, mistily blue. All that forenoon Hazel prowled restlessly out of doors without cap or coat. There was a new feel in the air. The deep winter snow had suddenly lost its harshness. A tentative stillness wrapped the North as if the land rested a moment, gathering its force for some titanic effort.

Toward evening a mild breeze freshened from the southwest. The tender blue of the sky faded at sundown to a slaty gray. Long wraiths of cloud floated up with the rising wind. At ten o'clock a gale whooped riotously through the trees. And at midnight Hazel wakened to a sound that she had not heard in months. She rose and groped her way to the window. The encrusting frost had vanished from the panes. They were wet to the touch of her fingers. She unhooked the fastening, and swung the window out. A great gust of damp, warm wind blew strands of hair across her face. She leaned through the casement, and drops of cold water struck her bare neck. That which she had heard was the dripping eaves. The chinook wind droned its spring song, and the bare boughs of the tree beside the cabin waved and creaked the time. Somewhere distantly a wolf lifted up his voice, and the long, throaty howl swelled in a lull of the wind. It was black and ghostly outside, and strange, murmuring sounds rose and fell in the surrounding forests, as though all the dormant life of the North was awakening at the seasonal change. She closed the window and went back to bed.

At dawn the eaves had ceased their drip, and the dirt roof laid bare to the cloud-banked sky. From the southwest the wind still blew strong and warm. The thick winter garment of the earth softened to slush, and vanished with amazing swiftness. Streams of water poured down every depression. Pools stood between the house and stable. Spring had leaped strong-armed upon old Winter and vanquished him at the first onslaught.

All that day the chinook blew, working its magic upon the land. When day broke again with a clearing sky, and the sun peered between the cloud rifts, his beams fell upon vast areas of brown and green, where but forty-eight hours gone there was the cold revelry of frost sprites upon far-flung fields of snow. Patches of earth steamed wherever a hillside lay bare to the sun. From some mysterious distance a lone crow winged his way, and, perching on a near-by treetop, cawed raucous greeting.

Hazel cleared away the breakfast things, and stood looking out the kitchen window. Roaring Bill sat on a log, shirt-sleeved, smoking his pipe. Presently he went over to the stable, led out his horses, and gave them their liberty. For twenty minutes or so he stood watching their mad capers as they ran and leaped and pranced back and forth over the clearing. Then he walked off into the timber, his rifle over one shoulder.

Hazel washed her dishes and went outside. The cabin sat on a benchlike formation, a shoulder of the mountain behind, and she could look away westward across miles and miles of timber, darkly green and merging into purple in the distance. It was a beautiful land — and lonely. She did not know why, but all at once a terrible feeling of utter forlornness seized her. It was spring — and also it was spring in other lands. The wilderness suddenly took on the characteristics of a prison, in which she was sentenced to solitary confinement. She rebelled against it, rebelled against her surroundings, against the manner of her being there, against everything. She hated the North, she wished to be gone from it, and most of all she hated Bill Wagstaff for constraining her presence there. In six months she had not seen a white face, nor spoken to a woman of her own blood. Out beyond that sea of forest lay the big, active world in which she belonged, of which she was a part, and she felt that she must get somewhere, do something, or go mad.

All the heaviness of heart, all the resentment she had felt in the first few days when she followed him perforce away from Cariboo Meadows, came back to her with redoubled force that forenoon. She went back into the house, now gloomy without a fire, slumped forlornly into a chair, and cried herself into a condition approaching hysteria. And she was sitting there, her head bowed on her hands, when Bill returned from his hunting. The sun sent a shaft through the south window, a shaft which rested on her drooping head. Roaring Bill walked softly up behind her and put his hand on her shoulder.

"What is it, little person?" he asked gently.

She refused to answer.

"Say," he bent a little lower, "you know what the Tentmaker said:

"'Come fill the cup, and in the fire of Spring
    Your Winter garment of Repentance fling;
The Bird of Time has but a little way
    To flutter — and the Bird is on the Wing.'

"Life's too short to waste any of it in being uselessly miserable. Come on out and go for a ride on Silk. I'll take you up on a mountainside, and show you a waterfall that leaps three hundred feet in the clear. The woods are waking up and putting on their Easter bonnets. There's beauty everywhere. Come along!"

She wrenched herself away from him.

"I want to go home!" she wailed. "I hate you and the North, and everything in it. If you've got a spark of manhood left in you, you'll take me out of here."

Roaring Bill backed away from her. "Do you mean that? Honest Injun?" he asked incredulously.

"I do — I do!" she cried vehemently. "Haven't I told you often enough? I didn't come here willingly, and I won't stay. I will not! I have a right to live my life in my own way, and it's not this way."

142

"So," Roaring Bill began evenly, "springtime with you only means getting back to work. You want to get back into the muddled rush of peopled places, do you? For what? To teach a class in school, or to be some business shark's slave of the typewriter at ten dollars a week? You want to be where you can associate with fluffy-ruffle, pompadoured girls, and be properly introduced to equally proper young men. Lord, but I seem to have made a mistake! And, by the same token, I'll probably pay for it — in a way you wouldn't understand if you lived a thousand years. Well, set your mind at rest. I'll take you out. I'll take you back to your stamping-ground if that's what you crave. Ye gods and little fishes, but I have sure been a fool!"

He sat down on the edge of the table, and Hazel blinked at him, half scared, and full of wonder. She had grown so used to seeing him calm, imperturbable, smiling cheerfully no matter what she said or did, that his passionate outbreak amazed her. She could only sit and look at him.

He got out his cigarette materials. But his fingers trembled, spilling the tobacco. And when he tore the paper in his efforts to roll it, he dashed paper and all into the fireplace with something that sounded like an oath, and walked out of the house. Nor did he return till the sun was well down toward the tree-rimmed horizon. When he came back he brought in an armful of wood and kindling, and began to build a fire. Hazel came out of her room. Bill greeted her serenely.

"Well, little person," he said, "I hope you'll perk up now."

143

"I'll try," she returned. "Are you really going to take me out?"

Bill paused with a match blazing in his fingers.

"I'm not in the habit of saying things I don't mean," he answered dryly. "We'll start in the morning."

The dark closed in on them, and they cooked and ate supper in silence. Bill remained thoughtful and abstracted. He slouched for a time in his chair by the fire. Then from some place among his books he unearthed a map, and, spreading it on the table, studied it a while. After that he dragged in his kyaks from outside, and busied himself packing them with supplies for a journey — tea and coffee and flour and such things done up in small canvas sacks.

And when these preparations were complete he got a sheet of paper and a pencil, and fell to copying something from the map. He was still at that, sketching and marking, when Hazel went to bed.

By all the signs and tokens, Roaring Bill Wagstaff slept none that night. Hazel herself tossed wakefully, and during her wakeful moments she could hear him stir in the outer room. And a full hour before daylight he called her to breakfast.

CHAPTER
THIRTEEN

The Out Trail

"This time last spring," Bill said to her, "I was piking away north of those mountains, bound for the head of the Naas to prospect for gold."

They were camped in a notch on the tiptop of a long divide, a thousand feet above the general level. A wide valley rolled below, and from the height they overlooked two great, sinuous lakes and a multitude of smaller ones. The mountain range to which Bill pointed loomed seventy miles distance, angling northwest. The sun glinted on the snow-capped peaks, though they themselves were in the shadow.

"I've been wondering," Hazel said. "This country somehow seems different. You're not going back to Cariboo Meadows, are you?"

Bill bestowed a look of surprise on her.

"I should say not!" he drawled. "Not that it would make any difference to me. But I'm very sure *you* don't want to turn up there in my company."

"That's true," she observed. "But all the clothes and all the money I have in the world are there."

"Don't let money worry you," he said briefly. "I have got plenty to see you through. And you can easily buy clothes."

They were now ten days on the road. Their course had lain across low, rolling country, bordered by rugged hills, spotted with lakes, and cut here and there by streams that put Bill Wagstaff to many strange shifts in crossing. But upon leaving this camp they crossed a short stretch of low country, and then struck straight into the heart of a mountainous region. Steadily they climbed, reaching up through gloomy cañons where foaming cataracts spilled themselves over sheer walls of granite, where the dim and narrow pack trail was crossed and recrossed with the footprints of bear and deer and the snowy-coated mountain goat. The spring weather held its own, and everywhere was the pleasant smell of growing things. Overhead the wild duck winged his way in aërial squadrons to the vast solitudes of the North.

Roaring Bill lighted his evening fire at last at the apex of the pass. He had traveled long after sundown, seeking a camp ground where his horses could graze. The fire lit up huge firs, and high above the fir tops the sky was studded with stars, brilliant in the thin atmosphere. They ate, and, being weary, lay down to sleep. At sunrise Hazel sat up and looked about her in silent, wondering appreciation. All the world spread east and west below. Bill squatted by the fire, piling on wood, and he caught the expression on her face.

"Isn't it great?" he said. "I ran across some verses in a magazine a long time ago. They just fit this, and they've been running in my head ever since I woke up:

> " 'All night long my heart has cried
>   For the starry moors
> And the mountain's ragged flank
>   And the plunge of oars.
>
> 'Oh, to feel the Wind grow strong
>   Where the Trail leaps down.
> *I* could never learn the way
>   And wisdom of the town.
>
> 'Where the hill heads split the Tide
>   Of green and living air
> I would press Adventure hard
>   To her deepest lair.'

"The last verse is the best of all," he said thoughtfully. "It has been my litany ever since I first read it:

> " 'I would let the world's rebuke
>   Like a wind go by,
> With my naked soul laid bare
>   To the naked Sky.'

"And here you are," he murmured, "hotfooting it back to where the world's rebuke is always in evidence, always ready to sting you like a hot iron if you should

147

chance to transgress one of its petty-larceny dictums. Well, you'll soon be there. Can you see a glint of blue away down there? No? Take the glasses."

She adjusted the binoculars and peered westward from the great height where the camp sat. Distantly, and far below, the green of the forest broke down to a hazy line of steel-blue that ran in turn to a huge fog bank, snow-white in the rising sun.

"Yes, I can see it now," she said. "A lake?"

"No. Salt water — a long arm of the Pacific," he replied. "That's where you and I part company — to your very great relief, I dare say. But look off in the other direction. Lord, you can see two hundred miles! If it weren't for the Babine Range sticking up you could look clear to where my cabin stands. What an outlook! Tens of thousands of square miles of timber and lakes and rivers! Sunny little valleys; fish and game everywhere; soil that will grow anything. And scarcely a soul in it all, barring here and there a fur post or a stray prospector. Yet human beings by the million herd in filthy tenements, and never see a blade of green grass the year around.

"I told you, I think, about prospecting on the head of the Naas last spring. I fell in with another fellow up there, and we worked together, and early in the season made a nice little clean-up on a gravel bar. I have another place spotted, by the way, that would work out a fortune if a fellow wanted to spend a couple of thousand putting in some simple machinery. However, when the June rise drove us off our bar, I pulled clear out of the country. Just took a notion to see the bright lights again. And I didn't stop short of New York. Do you know, I lasted there just one week by the calendar. It seems funny, when you think of it, that a man with three thousand dollars to spend should get lonesome in a place like New York. But I did. And at the end of a week I flew. The sole memento of that trip was a couple of Russell prints — and a very bad taste in my mouth. I had all that money burning my pockets — and, all told, I didn't spend five hundred. Fancy a man jumping over four thousand miles to have a good time, and then running away from it. It was very foolish of me, I think now. If I had stuck and got acquainted with somebody, and taken in all the good music, the theaters, and the giddy cafés I wouldn't have got home and blundered into Cariboo Meadows at the psychological moment to make a different kind of fool of myself. Well, the longer we live the more we learn. Day after to-morrow you'll be in Bella Coola. The cannery steamships carry passengers on a fairly regular schedule to Vancouver. How does that suit you?"

"Very well," she answered shortly.

"And you haven't the least twinge of regret at leaving all this?" He waved his hand in a comprehensive sweep.

"I don't happen to have your peculiar point of view," she returned. "The circumstances connected with my coming into this country and with my staying here are such as to make me anxious to get away."

"Same old story," Bill muttered under his breath.

"What is it?" she asked sharply.

"Oh, nothing," he said carelessly, and went on with his breakfast preparations.

They finished the meal. Bill got his horses up beside the fire, loading on the packs. Hazel sat on the trunk of a winter-broken fir, waiting his readiness to start. She heard no sound behind her. But she did see Roaring Bill stiffen and his face blanch under its tan. Twenty feet away his rifle leaned against a tree; his belt and six-shooter hung on a limb above it. He was tucking a keen-edged hatchet under the pack lashing. And, swinging this up, he jumped — it seemed — straight at her. But his eyes were fixed on something beyond.

Before she could move, or even turn to look, so sudden was his movement, Bill was beside her. The sound of a crunching blow reached her ears. In the same instant a heavy body collided with her, knocking her flat. A great weight, a weight which exhaled a rank animal odor, rolled over her. Her clutching hands briefly encountered some hairy object. Then she was slammed against the fallen tree with a force that momentarily stunned her.

When she opened her eyes again Roaring Bill had her head in his lap, peering anxiously down. She caught a glimpse of the unsteady hand that held a cup of water, and she struggled to a sitting posture with a shudder. Bill's shirt was ripped from the neckband to the wrist, baring his sinewy arm. And hand, arm, and shoulder were spattered with fresh blood. His face was spotted where he had smeared it with his bloody hand. Close by, so close that she could almost reach it, lay the grayish-black carcass of a bear, Bill's hatchet buried in the skull, as a woodsman leaves his ax blade stuck in a log.

150

"Feel all right?" Bill asked. His voice was husky.

"Yes, yes," she assured him. "Except for a sort of sickening feeling. Are you hurt?"

He shook his head.

"I thought you were broken in two," he muttered. "We both fell right on top of you. Ugh!"

He sat down on the tree and rested his head on his bloodstained hands, and Hazel saw that he was quivering from head to foot. She got up and went over to him.

"Are you sure you aren't hurt?" she asked again.

He looked up at her; big sweat drops were gathering on his face.

"Hurt? No," he murmured; "I'm just plain scared. You looked as if you were dead, lying there so white and still."

He reached out one long arm and drew her up close to him.

"Little person," he whispered, "if you just cared one little bit as much as I do, it would be all right. Look at me. Just the thought of what might have happened to you has set every nerve in my body jumping. I'm Samson shorn. Why can't you care? I'd be gooder than gold to *you*."

She drew herself away from him without answering — not in fear, but because her code of ethics, the repressive conventions of her whole existence urged her to do so in the face of a sudden yearning to draw his bloody face up close to her and kiss it. The very thought, the swift surge of the impulse frightened her, shocked her. She could not understand it, and so she took refuge behind the woman instinct to hold back, that strange feminine paradox which will deny and shrink from the dominant impulses of life. And Roaring Bill made no effort to hold her. He let her go, and fumbled for a handkerchief to wipe his glistening face. And presently he went over to where a little stream bubbled among the tree roots and washed his hands and face. Then he got a clean shirt out of his war bag and disappeared into the brush to change. When he came out he was himself again, if a bit sober in expression.

He finished his packing without further words. Not till the pack horses were ready, and Silk saddled for her, did he speak again. Then he cast a glance at the dead bear.

"By Jove!" he remarked. "I'm about to forget my tomahawk."

He poked tentatively at the furry carcass with his toe. Hazel came up and took a curious survey of fallen Bruin. Bill laid hold of the hatchet and wrenched it loose.

"I've hunted more or less all my life," he observed, "and I've seen bear under many different conditions. But this is the first time I ever saw a bear tackle anybody without cause or warning. I guess this beggar was strictly on the warpath, looking for trouble on general principles."

"Was he after me?" Hazel asked.

"Well, I don't know whether he had a grudge against you," Bill smiled. "But he was sure coming with his mouth open and his arms spread wide. You notice I didn't take time to go after my rifle, and I'm not a foolhardy person as a rule. I don't tackle a grizzly with a hatchet unless I'm cornered, believe me. It was lucky he wasn't overly big. At that, I can feel my hair stand up when I think how he would have mussed us up if I'd missed that first swing at his head. You'll never have a closer call. And the same thing might not happen again if you lived in a bear country for thirty years.

"It's a pity to let that good skin rot here," Bill concluded slowly; "but I guess I will. I don't want his pelt. It would always be a reminder of things — things I'd just as soon forget."

He tucked the hatchet in its place on the pack. Hazel swung up on Silk. They tipped over the crest of the mountain, and began the long descent.

The evening of the third day from there Bill traveled till dusk. When camp was made and the fire started, he called Hazel to one side, up on a little rocky knoll, and pointed out a half dozen pin points of yellow glimmering distantly in the dark.

"That's Bella Coola," he told her. "And unless they've made a radical change in their sailing schedules there should be a boat clear to-morrow at noon."

CHAPTER
FOURTEEN

The Drone of the Hive

A black cloud of smoke was rolling up from the funnel of the *Stanley D.* as Bill Wagstaff piloted Hazel from the grimy Bella Coola hotel to the wharf.

"There aren't many passengers," he told her. "They're mostly cannery men. But you'll have the captain's wife to chaperon you. She happens to be making the trip."

When they were aboard and the cabin boy had shown them to what was dignified by the name of stateroom, Bill drew a long envelope from his pocket.

"Here," he said, "is a little money. I hope you won't let any foolish pride stand in the way of using it freely. It came easy to me. I dug it out of Mother Earth, and there's plenty more where it came from. Seeing that I deprived you of access to your own money and all your personal belongings, you are entitled to this any way you look at it. And I want to throw in a bit of gratuitous advice — in case you should conclude to go back to the Meadows. They probably looked high and low for you. But there is no chance for them to learn where you actually did get to unless you yourself tell them. The most plausible explanation — and if you go there you must make some explanation — would be for you to say that you got lost — which is true enough — and that you eventually fell in with a party of Indians, and later on connected up with a party of white people who were traveling coastward. That you wintered with them, and they put you on a steamer and sent you to Vancouver when spring opened.

"That, I guess, is all," he concluded slowly. "Only I wish" — he caught her by the shoulders and shook her gently — "I sure do wish it could have been different, little person. Maybe you'll have a kindlier feeling for this big old North when you get back into your cities and towns, with their smoke and smells and business sharks, where it's everybody for himself and the devil take the hindmost. Maybe some time when I get restless for human companionship and come out to cavort in the bright lights for a while, I may pass you on a street somewhere. This world is very small. Oh, yes — when you get to Vancouver go to the Ladysmith. It's a nice, quiet hotel in the West End. Any hack driver knows the place."

He dropped his hands, and looked steadily at her for a few seconds, steadily and longingly.

"Good-by!" he said abruptly — and walked out, and down the gangplank that was already being cast loose, and away up the wharf without a backward glance.

The *Stanley D.*'s siren woke the echoes along the wooded shore. A throbbing that shook her from stem to stern betokened the first turnings of the screw. And slowly she backed into deep water and swung wide for the outer passage.

155

Hazel went out to the rail. Bill Wagstaff had disappeared, but presently she caught sight of him standing on the shore end of the wharf, his hands thrust deep in his coat pockets, staring after the steamer. Hazel waved the envelope that she still held in her hand. Now that she was independent of him, she felt magnanimous, forgiving — and suddenly very much alone, as if she had dropped back into the old, depressing Granville atmosphere. But he gave no answering sign save that he turned on the instant and went up the hill to where his horses stood tied among the huddled buildings. And within twenty minutes the *Stanley D.* turned a jutting point, and Bella Coola was lost to view.

Hazel went back into her stateroom and sat down on the berth. Presently she opened the envelope. There was a thick fold of bills, her ticket, and both were wrapped in a sheet of paper penciled with dots and crooked lines. She laid it aside and counted the money.

"Heavens!" she whispered. "I wish he hadn't given me so much. I didn't need all that."

For Roaring Bill had tucked a dozen one-hundred-dollar notes in the envelope. And, curiously enough, she was not offended, only wishful that he had been less generous. Twelve hundred dollars was a lot of money, far more than she needed, and she did not know how she could return it. She sat a long time with the money in her lap, thinking. Then she took up the map, recognizing it as the sheet of paper Bill had worked over so long their last night at the cabin.

It made the North more clear — a great deal more clear — to her, for he had marked Cariboo Meadows, the location of his cabin, and Bella Coola, and drawn dotted lines to indicate the way he had taken her in and brought her out. The Fraser and its tributaries, some of the crossings that she remembered were sketched in, the mountains and the lakes by which his trail had wound.

"I wonder if that's a challenge to my vindictive disposition?" she murmured. "I told him so often that I'd make him sweat for his treachery if ever I got a chance. Ah well —"

She put away the money and the map, and bestowed a brief scrutiny upon herself in the cabin mirror. Six months in the wild had given her a ruddy color, the glow of perfect physical condition. But her garments were tattered and sadly out of date. The wardrobe of the steamer-trunk lady had suffered in the winter's wear. She was barely presentable in the outing suit of corduroy. So that she was inclined to be diffident about her appearance, and after a time when she was not thinking of the strange episodes of the immediate past, her mind, womanlike, began to dwell on civilization and decent clothes.

The *Stanley D.* bore down Bentick Arm and on through Burke Channel to the troubled waters of Queen Charlotte Sound, where the blue Pacific opens out and away to far Oriental shores. After that she plowed south between Vancouver Island and the rugged foreshores where the Coast Range dips to the sea, past pleasant isles, and through narrow passes where the cliffs towered sheer on either hand, and, upon the evening of the third day, she turned into Burrard Inlet and swept across a harbor speckled with shipping from all the Seven Seas to her berth at the dock.

So Hazel came again to a city — a city that roared and bellowed all its manifold noises in her ears, long grown accustomed to a vast and brooding silence. Mindful of Bill's parting word, she took a hack to the Ladysmith. And even though the hotel was removed from the business heart of the city, the rumble of the city's herculean labors reached her far into the night. She lay wakefully, staring through her open window at the arc lights winking in parallel rows, listening to the ceaseless hum of man's activities. But at last she fell asleep, and dawn of a clear spring day awakened her.

She ate her breakfast, and set forth on a shopping tour. To such advantage did she put two of the hundred-dollar bills that by noon she was arrayed in a semi-tailored suit of gray, spring hat, shoes, and gloves to match. She felt once more at ease, less conscious that people stared at her frayed and curious habiliments. With a complete outfit of lingerie purchased, and a trunk in which to store it forwarded to her hotel, her immediate activity was at an end, and she had time to think of her next move.

And, brought face to face with that, she found herself at something of a loss. She had no desire to go back to Cariboo Meadows, even to get what few personal treasures she had left behind. Cariboo Meadows was wiped off the slate as far as she was concerned. Nevertheless, she must make her way. Somehow she must find a means to return the unused portion of the — to her — enormous sum Roaring Bill had placed in her hands. She must make her own living. The question that troubled her was: How, and where? She had her trade at her finger ends, and the storied office buildings of Vancouver assured her that any efficient stenographer could find work. But she looked up as she walked the streets at the high, ugly walls of brick and steel and stone, and her heart misgave her.

So for the time being she promised herself a holiday. In the afternoon she walked the length of Hastings Street, where the earth trembled with the roaring traffic of street cars, wagons, motors, and where folk scuttled back and forth across the way in peril of their lives. She had seen all the like before, but now she looked upon it with different eyes; it possessed somehow a different significance, this bustle and confusion which had seemingly neither beginning nor end, only sporadic periods of cessation.

She sat in a candy parlor and watched people go by, swarming like bees along the walk. She remembered having heard or read somewhere the simile of a human hive. The shuffle of their feet, the hum of their voices droned in her ears, confusing her, irritating her, and she presently found herself hurrying away from it, walking rapidly eastward toward a thin fringe of trees which showed against a distant sky-line over a sea of roofs. She walked fast, and before long the jar of solid heels on the concrete pavement bred an ache in her knees. Then she caught a car passing in that direction, and rode to the end of the line, where the rails ran out in a wilderness of stumps.

Crossing through these, she found a rudely graded highway, which in turn dwindled to a mere path. It led her through a pleasant area of second-growth fir, slender offspring of the slaughtered forest monarchs, whose great stumps dotted the roll of the land, and up on a little rise whence she could overlook the city and the inlet where rode the tall-masted ships and seascarred tramps from deep salt water. And for the time being she was content.

But a spirit of restlessness drove her back into the city. And at nightfall she went up to her room and threw herself wearily on the bed. She was tired, body and spirit, and lonely. Nor was this lightened by the surety that she would be lonelier still before she found a niche to fit herself in and gather the threads of her life once more into some orderly pattern.

In the morning she felt better, even to the point of going over the newspapers and jotting down several advertisements calling for office help. Her brief experience in Cariboo Meadows had not led her to look kindly on teaching as a means of livelihood. And stenographers seemed to be in demand. Wherefore, she reasoned that wages would be high. With the list in her purse, she went down on Hastings — which runs like a huge artery through the heart of the city, with lesser streets crossing and diverging.

But she made no application for employment. For on the corner of Hastings and Seymour, as she gathered

160

her skirt in her hand to cross the street, some one caught her by the arm, and cried:

"Well, forevermore, if it isn't Hazel Weir!"

And she turned to find herself facing Loraine Marsh — a Granville school chum — and Loraine's mother. Back of them, with wide and startled eyes, loomed Jack Barrow.

He pressed forward while the two women overwhelmed Hazel with a flood of exclamations and questions, and extended his hand. Hazel accepted the overture. She had long since gotten over her resentment against him. She was furthermore amazed to find that she could meet his eye and take his hand without a single flutter of her pulse. It seemed strange, but she was glad of it. And, indeed, she was too much taken up with Loraine Marsh's chatter, and too genuinely glad to hear a friendly voice again, to dwell much on ghosts of the past.

They stood a few minutes on the corner; then Mrs. Marsh proposed that they go to the hotel, where they could talk at their leisure and in comfort. Loraine and her mother took the lead. Barrow naturally fell into step with Hazel.

"I've been wearing sackcloth and ashes, Hazel," he said humbly. "And I guess you've got about a million apologies coming from everybody in Granville for the shabby way they treated you. Shortly after you left, somebody on one of the papers ferreted out the truth of that Bush affair, and the vindictive old hound's reasons for that compromising legacy were set forth. It seems this newspaper fellow connected up with Bush's secretary and the nurse. Also, Bush appears to have kept a diary — and kept it posted up to the day of his death — poured out all his feelings on paper, and repeatedly asserted that he would win you or ruin you. And it seems that that night after you refused to come to him when he was hurt, he called in his lawyer and made that codicil — and spent the rest of the time till he died gloating over the chances of it besmirching your character."

"I've grown rather indifferent about it," Hazel replied impersonally. "But he succeeded rather easily. Even you, who should have known me better, were ready to believe the very worst."

"I've paid for it," Barrow pleaded. "You don't know how I've hated myself for being such a cad. But it taught me a lesson — if you'll not hold a grudge against me. I've wondered and worried about you, disappearing the way you did. Where have you been, and how have you been getting on? You surely look well." He bent an admiring glance on her.

"Oh, I've been every place, and I can't complain about not getting on," she answered carelessly.

For the life of her, she could not help making comparisons between the man beside her and another who she guessed would by now be bearing up to the crest of the divide that overlooked the green and peaceful vista of forest and lake, with the Babine Range lying purple beyond. She wondered if Roaring Bill Wagstaff would ever, under any circumstances, have looked on her with the scornful, angry distrust that Barrow had once betrayed. And she could not conceive of Bill Wagstaff ever being humble or penitent for anything he had done. Barrow's attitude was that of a little boy who had broken some plaything in a fit of anger and was now woefully trying to put the pieces together again. It amused her. Indeed, it afforded her a distinctly un-Christian satisfaction, since she was not by nature of a meek or forgiving spirit. He had made her suffer; it was but fitting that he should know a pang or two himself.

Hazel visited with the three of them in the hotel parlor for a matter of two hours, went to luncheon with them, and at luncheon Loraine Marsh brought up the subject of her coming home to Granville with them. The Bush incident was discussed and dismissed. On the question of returning, Hazel was noncommittal. The idea appealed strongly to her. Granville was home. She had grown up there. There were a multitude of old ties, associations, friends to draw her back. But whether her home town would seem the same, whether she would feel the same toward the friends who had held aloof in the time when she needed a friend the most, even if they came flocking back to her, was a question that she thought of if she did not put it in so many words. On the other hand, she knew too well the drear loneliness that would close upon her in Vancouver when the Marshes left.

"Of course you'll come! We won't hear of leaving you behind. So you can consider that settled." Loraine Marsh declared at last. "We're going day after to-morrow. So is Mr. Barrow."

Jack walked with her out to the Ladysmith, and, among other things, told her how he happened to be in the coast city.

"I've been doing pretty well lately," he said. "I came out here on a deal that involved about fifty thousand dollars. I closed it up just this morning — and the commission would just about buy us that little house we had planned once. Won't you let bygones be by-gones, Hazie?"

"It might be possible, Jack," she answered slowly, "if it were not for the fact that you took the most effective means a man could have taken to kill every atom of affection I had for you. I don't feel bitter any more — I simply don't feel at all."

"But you will," he said eagerly. "Just give me a chance. I was a hot-headed, jealous fool, but I never will be again. Give me a chance, Hazel."

"You'll have to make your own chances," she said deliberately. "I refuse to bind myself in any way. Why should I put myself out to make you happy when you destroyed all the faith I had in you? You simply didn't trust me. You wouldn't trust me again. If slander could turn you against me once it might a second time. Besides, I don't care for you as a man wants a woman to care for him. And I don't think I'm going to care — except, perhaps, in a friendly way."

And with that Barrow had to be content.

He called for her the next day, and took her, with the Marshes, out for a launch ride, and otherwise devoted himself to being an agreeable cavalier. On the launch excursion it was settled definitely that Hazel should

164

accompany them East. She had no preparations to make. The only thing she would like to have done — return Roaring Bill's surplus money — she could not do. She did not know how or where to reach him with a letter. So far as Granville was concerned, she could always leave it if she desired, and she was a trifle curious to know how all her friends would greet her now that the Bush mystery was cleared up and the legacy explained.

So that at dusk of the following day she and Loraine Marsh sat in a Pullman, flattening their noses against the car window, taking a last look at the environs of Vancouver as the train rolled through the outskirts of the city. Hazel told herself that she was going home. Barrow smiled friendly assurance over the seat.

Even so, she was restless, far from content. There was something lacking. She grew distrait, monosyllabic, sat for long intervals staring absently into the gloom beyond the windowpane. The Limited was ripping through forested land. She could see now and then tall treetops limned against the starlit sky. The ceaseless roar of the trucks and the buzz of conversation in the car irritated her. At half after eight she called the porter and had him arrange her section for the night. And she got into bed, thankful to be by herself, depressed without reason.

She slept for a time, her sleep broken into by morbid dreams, and eventually she wakened to find her eyes full of tears. She did not know why she should cry, but cry she did till her pillow grew moist — and the heavy feeling in her breast grew, if anything, more intense.

165

She raised on one elbow and looked out the window. The train slowed with a squealing of brakes and the hiss of escaping air to a station. On the signboard over the office window she read the name of the place and the notation: "Vancouver, 180 miles."

Her eyes were still wet. When the Limited drove east again she switched on the tiny electric bulb over her head, and fumbled in her purse for another handkerchief. Her fingers drew forth, with the bit of linen, a folded sheet of paper, which seemed to hypnotize her, so fixedly did she remain looking at it. A sheet of plain white paper, marked with dots and names and crooked lines that stood for rivers, with shaded patches that meant mountain ranges she had seen — Bill Wagstaff's map.

She stared at it a long time. Then she found her time-table, and ran along the interminable string of station names till she found Ashcroft, from whence northward ran the Appian Way of British Columbia, the Cariboo Road, over which she had journeyed by stage. She noted the distance, and the Limited's hour of arrival, and looked at her watch. Then a feverish activity took hold of her. She dressed, got her suit case from under the berth, and stuffed articles into it, regardless of order. Her hat was in a paper bag suspended from a hook above the upper berth. Wherefore, she tied a silk scarf over her head.

That done, she set her suit case in the aisle, and curled herself in the berth, with her face pressed close against the window. A whimsical smile played about her

166

mouth, and her fingers tap-tapped steadily on the purse, wherein was folded Bill Wagstaff's map.

And then out of the dark ahead a cluster of lights winked briefly, the shriek of the Limited's whistle echoed up and down the wide reaches of the North Thompson, and the coaches came to a stop. Hazel took one look to make sure. Then she got softly into the aisle, took up her suit case, and left the car. At the steps she turned to give the car porter a message.

"Tell Mrs. Marsh — the lady in lower five," she said, with a dollar to quicken his faculties, "that Miss Weir had to go back. Say that I will write soon and explain."

She stood back in the shadow of the station for a few seconds. The Limited's stop was brief. When the red lights went drumming down the track, she took up her suit case and walked uptown to the hotel where she had tarried overnight once before.

The clerk showed her to a room. She threw her suit case on the bed and turned the key in the lock. Then she went over, and, throwing up the window to its greatest height, sat down and looked steadily toward the north, smiling to herself.

"I can find him," she suddenly said aloud. "Of course I can find him!"

And with that she blew a kiss from her finger-tips out toward the dark and silent North, pulled down the shade, and went quietly to bed.

CHAPTER FIFTEEN

An Ending and a Beginning

Unconsciously, by natural assimilation, so to speak, Hazel Weir had absorbed more woodcraft than she realized in her over-winter stay in the high latitudes. Bill Wagstaff had once told her that few people know just what they can do until they are compelled to try, and upon this, her second journey northward, the truth of that statement grew more patent with each passing day. Little by little the vast central interior of British Columbia unfolded its orderly plan of watercourses, mountain ranges, and valleys. She passed camping places, well remembered of that first protesting journey. And at night she could close her eyes beside the camp fires and visualize the prodigious setting of it all — eastward the pyramided Rockies, westward lesser ranges, the Telegraph, the Babine; and through the plateau between the turbulent Frazer, bearing eastward from the Rockies and turning abruptly for its long flow south, with its sinuous doublings and turnings that were marked in bold lines on Bill Wagstaff's map.

So trailing north with old Limping George, his fat *klootch*, and two half-grown Siwash youths, Hazel bore steadily across country, driving as straight as the rolling land allowed for the cabin that snuggled in a woodsy basin close up to the peaks that guard Pine River Pass.

There came a day when brief uncertainty became sure knowledge at sight of an L-shaped body of water glimmering through the fire-thinned spruce. Her heart fluttered for a minute. Like a homing bird, by grace of the rude map and Limping George, she had come to the lake where the Indians had camped in the winter, and she could have gone blindfolded from the lake to Roaring Bill's cabin.

On the lake shore, where the spruce ran out to birch and cottonwood, she called a halt.

"Make camp," she instructed. "Cabin over there," she waved her hand. "I go. Byemby come back."

Then she urged her pony through the light timber growth and across the little meadows where the rank grass and strange varicolored flowers were springing up under the urge of the warm spring sun. Twenty minutes brought her to the clearing. The grass sprang lush there, and the air was pleasant with odors of pine and balsam wafted down from the mountain height behind. But the breath of the woods was now a matter of small moment, for Silk and Satin and Nigger loafing at the sunny end of the stable pricked up their ears at her approach, and she knew that Roaring Bill was home again. She tied her horse to a sapling and drew nearer. The cabin door stood wide.

169

A brief panic seized her. She felt a sudden shrinking, a wild desire for headlong flight. But it passed. She knew that for good or ill she would never turn back. And so, with her heart thumping tremendously and a tentative smile curving her lips, she ran lightly across to the open door.

On the soft turf her footsteps gave forth no sound. She gained the doorway as silently as a shadow. Roaring Bill faced the end of the long room, but he did not see her, for he was slumped in the big chair before the fireplace, his chin sunk on his breast, staring straight ahead with absent eyes.

In all the days she had been with him she had never seen him look like that. It had been his habit, his defense, to cover sadness with a smile, to joke when he was hurt. That weary, hopeless expression, the wry twist of his lips, wrung her heart and drew from her a yearning little whisper:

"Bill!"

He came out of his chair like a panther. And when his eyes beheld her in the doorway he stiffened in his tracks, staring, seeing, yet reluctant to believe the evidence of his vision. His brows wrinkled. He put up one hand and absently ran it over his cheek.

"I wonder if I've got to the point of seeing things," he said slowly. "Say, little person, is it your astral body, or is it really you?"

"Of course it's me," she cried tremulously, and with fine disregard for her habitual preciseness of speech.

He came up close to her and pinched her arm with a gentle pressure, as if he had to feel the material

170

substance of her before he could believe. And then he put his hands on her shoulders, as he had done on the steamer that day at Bella Coola, and looked long and earnestly at her — looked till a crimson wave rose from her neck to the roots of her dark, glossy hair. And with that Roaring Bill took her in his arms, cuddled her up close to him, and kissed her, not once but many times.

"You really and truly came back, little person," he murmured. "Lord, Lord — and yet they say the day of miracles is past."

"You didn't think I would, did you?" she asked, with her blushing face snuggled against his sturdy breast. "Still, you gave me a map so that I could find the place?"

"That was just taking a desperate chance. No, I never expected to see you again, unless by accident," he said honestly. "And I've been crying the hurt of it to the stars all the way back from the coast. I only got here yesterday. I pretty near passed up coming back at all. I didn't see how I could stay, with everything to remind me of you. Say, but it looked like a lonesome hole. I used to love this place — but I didn't love it last night. It seemed about the most cheerless and depressing spot I could have picked. I think I should have ended up by touching a match to the whole business and hitting the trail to some new country. I don't know. I'm not weak. But I don't think I could have stayed here long."

They stood silent in the doorway for a long interval. Bill holding her close to him, and she blissfully contented, careless and unthinking of the future, so filled was she with joy of the present.

"Do you love me much, little person?" Bill asked, after a little.

She nodded vigorous assent.

"Why?" he desired to know.

"Oh, just because — because you're a man, I suppose," she returned mischievously.

"The world's chuck-full of men," Bill observed.

"Surely," she looked up at him. "But they're not like you. Maybe it's bad policy to start in flattering you, but there aren't many men of your type, Billy-boy; big and strong and capable, and at the same time kind and patient and able to understand things, things a woman can't always put into words. Last fall you hurt my pride and nearly scared me to death by carrying me off in that lawless, headlong fashion of yours. But you seemed to know just how I felt about it, and you played fairer than any man I ever knew would have done under the same circumstances. I didn't realize it until I got back into the civilized world. And then all at once I found myself longing for you — and for these old forests and the mountains and all. So I came back."

"Wise girl," he kissed her. "You'll never be sorry, I hope. It took some nerve, too. It's a long trail from here to the outside. But this North country — it gets in your blood — if your blood's red — and I don't think there's any water in your veins, little person. Lord! I'm afraid to let go of you for fear you'll vanish into nothing, like a Hindu fakir stunt."

"No fear," Hazel laughed. "I've got a pony tied to a tree out there, and four Siwashes and a camp outfit

172

over by Crooked Lake. If I should vanish I'd leave a plain trail for you to follow."

"Well," Bill said, after a short silence, "it's a hundred and forty miles to a Hudson's Bay post where there's a mission and a preacher. Let's be on our way and get married. Then we'll come back here and spend our honeymoon. Eh?"

She nodded assent.

"Are you game to start in half an hour?" he asked, holding her off at arm's length admiringly.

"I'm game for anything, or I wouldn't be here," she retorted.

"All right. You just watch an exhibition of speedy packing," Bill declared — and straightway fell to work.

Hazel followed him about, helping to get the kyaks packed with food. They caught the three horses, and Bill stripped the pony of Hazel's riding gear and placed a pack on him. Then he put her saddle on Silk.

"He's your private mount henceforth," Bill told her laughingly. "You'll ride him with more pleasure than you did the first time, won't you?"

Presently they were ready to start, planning to ride past Limping George's camp and tell him whither they were bound. Hazel was already mounted. Roaring Bill paused, with his toe in the stirrup, and smiled whimsically at her over his horse's back.

"I forgot something," said he, and went back into the cabin — whence he shortly emerged, bearing in his hand a sheet of paper upon which something was written in bold, angular characters. This he pinned on the door. Hazel rode Silk close to see what it might be, and laughed amusedly, for Bill had written:

"Mr. and Mrs. William Wagstaff will be at home to their friends on and after June the twentieth."

He swung up into his saddle, and they jogged across the open. In the edge of the first timber they pulled up and looked backward at the cabin drowsing silently under its sentinel tree. Roaring Bill reached out one arm and laid it across Hazel's shoulders.

"Little person," he said soberly, "here's the end of one trail, and the beginning of another — the longest trail either of us has ever faced. How does it look to you?"

She caught his fingers with a quick, hard pressure.

"All trails look alike to me," she said, with shining eyes, "just so we hit them together."

CHAPTER
SIXTEEN

A Brief Time
of Planning

"What day of the month is this, Bill?" Hazel asked.

"Haven't the least idea," he answered lazily. "Time is of no consequence to me at the present moment."

They were sitting on the warm earth before their cabin, their backs propped comfortably against a log, watching the sun sink behind a distant sky-line all notched with purple mountains upon which snow still lingered. Beside them a smudge dribbled a wisp of smoke sufficient to ward off a pestilential swarm of mosquitoes and black flies. In the clear, thin air of that altitude the occasional voices of what bird and animal life was abroad in the wild broke into the evening hush with astonishing distinctness — a lone goose winged above in wide circles, uttering his harsh and solitary cry. He had lost his mate, Bill told her. Far off in the bush a fox barked. The evening flight of the wild duck from Crooked Lake to a chain of swamps passed intermittently over the clearing with a sibilant whistle of wings. To all the wild things, no less than to the two who watched and listened to the forest traffic, it was a land of peace and plenty.

"We ought to go up to the swamps to-morrow and rustle some duck eggs," Bill observed irrelevantly — his eyes following the arrow flight of a mallard flock. But his wife was counting audibly, checking the days off on her fingers.

"This is July the twenty-fifth, Mr. Roaring Bill Wagstaff," she announced. "We've been married exactly one month."

"A whole month?" he echoed, in mock astonishment. "A regular calendar month of thirty-one days, huh? You don't say so? Seems like it was only day before yesterday, little person."

"I wonder," she snuggled up a little closer to him, "if any two people were ever as happy as we've been?"

Bill put his arm across her shoulders and tilted her head back so that he could smile down into her face.

"They have been a bunch of golden days, haven't they?" he whispered. "We haven't come to a single bump in the road yet. You won't forget this joy time if we ever do hit real hard going, will you, Hazel?"

"The bird of ill omen croaks again," she reproved. "Why should we come to hard going, as you call it?"

"We shouldn't," he declared. "But most people do. And we might. One never can tell what's ahead. Life takes queer and unexpected turns sometimes. We've got to live pretty close to each other, depend absolutely on each other in many ways — and that's the acid test of human companionship. By and by, when the novelty wears off — maybe you'll get sick of seeing the same

176

old Bill around and nobody else. You see I've always been on my good behavior with you. Do you like me a lot?"

His arm tightened with a quick and powerful pressure, then suddenly relaxed to let her lean back and stare up at him tenderly.

"I ought to punish you for saying things like that," she pouted. "Only I can't think of any effective method. Sufficient unto the day is the evil thereof — and there is no evil in *our* days."

"Amen," he whispered softly — and they fell to silent contemplation of the rose and gold that spread in a wonderful blazon over all the western sky.

"Twenty-fifth of July, eh?" he mused presently. "Summer's half gone already. I didn't realize it. We ought to be stirring pretty soon, lady."

"Let's stir into the house, then," she suggested. "These miserable little black flies have found a tender place on me. My, but they're bloodthirsty insects."

Bill laughed, and they took refuge in the cabin, the doorways and windows of which were barricaded with cotton mosquito net against the winged swarms that buzzed hungrily without. Ensconced in the big chair by the fireplace, with Bill sprawled on the bearskin at her feet, Hazel came back to his last remark.

"Why did you say it was time for us to be stirring, Billum?"

"Because these Northern seasons are so blessed short," he answered. "We ought to try and do a little good for ourselves — make hay while the sun shines. We'll needa da mon'."

"Needa fiddlesticks," she laughed. "What do we need money for? It costs practically nothing to live up here. Why this sudden desire to pursue the dollar? Besides, how are you going to pursue it?"

"Go prospecting," he replied promptly. "Hit the trail for a place I know where there's oodles of coarse gold, if you can get to it at low water. How'd you like to go into the Upper Naas country this fall, trap all winter, work the sand bars in the spring, and come out next fall with a sack of gold it would take a horse to pack?"

Hazel clapped her hands.

"Oh, Bill, wouldn't that be fine?" she cried. Across her mind flashed a vivid picture of the journey, pregnant with adventure, across the wild hinterlands — they two together. "I'd love to."

"It won't be all smooth sailing," he warned. "It's a long trip and a hard one, and the winter will be longer and harder than the trip. We won't have the semiluxuries we've got here in this cabin. Not by a long shot. Still, there's a change for a good big stake, right in that one trip."

"But why the necessity for making a stake?" she inquired thoughtfully, after a lapse of five minutes. "I thought you didn't care anything about money so long as you had enough to get along on? And we surely have that. We've got over two thousand dollars in real money — and no place to spend it — so we're compelled to save."

Bill blew a smoke ring over his head and watched it vanish up toward the dusky roof beams before he answered.

178

"Well, little person," said he, "that's very true, and we can't truthfully say that stern necessity is treading on our heels. The possession of money has never been a crying need with me. But I hadn't many wants when I was playing a lone hand, and I generally let the future take care of itself. It was always easy to dig up money enough to buy books and grub or anything I wanted. Now that I've assumed a certain responsibility, it has begun to dawn on me that we'd enjoy life better if we were assured of a competence. We can live on the country here indefinitely. But we won't stay here always. I'm pretty much contented just now. So are you. But I know from past experience that the outside will grow more alluring as time passes. You'll get lonesome for civilization. It's the most natural thing in the world. And when we go out to mix with our fellow humans we want to meet them on terms of worldly equality. Which is to say with good clothes on, and a fat bank roll in our pocket. The best is none too good for us, lady. And the best costs money. Anyway, I'll plead guilty to changing, or, rather, modifying my point of view — getting married has opened up new vistas of pleasure for us that call for dollars. And last, but not least, old girl, while I love to loaf, I can only loaf about so long in contentment. Sabe? I've got to be doing *something*; whether it was profitable or not has never mattered, just so it was action."

"I sabe, as you call it," Hazel smiled. "Of course I do. Only lazy people like to loaf all the time. I love this place, and we might stay here for years and be satisfied. But —"

179

"But we'd be better satisfied to stay if we knew that we could leave it whenever we wanted to," he interrupted. "That's the psychology of the human animal, all right. We don't like to be coerced, even by circumstances. Well, granted health, one can be boss of old Dame Circumstance, if one has the price in cold cash. It's a melancholy fact that the good things of the world can only be had for a consideration."

"If you made a lot of money mining, we could travel — one could do lots of things," she reflected. "I don't think I'd want to live in a city again. But it would be nice to go there sometimes."

"Yes, dear girl, it would," Bill agreed. "With a chum to help you enjoy things. I never got much fun out of the bright lights by myself — it was too lonesome. I used to prowl around by myself with an analytical eye upon humanity, and I was always bumping into a lot of sordidness and suffering that I couldn't in the least remedy, and it often gave me a bad taste in my mouth. Then I'd beat it for the woods — and they always looked good to me. The trouble was that I had too much time to think, and nothing to do when I hit a live town. It would be different now. We can do things together that I couldn't do alone, and you couldn't do alone. Remains only to get the where-withal. And since I know how to manage that with a minimum amount of effort, I'd like to be about it before somebody else gets ahead of me. Though there's small chance of that."

"We'll be partners," said she. "How will we divide the profits, Billum?"

180

"We'll split even," he declared. "That is, I'll make the money, and you'll spend it."

They chuckled over this conceit, and as the dusk closed in slowly they fell to planning the details. Hazel lit the lamp, and in its yellow glow pored over maps while Bill idly sketched their route on a sheet of paper. His objective lay east of the head of the Naas proper, where amid a wild tangle of mountains and mountain torrents three turbulent rivers, the Stikine, the Skeena, and the Naas, took their rise. A God-forsaken region, he told her, where few white men had penetrated. The peaks flirted with the clouds, and their sides were scarred with glaciers. A lonesome, brooding land, the home of a vast and seldom-broken silence.

"But there's all kinds of game and fur in there," Bill remarked thoughtfully. "And gold. Still, it's a fierce country for a man to take his best girl into. I don't know whether I ought to tackle it."

"We couldn't be more isolated than we are here," Hazel argued, "if we were in the arctic. Look at that poor woman at Pelt House. Three babies born since she saw a doctor or another woman of her own color! What's a winter by ourselves compared to that. And *she* didn't think it so great a hardship. Don't you worry about me, Mr. Bill. I think it will be fun. I'm a real pioneer at heart. The wild places look good to me — when you're along."

She received her due reward for that, and then, the long twilight having brought the hour to a lateness that manifested itself by sundry yawns on their part, they went to bed.

With breakfast over, Bill put a compass in his pocket, after having ground his ax blade to a keen edge.

"Come on," said he, then; "I'm going to transact some important business."

"What is it?" she promptly demanded with much curiosity.

"This domicile of ours, girl," he told her, while he led the way through the surrounding timber, "is ours only by grace of the wilderness. It's built on unsurveyed government land — land that I have no more legal claim to than any passing trapper. I never thought of it before — which goes to show that this double-harness business puts a different face on 'most everything. But I'm going to remedy that. Of course, it may be twenty years before this country begins to settle up enough so that some individual may cast a covetous eye on this particular spot — but I'm not going to take any chances. I'm going to formally stake a hundred and sixty acres of this and apply for its purchase. Then we'll have a cinch on our home. We'll always have a refuge to fly to, no matter where we go."

She nodded appreciation of this. The cabin in the clearing stood for some of those moments that always loom large and unforgettable in every woman's experience. She had come there once in hot, shamed anger, and she had come again as a bride. It was the handiwork of a man she loved with a passion that sometimes startled her by its intensity. She had plumbed depths of bitterness there, and, contrariwise, reached a point of happiness she had never believed possible. Just the mere possibility of that place being

182

given over to others roused in her a pang of resentment. It was theirs, hers and Bill's, and, being a woman, she viewed its possession jealously.

So she watched with keen interest what he did. Which, in truth, was simple enough. He worked his way to a point southeast of the clearing till they gained a little rise whence through the treetops they could look back and see the cabin roof. There Bill cut off an eight-inch jack pine, leaving the stump approximately four feet high. This he hewed square, the four flat sides of the post facing respectively the cardinal points of the compass. On one smoothed surface Bill set to work with his pocketknife. Hazel sat down and watched while he busied himself at this. And when he had finished she read, in deep-carved letters:

W. WAGSTAFF'S S. E. CORNER.

Then he penned on a sheet of letter paper a brief notice to the effect that he, William Wagstaff, intended to apply for the purchase of the land embraced in an area a half mile square, of which the post was the southeast corner mark. This notice he fastened to the stump with a few tacks, and sat down to rest from his labors.

"How long do you suppose that will stay there, and who is there to read it, if it does?" Hazel observed.

"Search me. The moose and the deer and the timber wolves, I guess," Bill grinned. "The chances are the paper won't last long, with winds and rains. But it doesn't matter. It's simply a form prescribed by the

183

Land Act of British Columbia, and, so long as I go through the legal motions, that lets me out. Matter of form, you know."

"Then what else do you have to do?"

"Nothing but furnish the money when the land department gets around to accept my application," he said. "I can get an agent to attend to all the details. Oh, I have to furnish a description of the land by natural boundaries, to give them an idea of about where it's situated. Well, let's take a look at our estate from another corner."

This, roughly ascertained by sighting a line with the compass and stepping off eight hundred and eighty yards, brought them up on a knoll that commanded the small basin of which the clearing was practically in the center.

"Aha!" Bill exclaimed. "Look at our ranch, would you; our widespread acres basking in the sun. A quarter section is quite a chunk. Do you know I never thought much about it before, but there's a piece of the finest land that lies outdoors. I wasn't looking for land when I squatted there. It was a pretty place, and there was hay for our horses in that meadow, and trout in the creek back of the cabin. So I built the old shack largely on the conveniences and the natural beauty of the spot. But let me tell you, if this country should get a railroad and settle up, that quarter section might produce all the income we'd need, just out of hay and potatoes. How'd you like to be a farmer's wife, huh?"

"Fine," she smiled. "Look at the view — it isn't gorgeous. It's — it's simply peaceful and quiet and soothing. I hate to leave it."

"Better be sorry to leave a place than glad to get away," he answered lightly. "Come on, let's pike home and get things in order for the long trail, woman o' mine. I'll teach you how to be a woodland vagabond."

CHAPTER
SEVENTEEN

En Route

Long since Hazel had become aware that whatsoever her husband set about doing he did swiftly and with inflexible purpose. There was no malingering or doubtful hesitation. Once his mind was made up, he acted. Thus, upon the third day from the land staking they bore away eastward from the clearing, across a trackless area, traveling by the sun and Bill's knowledge of the country.

"Some day there'll be trails blazed through here by a paternal government," he laughed over his shoulder, "for the benefit of the public. But *we* don't need 'em, thank goodness."

The buckskin pony Hazel had bought for the trip in with Limping George ambled sedately under a pack containing bedding, clothes, and a light shelter tent. The black horse, Nigger, he of the cocked ear and the rolling eye, carried in a pair of kyaks six weeks' supply of food. Bill led the way, seconded by Hazel on easygaited Silk. Behind her trailed the pack horses like dogs well broken to heel, patient under their heavy burdens. Off in the east the sun was barely clear of the towering Rockies, and the woods were still cool and shadowy, full of aromatic odors from plant and tree.

Hazel followed her man contentedly. They were together upon the big adventure, just as she had seen it set forth in books, and she found it good. For her there was no more diverging of trails, no more problems looming fearsomely at the journey's end. To jog easily through woods and over open meadows all day, and at night to lie with her head pillowed on Bill's arm, peering up through interlocked branches at a myriad of gleaming stars — that was sufficient to fill her days. To live and love and be loved, with all that had ever seemed hateful and sordid and mean thrust into a remote background. It was almost too good to be true, she told herself. Yet it was indubitably true. And she was grateful for the fact. Touches of the unavoidable bitterness of life had taught her the worth of days that could be treasured in the memory.

Occasionally she would visualize the cabin drowsing lifeless in its emerald setting, haunted by the rabbits that played timidly about in the twilight, or perhaps a wandering deer peering his wide-eyed curiosity from the timber's edge. The books and rugs and curtains were stowed in boxes and bundles and hung by wires to the ridge log to keep them from the busy bush-tailed rats. Everything was done up carefully and put away for safekeeping, as became a house that is to be long untenanted.

The mother instinct to keep a nest snug and cozy gave her a tiny pang over the abandoned home. The dust of many months would gather on the empty chairs and shelves. Still it was only a passing absence. They would come back, with treasure wrested from the strong box of the wild. Surely Fortune could not forbear smiling on a mate like hers?

There was no monotony in the passing days. Rivers barred their way. These they forded or swam, or ferried a makeshift raft of logs, as seemed most fit. Once their raft came to grief in the maw of a snarling current, and they laid up two days to dry their saturated belongings. Once their horses, impelled by some mysterious home yearning, hit the back trail in a black night of downpour, and they trudged half a day through wet grass and dripping scrub to overtake the truants. Thunderstorms drove up, shattering the hush of the land with ponderous detonations, assaulting them with fierce bursts of rain. Haps and mishaps alike they accepted with an equable spirit and the true philosophy of the trail — to take things as they come. When rain deluged them, there was always shelter to be found and fire to warm them. If the flies assailed too fiercely, a smudge brought easement of that ill. And when the land lay smiling under a pleasant sun, they rode light-hearted and care-free, singing or in silent content, as the spirit moved. If they rode alone, they felt none of that loneliness which is so integral a part of the still, unpeopled places. Each day was something more than a mere toll of so many miles traversed. The unexpected, for which both were eager-eyed, lurked on the shoulder of each mountain, in the hollow of every cool cañon, or met them boldly in the open, naked and unafraid.

188

Bearing up to where the Nachaco debouches from Fraser Lake, with a Hudson's Bay fur post and an Indian mission on its eastern fringe, they came upon a blazed line in the scrub timber. Roaring Bill pulled up, and squinted away down the narrow lane fresh with ax marks.

"Well," said he, "I wonder what's coming off now? That looks like a survey line of some sort. It isn't a trail — too wide. Let's follow it a while.

"I'll bet a nickel," he asserted next, "that's a railroad survey." They had traversed two miles more or less, and the fact was patent that the blazed line sought a fairly constant level across country. "A land survey runs all same latitude and longitude. Huh!"

Half an hour of easy jogging set the seal of truth on his assertion. They came upon a man squinting through a brass instrument set on three legs, directing, with alternate wavings of his outspread hands, certain activities of other men ahead of him.

"Well, I'll be —" he bit off the sentence, and stared a moment in frank astonishment at Hazel. Then he took off his hat and bowed. "Good morning," he greeted politely.

"Sure," Bill grinned. "We have mornings like this around here all the time. What all are you fellows doing in the wilderness, anyway? Railroad?"

"Cross-section work for the G. T. P.," the surveyor replied.

"Huh," Bill grunted. "Is it a dead cinch, or is it something that may possibly come to pass in the misty future?"

189

"As near a cinch as anything ever is," the surveyor answered. "Construction has begun — at both ends. I thought the few white folks in this country kept tab on anything as important as a new railroad."

"We've heard a lot, but none of 'em has transpired yet; not in my time, anyway," Bill replied dryly. "However, the world keeps right on moving. I've heard more or less talk of this, but I didn't know it had got past the talking stage. What's their Pacific terminal?"

"Prince Rupert — new town on a peninsula north of the mouth of the Skeena," said the surveyor. "It's a rush job all the way through, I believe. Three years to spike up the last rail. And that's going some for a transcontinental road. Both the Dominion and B. C. governments have guaranteed the company's bonds away up into millions."

"Be a great thing for this country — say, where does it cross the Rockies? — what's the general route?" Bill asked abruptly.

"Goes over the range through Yellowhead Pass. From here it follows the Nachaco to Fort George, then up the Fraser by Tete Juan Cache, through the pass, then down the Athabasca till it switches over to strike Edmonton."

"Uh-huh," Bill nodded. "One of the modern labors of Hercules. Well, we've got to peg. So long."

"Our camp's about five miles ahead. Better stop in and noon," the surveyor invited, "if it's on your road."

"Thanks. Maybe we will," Bill returned.

190

The surveyor lifted his hat, with a swift glance of admiration at Hazel, and they passed with a mutual "so long."

"What do you think of that, old girl?" Bill observed presently. "A real, honest-to-God railroad going by within a hundred miles of our shack. Three years. It'll be there before we know it. We'll have neighbors to burn."

"A hundred miles!" Hazel laughed. "Is that your idea of a neighborly distance?"

"What's a hundred miles?" he defended. "Two days' ride, that's all. And the kind of people that come to settle in a country like this don't stick in sight of the cars. They're like me — need lots of elbow room. There'll be hardy souls looking for a location up where we are before very long. You'll see."

They passed other crews of men, surveyors with transits, chainmen, stake drivers, ax gangs widening the path through the timber. Most of them looked at Hazel in frank surprise, and stared long after she passed by. And when an open bottom beside a noisy little creek showed the scattered tents of the survey camp, Hazel said:

"Let's not stop, Bill."

He looked back over his shoulder with a comprehending smile.

"Getting shy? Make you uncomfortable to have all these boys look at you, little person?" he bantered. "All right, we won't stop. But all these fellows probably haven't seen a white woman for months. You can't

191

blame them for admiring. You do look good to other men besides me, you know."

So they rode through the camp with but a nod to the aproned cook, who thrust out his head, and a gray-haired man with glasses, who humped over a drafting board under an awning. Their noon fire they built at a spring five miles beyond.

Thereafter they skirted three lakes in succession, Fraser, Burns, and Decker, and climbed over a low divide to drop into the Bulkley Valley — a pleasant, rolling country, where the timber was interspersed with patches of open grassland and set with small lakes, wherein schools of big trout lived their finny lives unharried by anglers — save when some wandering Indian snared one with a primitive net.

Far down this valley they came upon the first sign of settlement. Hardy souls, far in advance of the coming railroad, had built here and there a log cabin and were hard at it clearing and plowing and getting the land ready for crops. Four or five such lone ranches they passed, tarrying overnight at one where they found a broad-bosomed woman with a brood of tow-headed children. Her husband was out after supplies — a week's journey. She kept Hazel from her bed till after midnight, talking. They had been there over winter, and Hazel Wagstaff was the first white woman she had bespoken in seven months. There were other women in the valley farther along; but fifty or sixty miles leaves scant opportunity for visiting when there is so much work to be done ere wild acres will feed hungry mouths.

At length they fared into Hazleton, which is the hub of a vast area over which men pursue gold and furs. Some hundred odd souls were gathered there, where the stern-wheel steamers that ply the turgid Skeena reach the head of navigation. A land-recording office and a mining recorder Hazleton boasted as proof of its civic importance. The mining recorder, who combined in himself many capacities besides his governmental function, undertook to put through Bill's land deal. He knew Bill Wagstaff.

"Wise man," he nodded, over the description. "If some more uh these boys that have blazed trails through this country would do the same thing, they'd be better off. A chunk of land anywhere in this country is a good bet now. We'll have rails here from the coast in a year. Better freeze onto a couple uh lots here in Hazleton, while they're low. Be plumb to the skies in ten years. Natural place for a city, Bill. It's astonishin' how the settlers is comin'."

There was ocular evidence of this last, for they had followed in a road well rutted from loaded wagons. But Bill invested in no real estate, notwithstanding the positive assurance that Hazleton was on the ragged edge of a boom.

"Maybe, maybe," he admitted. "But I've got other fish to fry. That one piece up by Pine River will do me for a while."

Here where folk talked only of gold and pelts and railroads and settlement and the coming boom that would make them all rich, Bill Wagstaff added two more ponies to his pack train. These he loaded down with food, staples only, flour, sugar, beans, salt, tea and coffee, and a sack of dried fruit. Also he bestowed upon Nigger a further burden of six dozen steel traps.

And in the cool of a midsummer morning, before Hazleton had rubbed the sleep out of its collective eyes and taken up the day's work of discussing its future greatness, Roaring Bill and his wife draped the mosquito nets over their heads and turned their faces north.

They bore out upon a wagon road. For a brief distance only did this endure, then dwindled to a path. A turn in this hid sight of the clustered log houses and tents, and the two steamers that lay up against the bank. The river itself was soon lost in the far stretches of forest. Once more they rode alone in the wilderness. For the first time Hazel felt a quick shrinking from the North, an awe of its huge, silent spaces, which could so easily engulf thousands such as they and still remain a land untamed.

But this feeling passed, and she came again under the spell of the trail, riding with eyes and ears alert, sitting at ease in the saddle, and taking each new crook in the way with quickened interest.

CHAPTER
EIGHTEEN

The Wintering Place

On the second day they crossed the Skeena, a risky and tedious piece of business, for the river ran deep and strong. And shortly after this crossing they came to a line of wire strung on poles. Originally a fair passageway had been cleared through low brush and dense timber alike. A pathway of sorts still remained, though dim and little trodden and littered with down trees of various sizes. Bill followed this.

"What is the wire? A rural telephone? Oh, I remember you told me once — that Yukon telegraph," Hazel remarked.

"Uh-huh. That's the famous Telegraph Trail," Bill answered. "Runs from Ashcroft clear to Dawson City, on the Yukon; that is, the line does. There's a lineman's house every twenty miles or so, and an operator every forty miles. The best thing about it is that it furnishes us with a sort of a road. And that's mighty lucky, for there's some tough going ahead of us."

So long as they held to the Telegraph Trail the way led through fairly decent country. In open patches there was ample grazing for their horses. Hills there were, to be sure; all the land rolled away in immense forested billows, but the mountains stood off on the right and left, frowning in the distance. A plague of flies harassed them continually, Hazel's hands suffering most, even though she kept religiously to thick buckskin gloves. The poisonous bites led to scratching, which bred soreness. And as they gained a greater elevation and the timbered bottoms gave way to rocky hills over which she must perforce walk and lead her horse, the sweat of the exertion stung and burned intolerably, like salt water on an open wound.

Minor hardships, these; scarcely to be dignified by that name, more in the nature of aggravated discomforts they were. But they irked, and, like any accumulation of small things, piled up a disheartening total. By imperceptible degrees the glamour of the trail, the lure of gypsying, began to lessen. She found herself longing for the Pine River cabin, for surcease from this never-ending journey. But she would not have owned this to Roaring Bill; not for the world. It savored of weakness, disloyalty. She felt ashamed. Still — it was no longer a pleasure jaunt. The country they bore steadily up into grew more and more forbidding. The rugged slopes bore no resemblance to the kindly, peaceful land where the cabin stood. Swamps and reedy lakes lurked in low places. The hills stood forth grim and craggy, gashed with deep-cleft gorges, and rising to heights more grim and desolate at the uttermost reach of her vision. And into the heart of this, toward a far-distant area where she could faintly distinguish virgin snow on peaks that pierced the sky, they traveled day after day.

196

Shortly before reaching Station Six they crossed the Naas, foaming down to the blue Pacific. And at Station Seven, Bill turned squarely off the Telegraph Trail and struck east by north. It had been a break in the monotony of each day's travel to come upon the lonely men in their little log houses. When they turned away from the single wire that linked them up with the outer world, it seemed to Hazel as if the profound, disquieting stillness of the North became intensified.

Presently the way grew rougher. If anything, Roaring Bill increased his pace. He himself no longer rode. When the steepness of the hills and cañons made the going hard the packs were redivided, and henceforth Satin bore on his back a portion of the supplies. Bill led the way tirelessly. Through flies, river crossings, camp labor, and all the petty irritations of the trail he kept an unruffled spirit, a fine, enduring patience that Hazel marveled at and admired. Many a time, wakening at some slight stir, she would find him cooking breakfast. In every way within his power he saved her.

"I got to take good care of you, little person," he would say. "I'm used to this sort of thing, and I'm tough as buckskin. But it sure isn't proving any picnic for you. It's a lot worse in this way than I thought it would be. And we've got to get in there before the snow begins to fly, or it will play the dickens with us."

Many a strange shift were they put to. Once Bill had to fell a great spruce across a twenty-foot crevice. It took him two days to hew it flat so that his horses could be led over. The depth was bottomless to the eye, but from far below rose the cavernous growl of rushing

197

water, and Hazel held her breath as each animal stepped gingerly over the narrow bridge. One misstep —

Once they climbed three weary days up a precipitous mountain range, and, turned back in sight of the crest by an impassable cliff, were forced to back track and swing in a fifty-mile detour.

In an air line Roaring Bill's destination lay approximately two hundred miles north — almost due north — of Hazleton. By the devious route they were compelled to take the distance was doubled, more than doubled. And their rate of progress now fell short of a ten-mile average. September was upon them. The days dwindled in length, and the nights grew to have a frosty nip.

Early and late he pushed on. Two camp necessities were fortunately abundant, grass and water. Even so, the stress of the trail told on the horses. They lost flesh. The extreme steepness of succeeding hills bred galls under the heavy packs. They grew leg weary, no longer following each other with sprightly step and heads high. Hazel pitied them, for she herself was trail weary beyond words. The vagabond instinct had fallen asleep. The fine aura of romance no longer hovered over the venture.

Sometimes when dusk ended the day's journey and she swung her stiffened limbs out of the saddle, she would cheerfully have foregone all the gold in the North to be at her ease before the fireplace in their distant cabin, with her man's head nesting in her lap, and no toll of weary miles looming sternly on the morrow's horizon. It was all work, trying work, the more trying because she sensed a latent uneasiness on her husband's part, an uneasiness she could never induce him to embody in words. Nevertheless, it existed, and she resented its existence — a trouble she could not share. But she could not put her finger on the cause, for Bill merely smiled a denial when she mentioned it.

Nor did she fathom the cause until upon a certain day which fell upon the end of a week's wearisome traverse of the hardest country yet encountered. Up and up and still higher he bore into a range of beetling crags, and always his gaze was fixed steadfastly and dubiously on the serrated backbone toward which they ascended with infinite toil and hourly risk, skirting sheer cliffs on narrow rock ledges, working foot by foot over declivities where the horses dug their hoofs into a precarious toe hold, and where a slip meant broken bones on the ragged stones below. But win to the uppermost height they did, where an early snowfall lay two inches deep in a thin forest of jack pine.

They broke out of a cañon up which they had struggled all day onto a level plot where the pine stood in somber ranks. A spring creek split the flat in two. Beside this tiny stream Bill unlashed his packs. It still lacked two hours of dark. But he made no comment and Hazel forbore to trouble him with questions. Once the packs were off and the horses at liberty, Bill caught up his rifle.

"Come on, Hazel," he said. "Let's take a little hike."

199

The flat was small, and once clear of it the pines thinned out on a steep, rocky slope so that westward they could overlook a vast network of cañons and mountain spurs. But ahead of them the mountain rose to an upstanding backbone of jumbled granite, and on this backbone Bill Wagstaff bent an anxious eye. Presently they sat down on a bowlder to take a breathing spell after a stiff stretch of climbing. Hazel slipped her hand in his and whispered:

"What is it, Billy-boy?"

"I'm afraid we can't get over here with the horses," he answered slowly. "And if we can't find a pass of some kind — well, come on! It isn't more than a quarter of a mile to the top."

He struck out again, clambering over great bowlders, clawing his way along rocky shelves, with a hand outstretched to help her now and then. Her perceptions quickened by the hint he had given, Hazel viewed the long ridge for a possible crossing, and she was forced to the reluctant conclusion that no hoofed beast save mountain sheep or goat could cross that divide. Certainly not by the route they were taking. And north and south as far as she could see the backbone ran like a solid wall.

It was a scant quarter mile to the top, beyond which no farther mountain crests showed — only clear, blue sky. But it was a stretch that taxed her endurance to the limit for the next hour. Just short of the top Bill halted, and wiped the sweat out of his eyes. And as he stood his gaze suddenly became fixed, a concentrated stare at a point northward. He raised his glasses.

200

"By thunder!" he exclaimed. "I believe — it's me for the top."

He went up the few remaining yards with a haste that left Hazel panting behind. Above her he stood balanced on a bowlder, cut sharp against the sky, and she reached him just as he lowered the field glasses with a long sigh of relief. His eyes shone with exultation.

"Come on up on the perch," he invited, and reached forth a long, muscular arm, drawing her up close beside him on the rock.

"Behold the Promised Land," he breathed, "and the gateway thereof, lying a couple of miles to the north."

They were, it seemed to Hazel, roosting precariously on the very summit of the world. On both sides the mountain pitched away sharply in rugged folds. Distance smoothed out the harsh declivities, blurred over the tremendous cañons. Looking eastward, she saw an ample basin, which gave promise of level ground on its floor. True, it was ringed about with sky-scraping peaks, save where a small valley opened to the south. Behind them, between them and the far Pacific rolled a sea of mountains, snow-capped, glacier-torn, gigantic.

"Down there," Roaring Bill waved his hand, "there's a little meadow, and turf to walk on. Lord, I'll be glad to get out of these rocks! You'll never catch me coming in this way again. It's sure tough going. And I've been scared to death for a week, thinking we couldn't get through."

"But we can?"

"Yes, easy," he assured. "Take the glasses and look. That flat we left our outfit in runs pretty well to the top, about two miles along. Then there's a notch in the ridge that you can't get with the naked eye, and a wider cañon running down into the basin. It's the only decent break in the divide for fifty miles so far as I can see. This backbone runs to high mountains both north and south of us — like the great wall of China. We're lucky to hit this pass."

"Suppose we couldn't get over here?" Hazel asked. "What if there hadn't been a pass?"

"That was beginning to keep me awake nights," he confessed. "I've been studying this rock wall for a week. It doesn't look good from the east side, but it's worse on the west, and I couldn't seem to locate the gap I spotted from the basin one time. And if we couldn't get through, it meant a hundred miles or more back south around that white peak you see. Over a worse country than we've come through — and no cinch on getting over at that. Do you realize that it's getting late in the year? Winter may come — bing! — inside of ten days. And me caught in a rock pile, with no cabin to shelter my best girl, and no hay up to feed my horses! You bet it bothered me."

She hugged him sympathetically, and Bill smiled down at her.

"But it's plain sailing now," he continued. "I know that basin and all the country beyond it. It's a pretty decent camping place, and there's a fairly easy way out."

He bestowed a reassuring kiss upon her. They sat on the bowlder for a few minutes, then scrambled down-hill to the jack-pine flat, and built their evening fire. And for the first time in many days Roaring Bill whistled and lightly burst into snatches of song in the deep, bellowing voice that had given him his name back in the Cariboo country. His humor was infectious. Hazel felt the gods of high adventure smiling broadly upon them once more.

Before daybreak they were up and packed. In the dim light of dawn Bill picked his way up through the jack-pine flat. With easy traveling they made such time as enabled them to cross through the narrow gash — cut in the divide by some glacial offshoot when the Klappan Range was young — before the sun, a ball of molten fire, heaved up from behind the far mountain chain.

At noon, two days later, they stepped out of a heavy stand of spruce into a sun-warmed meadow, where ripe, yellow grasses waved to their horses' knees. Hazel came afoot, a fresh-killed deer lashed across Silk's back.

Bill hesitated, as if taking his bearings, then led to where a rocky spur of a hill jutted into the meadow's edge. A spring bubbled out of a pebbly basin, and he poked about in the grass beside it with his foot, presently stooping to pick up something which proved to be a short bit of charred stick.

"The remains of my last camp fire," he smiled reminiscently. "Packs off, old pal. We're through with the trail for a while."

CHAPTER
NINETEEN

Four Walls and a Roof

To such as view with a kindly eye the hushed areas of virgin forest and the bold cliffs and peaks of mountain ranges, it is a joy to tread unknown trails, camping as the spirit moves, journeying leisurely and in decent comfort from charming spot to spots more charming. With no spur of need to drive, such inconsequential wandering gives to each day and incident an added zest. Nature appears to have on her best bib and tucker for the occasion. The alluring finger of the unknown beckons alluringly onward, so that if one should betimes strain to physical exhaustion in pursuit, that is a matter of no moment whatever.

But it is a different thing to face the wilderness for a purpose, to journey in haste toward a set point, with a penalty swift and sure for failure to reach that point in due season. Especially is this so in the high latitudes. Natural barriers uprear before the traveler, barriers which he must scale with sweat and straining muscles. He must progress by devious ways, seeking always the line of least resistance. The season of summer is brief, a riot of flowers and vegetation. A certain number of weeks the land smiles and flaunts gay flowers in the shadow of the ancient glaciers. Then the frost and snow come back to their own, and the long nights shut down like a pall.

Brought to it by a kindlier road, Hazel would have found that nook in the Klappan Range a pleasant enough place. She could not deny its beauty. It snuggled in the heart of a wild tangle of hills all turreted and battlemented with ledge and pinnacle of rock, from which ran huge escarpments clothed with spruce and pine, scarred and gashed on every hand with slides and deep-worn watercourses, down which tumultuous streams rioted their foamy way. And nestled amid this, like a precious stone in its massive setting, a few hundred acres of level, grassy turf dotted with trees. Southward opened a narrow valley, as if pointing the road to a less rigorous land. No, she could not deny its beauty. But she was far too trail weary to appreciate the grandeur of the Klappan Range. She desired nothing so much as rest and comfort, and the solemn mountains were neither restful nor soothing. They stood too grim and aloof in a lonely land.

There was so much to be done, work of the hands; a cabin to build, and a stable; hay to be cut and stacked so that their horses might live through the long winter — which already heralded his approach with sharp, stinging frosts at night, and flurries of snow along the higher ridges.

Bill staked the tent beside the spring, fashioned a rude fork out of a pronged willow, and fitted a handle to the scythe he had brought for the purpose. From dawn to dark he swung the keen blade in the heavy grass which carpeted the bottom. Behind him Hazel piled it in little mounds with the fork. She insisted on this, though it blistered her hands and brought furious pains to her back. If her man must strain every nerve she would lighten the burden with what strength she had. And with two pair of hands to the task, the piles of hay gathered thick on the meadow. When Bill judged that the supply reached twenty tons, he built a rude sled with a rack on it, and hauled in the hay with a saddle horse.

"Amen!" said Bill, when he had emptied the rack for the last time, and the hay rose in a neat stack. "That's another load off my mind. I can build a cabin and a stable in six feet of snow if I have to, but there would have been a slim chance of haying once a storm hit us. And the caballos need a grubstake for the winter worse than we do, because they can't eat meat. We wouldn't go hungry — there's moose enough to feed an army ranging in that low ground to the south."

"There's everything that one needs, almost, in the wilderness, isn't there?" Hazel observed reflectively. "But still the law of life is awfully harsh, don't you think, Bill? Isolation is a terrible thing when it is so absolutely complete. Suppose something went wrong? There's no help, and no mercy — absolutely none. You could die here by inches and the woods and mountains would look calmly on, just as they have looked on everything for thousands of years. It's like prison regulations. You *must* do this, and you *must* do that, and there's no excuse for mistakes. Nature, when you get close to her, is so inexorable."

Bill eyed her a second. Then he put his arms around her, and patted her hair tenderly.

"Is it getting on your nerves already, little person?" he asked. "Nothing's going to go wrong. I've been in wild country too often to make mistakes or get careless. And those are the two crimes for which the North — or any wilderness — inflicts rather serious penalties. Life isn't a bit harsher here than in the human ant heaps. Only everything is more direct; cause and effect are linked up close. There are no complexities. It's all done in the open, and if you don't play the game according to the few simple rules you go down and out. That's all there is to it. There's no doctor in the next block, nor a grocer to take your order over the phone, and you can't run out to a café and take dinner with a friend. But neither is the air swarming with disease germs, nor are there malicious gossips to blast you with their tongues, nor rent and taxes to pay every time you turn around. Nor am I at the mercy of a job. And what does the old, settled country do to you when you have neither money nor job? It treats you worse than the worst the North can do; for, lacking the price, it denies you access to the abundance that mocks you in every shop window, and bars you out of the houses that line the streets. Here, everything needful is yours for the taking. If one is ignorant, or unable to convert wood and water and game to his own uses, he must learn how, or pay the penalty of incompetence. No, little person, I don't think the law of life is nearly so harsh here as it is where the mob struggles for its daily bread. It's more open and aboveboard here; more up to the individual. But it's lonely sometimes. I guess that's what ails you."

"Oh, pouf!" she denied. "I'm not lonely, so long as I've got you. But sometimes I think of something happening to you — sickness and accidents, and all that. One can't help thinking what *might* happen."

"Forget it!" Bill exhorted. "That's the worst of living in this big, still country — it makes one introspective, and so confoundedly conscious of what puny atoms we human beings are, after all. But there's less chance of sickness here than any place. Anyway, we've got to take a chance on things now and then, in the course of living our lives according to our lights. We're playing for a stake — and things that are worth having are never handed to us on a silver salver. Besides, I never had worse than a stomachache in my life — and you're a pretty healthy specimen yourself. Wait till I get that cabin built, with a big fireplace at one end. We'll be more comfortable, and things will look a little rosier. This thing of everlasting hurry and hard work gets on anybody's nerves."

The best of the afternoon was still unspent when the haystacking terminated, and Bill declared a holiday. He rigged a line on a limber willow wand, and with a fragment of venison for bait sought the pools of the stream which flowed out the south opening. He prophesied that in certain black eddies plump trout would be lurking, and he made his prophecy good at the first pool. Hazel elected herself gun-bearer to the expedition, but before long Bill took up that office while she snared trout after trout from the stream —

having become something of an angler herself under Bill's schooling. And when they were frying the fish that evening he suddenly observed:

"Say, they were game little fellows, these, weren't they? Wasn't that better sport than taking a street car out to the park and feeding the swans?"

"What an idea!" she laughed. "Who wants to feed swans in a park?"

But when the fire had sunk to dull embers, and the stars were peeping shyly in the open flap of their tent, she whispered in his ear:

"You mustn't think I'm complaining or lonesome or anything, Billy-boy, when I make remarks like I did to-day. I love you a heap, and I'd be happy *anywhere* with you. And I'm really and truly at home in the wilderness. Only — only sometimes I have a funny feeling; as if I were afraid. It seems silly, but this is all so different from our little cabin. I look up at these big mountains, and they seem to be scowling — as if we were trespassers or something."

"I know." Bill drew her close to him. "But that's just mood. I've felt that same sensation up here — a foolish, indefinable foreboding. All the out-of-the-way places of the earth produce that effect, if one is at all imaginative. It's the bigness of everything, and the eternal stillness. I've caught myself listening — when I knew there was nothing to hear. Makes a fellow feel like a small boy left by himself in some big, gloomy building — awesome. Sure, I know it. It would be hard on the nerves to live here always. But we're only after a stake — then all the pleasant places of the earth are open to us; with that little, old log house up by Pine River for a refuge whenever we get tired of the world at large. Cuddle up and go to sleep. You're a dead-game sport, or you'd have hollered long ago."

And, next day, to Hazel, sitting by watching him swing the heavy, double-bitted ax on the foundation logs of their winter home, it all seemed foolish, that heaviness of heart which sometimes assailed her. She was perfectly happy. In each of them the good, red blood of youth ran full and strong, offering ample security against illness. They had plenty of food. In a few brief months Bill would wrest a sack of gold from the treasure house of the North, and they would journey home by easy stages. Why should she brood? It was sheer folly — a mere ebb of spirit.

Fortune favored them to the extent of letting the October storms remain in abeyance until Bill finished his cabin, with a cavernous fireplace of rough stone at one end. He split planks for a door out of raw timber, and graced his house with two windows — one of four small panes of glass carefully packed in their bedding all the way from Hazleton, the other a two-foot square of deerskin scraped parchment thin; opaque to the vision, it still permitted light to enter. The floor was plain earth, a condition Bill promised to remedy with hides of moose, once his buildings were completed. Rudely finished, and lacking much that would have made for comfort, still it served its purpose, and Hazel made shift contentedly.

Followed then the erection of a stable to shelter the horses. Midway of its construction a cloud bank blew out of the northeast, and a foot of snow fell. Then it cleared to brilliant days of frost. Bill finished his stable. At night he tied the horses therein. By day they were turned loose to rustle their fodder from under the crisp snow. It was necessary to husband the stock of hay, for spring might be late.

After that they went hunting. The third day Bill shot two moose in an open glade ten miles afield. It took them two more days to haul in the frozen meat on a sled.

"Looks like one side of a butcher shop," Bill remarked, viewing the dressed meat where it hung on a pole scaffolding beyond reach of the wolves.

"It certainly does," Hazel replied. "We'll never eat all that."

"Probably not," he smiled. "But there's nothing like having plenty. The moose might emigrate, you know. I think I'll add a deer to that lot for variety — if I can find one."

He managed this in the next few days, and also laid in a stock of frozen trout by the simple expedient of locating a large pool, and netting the speckled denizens thereof through a hole in the ice.

So their larder was amply supplied. And, as the cold rigidly tightened its grip, and succeeding snows deepened the white blanket till snowshoes became imperative, Bill began to string out a line of traps.

CHAPTER
TWENTY

Boreas Chants His Lay

December winged by, the days succeeding each other like glittering panels on a black ground of long, drear nights. Christmas came. They mustered up something of the holiday spirit, dining gayly off a roast of caribou. For the occasion Hazel had saved the last half dozen potatoes. With the material at her command she evolved a Christmas pudding, serving it with brandy sauce. And after satisfying appetites bred of a morning tilt with Jack Frost along Bill's trap line, they spent a pleasant hour picturing their next Christmas. There would be holly and bright lights and music — the festival spirit freed of all restraint.

The new year was born in a wild smother of flying snow, which died at dawn to let a pale, heatless sun peer tentatively over the southern mountains, his slanting beams setting everything aglitter. Frost particles vibrated in the air, coruscating diamond dust. Underfoot, on the path beaten betwixt house and stable, the snow crunched and complained as they walked, and in the open where the mad winds had piled it in hard, white windrows. But in the thick woods it lay as it had fallen, full five foot deep, a downy wrapping

212

for the slumbering earth, over which Bill Wagstaff flitted on his snowshoes as silently as a ghost — a fur-clad ghost, however, who bore a rifle on his shoulder, and whose breath exhaled in white, steamy puffs.

Gold or no gold, the wild land was giving up its treasure to them. Already the catch of furs totaled ninety marten, a few mink, a dozen wolves — and two pelts of that rara avis, the silver fox. Around twelve hundred dollars, Bill estimated, with four months yet to trap. And the labor of tending the trap lines, of skinning and stretching the catch, served to keep them both occupied — Hazel as much as he, for she went out with him on all but the hardest trips. So that their isolation in the hushed, white world where the frost ruled with an iron hand had not so far become oppressive. They were too busy to develop that dour affliction of the spirit which loneliness and idleness breed through the long winters of the North.

A day or two after the first of the year Roaring Bill set out to go over one of the uttermost trap lines. Five minutes after closing the door he was back.

"Easy with that fire, little person," he cautioned. "She's blowing out of the northwest again. The sparks are sailing pretty high. Keep your eye on it, Hazel."

"All right, Billum," she replied. "I'll be careful."

Not more than fifty yards separated the house and stable. At the stable end stood the stack of hay, a low hummock above the surrounding drift. Except for the place where Bill daily removed the supply for his horses there was not much foothold for a spark, since a thin

213

coat of snow overlaid the greater part of the top. But there was that chance of catastrophe. The chimney of their fireplace yawned wide to the sky, vomiting sparks and ash like a miniature volcano when the fire was roughly stirred, or an extra heavy supply of dry wood laid on. When the wind whistled out of the northwest the line of flight was fair over the stack. It behooved them to watch wind and fire. By keeping a bed of coals and laying on a stick or two at a time a gale might roar across the chimney-top without sucking forth a spark large enough to ignite the hay. Hence Bill's warning. He had spoken of it before.

Hazel washed up her breakfast dishes, and set the cabin in order according to her housewifely instincts. Then she curled up in the chair which Bill had painstakingly constructed for her especial comfort with only ax and knife for tools. She was working up a pair of moccasins after an Indian pattern, and she grew wholly absorbed in the task, drawing stitch after stitch of sinew strongly and neatly into place. The hours flicked past in unseemly haste, so completely was she engrossed. When at length the soreness of her fingers warned her that she had been at work a long time, she looked at her watch.

"Goodness me! Bill's due home any time, and I haven't a thing ready to eat," she exclaimed. "And here's my fire nearly out."

She piled on wood, and stirring the coals under it, fanned them with her husband's old felt hat, forgetful of sparks or aught but that she should be cooking against his hungry arrival. Outside, the wind blew lustily, driving the loose snow across the open in long, wavering ribbons. But she had forgotten that it was in the dangerous quarter, and she did not recall that important fact even when she sat down again to watch her moose steaks broil on the glowing coals raked apart from the leaping blaze. The flames licked into the throat of the chimney with the purr of a giant cat.

No sixth sense warned her of impending calamity. It burst upon her with startling abruptness only when she opened the door to throw out some scraps of discarded meat, for the blaze of the burning stack shot thirty feet in the air, and the smoke rolled across the meadow in a sooty manner.

Bareheaded, in a thin pair of moccasins, without coat or mittens to fend her from the lance-toothed frost, Hazel ran to the stable. She could get the horses out, perhaps, before the log walls became their crematory. But Bill, coming in from his traps, reached the stable first, and there was nothing for her to do but stand and watch with a sickening self-reproach. He untied and clubbed the reluctant horses outside. Already the stable end against the hay was shooting up tongues of flame. As the blaze lapped swiftly over the roof and ate into the walls, the horses struggled through the deep drift, lunging desperately to gain a few yards, then turned to stand with ears pricked up at the strange sight, shivering in the bitter northwest wind that assailed their bare, unprotected bodies.

Bill himself drew back from the fire, and stared at it fixedly. He kept silence until Hazel timidly put her hand on his arm.

"You watched that fire all right, didn't you?" he said then.

"Bill, Bill!" she cried. But he merely shrugged his shoulders, and kept his gaze fixed on the burning stable.

To Hazel, shivering with the cold, even close as she was to the intense heat, it seemed an incredibly short time till a glowing mound below the snow level was all that remained; a black-edged pit that belched smoke and sparks. That and five horses humped tail to the driving wind, stolidly enduring. She shuddered with something besides the cold. And then Bill spoke absently, his eyes still on the smoldering heap.

"Five feet of caked snow on top of every blade of grass," she heard him mutter. "They can't browse on trees, like deer. Aw, hell!"

He had stuck his rifle butt first in the snow. He walked over to it; Hazel followed. When he stood, with the rifle slung in the crook of his arm, she tried again to break through this silent aloofness which cut her more deeply than any harshness of speech could have done.

"Bill, I'm so sorry!" she pleaded. "It's terrible, I know. What can we do?"

"Do? Huh!" he snorted. "If I ever have to die before my time, I hope it will be with a full belly and my head in the air — and mercifully swift."

Even then she had no clear idea of his intention. She looked up at him pleadingly, but he was staring at the horses, his teeth biting nervously at his under lip. Suddenly he blinked, and she saw his eyes moisten. In the same instant he threw up the rifle. At the thin, vicious crack of it, Silk collapsed.

She understood then. With her hand pressed hard over her mouth to keep back the hysterical scream that threatened, she fled to the house. Behind her the rifle spat forth its staccato message of death. For a few seconds the mountains flung whiplike echoes back and forth in a volley. Then the sibilant voice of the wind alone broke the stillness.

Numbed with the cold, terrified at the elemental ruthlessness of it all, she threw herself on the bed, denied even the relief of tears. Dry-eyed and heavy-hearted, she waited her husband's coming, and dreading it — for the first time she had seen her Bill look on her with cold, critical anger. For an interminable time she lay listening for the click of the latch, every nerve strung tight.

He came at last, and the thump of his rifle as he stood it against the wall had no more than sounded before he was bending over her. He sat down on the edge of the bed, and putting his arm across her shoulders, turned her gently so that she faced him.

"Never mind, little person," he whispered. "It's done and over. I'm sorry I slashed at you the way I did. That's a fool man's way — if he's hurt and sore he always has to jump on somebody else."

Then by some queer complexity of her woman's nature the tears forced their way. She did not want to cry — only the weak and mushy-minded wept. She had always fought back tears unless she was shaken to the roots of her soul. But it was almost a relief to cry with

217

Bill's arm holding her close. And it was brief. She sat up beside him presently. He held her hand tucked in between his own two palms, but he looked wistfully at the window, as if he were seeing what lay beyond.

"Poor, dumb devils!" he murmured. "I feel like a murderer. But it was pure mercy to them. They won't suffer the agony of frost, nor the slow pain of starvation. That's what it amounted to — they'd starve if they didn't freeze first. I've known men I would rather have shot. I bucked many a hard old trail with Silk and Satin. Poor, dumb devils!"

"D-don't, Bill!" she cried forlornly. "I know it's my fault. I let the fire almost go out, and then built it up big without thinking. And I know being sorry doesn't make any difference. But please — I don't want to be miserable over it. I'll never be careless again."

"All right; I won't talk about it, hon," he said. "I don't think you will ever be careless about such things again. The North won't let us get away with it. The wilderness is bigger than we are, and it's merciless if we make mistakes."

"I see that." She shuddered involuntarily. "It's a grim country. It frightens me."

"Don't let it," he said tenderly. "So long as we have our health and strength we can win out, and be stronger for the experience. Winter's a tough proposition up here, but you want to fight shy of morbid brooding over things that can't be helped. This everlasting frost and snow will be gone by and by. It'll be spring. And everything looks different when there's green grass and flowers, and the sun is warm. Buck up, old girl — Bill's still on the job."

"How can you prospect in the spring without horses to pack the outfit?" she asked, after a little. "How can we get out of here with all the stuff we'll have?"

"We'll manage it," he assured lightly. "We'll get out with our furs and gold, all right, and we won't go hungry on the way, even if we have no pack train. Leave it to me."

CHAPTER
TWENTY-ONE

Jack Frost Withdraws

All through the month of January each evening, as dusk folded its somber mantle about the meadow, the wolves gathered to feast on the dead horses, till Hazel's nerves were strained to the snapping point. Continually she was reminded of that vivid episode, of which she had been the unwitting cause. Sometimes she would open the door, and from out the dark would arise the sound of wolfish quarrels over the feast, disembodied snappings and snarlings. Or when the low-swimming moon shed a misty glimmer on the open she would peer through a thawed place on the window-pane, and see gray shapes circling about the half-picked skeletons. Sometimes, when Bill was gone, and all about the cabin was utterly still, one, bolder or hungrier than his fellows, would trot across the meadow, drawn by the scent of the meat. Two or three of these Hazel shot with her own rifle.

But when February marked another span on the calendar the wolves came no more. The bones were clean.

There was no impending misfortune or danger that she could point to or forecast with certitude.

Nevertheless, struggle against it as she might, knowing it for pure psychological phenomena arising out of her harsh environment, Hazel suffered continual vague forebodings. The bald, white peaks seemed to surround her like a prison from which there could be no release. From day to day she was harassed by dismal thoughts. She would wake in the night clutching at her husband. Such days as he went out alone she passed in restless anxiety. Something would happen. What it would be she did not know, but to her it seemed that the bleak stage was set for untoward drama, and they two the puppets that must play.

She strove against this impression with cold logic; but reason availed nothing against the feeling that the North had but to stretch forth its mighty hand and crush them utterly. But all of this she concealed from Bill. She was ashamed of her fears, the groundless uneasiness. Yet it was a constant factor in her daily life, and it sapped her vitality as surely and steadily as lack of bodily nourishment could have done.

Had there been in her make-up any inherent weakness of mentality, Hazel might perhaps have brooded herself into neurasthenia. Few save those who have actually experienced complete isolation for extended periods can realize the queer, warped outlook such an existence imposes on the human mind, if that mind is a trifle more than normally sensitive to impressions, and a nature essentially social both by inclination and habit. In the first months of their marriage she had assured herself and him repeatedly that she could be perfectly happy and contented any place on earth with Bill Wagstaff.

Emotion has blinded wiser folk, and perhaps that is merely a little device of nature's, for if one could look into the future with too great a clarity of vision there would be fewer matings. In the main her declaration still held true. She loved her husband with the same intensity; possibly even more, for she had found in him none of the flaws which every woman dreads that time and association may bring to light in her chosen mate.

When Bill drew her up close in his arms, the intangible menace of the wilderness and all the dreary monotony of the days faded into the background. But they, no more than others who have tried and failed for lack of understanding, could not live their lives with their heads in an emotional cloud. For every action there must be a corresponding reaction. They who have the capacity to reach the heights must likewise, upon occasion, plumb the depths. Life, she began to realize, resolved itself into an unending succession of little, trivial things, with here and there some great event looming out above all the rest for its bestowal of happiness or pain.

Bill knew. He often talked about such things. She was beginning to understand that he had a far more comprehensive grasp of the fundamentals of existence that she had. He had explained to her that the individual unit was nothing outside of his group affiliations, and she applied that to herself in a practical way in an endeavor to analyze herself. She was a group product, and only under group conditions could her life flow along nonirritant lines. Such being the case, it followed that if Bill persisted in living out of the world they would eventually drift apart, in spirit if not in actuality. And that was an absurd summing-up.

She rejected the conclusion decisively. For was not their present situation the net result of a concrete endeavor to strike a balance between the best of what both the wilderness and the humming cities had to offer them? It seemed treason to Bill to long for other voices and other faces. Yet she could not help the feeling. She wondered if he, too, did not sometimes long for company besides her own. And the thought stirred up a perverse jealousy. They two, perfectly mated in all things, should be able to make their own little world complete — but they could not, she knew. Life was altogether too complex an affair to be solved in so primitive a fashion. She felt that continued living under such conditions would drive her mad; that if she stayed long enough under the somber shadow of the Klappan Range she would hate the North and all it contained.

That would have been both unjust and absurd, so she set herself resolutely to overcome that feeling of oppression. She was too well-balanced to drift unwittingly along this perilous road of thought. She schooled herself to endure and to fight off introspection. She had absorbed enough of her husband's sturdy philosophy of life to try and make the best of a bad job. After all, she frequently assured herself, the badness of the job was mostly a state of mind. And she had a growing conviction that Bill sensed the struggle, and that it hurt him. For that reason, if for no other, she did her best to make light of the grim environment, and to wait patiently for spring.

February and March stormed a path furiously across the calendar. Higher and higher the drifts piled about the cabin, till at length it was banked to the eaves with snow save where Bill shoveled it away to let light to the windows. Day after day they kept indoors, stoking up the fire, listening to the triumphant whoop of the winds.

"Snow, snow!" Hazel burst out one day. "Frost that cuts you like a knife. I wonder if there's ever going to be an end to it? I wish we were home again — or some place."

"So do I, little person," Bill said gently. "But spring's almost at the door. Hang on a little longer. We've made a fair stake, anyway, if we don't wash an ounce of gold."

Hazel let her gaze wander over the pelts hanging thick from ridge log and wall. Bill had fared well at his trapping. Over two thousand dollars he estimated the value of his catch.

"How are we going to get it all out?" She voiced a troublesome thought.

"Shoulder pack to the Skeena," he answered laconically. "Build a dugout there, and float downstream. Portage the rapids as they come."

"Oh, Bill!" she came and leaned her head against him contritely. "Our poor ponies! And it was all my carelessness."

"Never mind, hon," he comforted. "They blinked out without suffering. And we'll make it like a charm. Be game — it'll soon be spring."

As if in verification of his words, with the last breath of that howling storm came a sudden softening of the atmosphere. The sharp teeth of the frost became swiftly blunted, and the sun, swinging daily in a wider arc, brought the battery of his rays into effective play on the mountainsides. The drifts lessened, shrunk, became moisture sodden. For ten days or more the gradual thaw increased. Then a lusty-lunged chinook wind came booming up along the Klappan Range, and stripped it to a bare, steaming heap. Overhead whistled the first flight of the wild goose, bound for the nesting grounds. Night and day the roar of a dozen cataracts droned on all sides of the basin, as the melting snow poured down in the annual spring flood.

By April the twentieth the abdication of Jack Frost was complete. A kindlier despot ruled the land, and Bill Wagstaff began to talk of gold.

CHAPTER
TWENTY-TWO

The Strike

". . . that precious yellow metal sought by men
  In regions desolate.
    Pursued in patient hope or furious toil;
  Breeder of discord, wars, and murderous hate;
    The victor's spoil."

So Hazel quoted, leaning over her husband's shoulder. In the bottom of his pan, shining among a film of black sand, lay half a dozen bright specks, varying from pin-point size to the bigness of a grain of wheat.

"That's the stuff," Bill murmured. "Only it seems rather far-fetched for your poet to blame inanimate matter for the cussedness of humanity in general. I suppose, though, he thought he was striking a highly dramatic note. Anyway, it looks as if we'd struck it pretty fair. It's time, too — the June rise will hit us like a whirlwind one of these days."

"About what is the value of those little pieces?" Hazel asked.

"Oh, fifty or sixty cents," he answered. "Not much by itself. But it seems to be uniform over the bar — and I can wash a good many pans in a day's work."

"I should think so," she remarked. "It didn't take you ten minutes to do that one."

"Whitey Lewis and I took out over two hundred dollars a day on that other creek last spring — no, a year last spring, it was," he observed reminiscently. "This isn't as good, but it's not to be sneezed at, either. I think I'll make me a rocker. I've sampled this bend quite a lot, and I don't think I can do any better than fly at this while the water stays low."

"I can help, can't I?" she said eagerly.

"Sure," he smiled. "You help a lot, little person, just sitting around keeping me company."

"But I want to work," she declared. "I've sat around now till I'm getting the fidgets."

"All right; I'll give you a job," he returned good-naturedly. "Meantime, let's eat that lunch you packed up here."

In a branch of the creek which flowed down through the basin, Bill had found plentiful colors as soon as the first big run-off of water had fallen. He had followed upstream painstakingly, panning colors always, and now and then a few grains of coarse gold to encourage him in the quest. The loss of their horses precluded ranging far afield to that other glacial stream which he had worked with Whitey Lewis when he was a free lance in the North. He was close to his base of supplies, and he had made wages — with always the prospector's lure of a rich strike on the next bar.

And now, with May well advanced, he had found definite indications of good pay dirt. The creek swung in a hairpin curve, and in the neck between the two sides of the loop the gold was sifted through wash gravel and black sand, piled there by God only knew how many centuries of glacial drift and flood. But it was there. He had taken panfuls at random over the bar, and uniformly it gave up coarse gold. With a rocker he stood a fair chance of big money before the June rise.

"In the morning," said he, when lunch was over, "I'll bring along the ax and some nails and a shovel, and get busy."

That night they trudged down to the cabin in high spirits. Bill had washed out enough during the afternoon to make a respectable showing on Hazel's outspread handkerchief. And Hazel was in a gleeful mood over the fact that she had unearthed a big nugget by herself. Beginner's luck, Bill said teasingly, but that did not diminish her elation. The old, adventurous glamour, which the long winter and moods of depression had worn threadbare, began to cast its pleasant spell over her again. The fascination of the gold hunt gripped her. Not for the stuff itself, but for what it would get. She wondered if the men who dared the impassive solitudes of the North for weary, lonesome years saw in every morsel of the gold they found a picture of what that gold would buy them in kindlier lands. And some never found any, never won the stake that would justify the gamble. It was a gamble, in a sense — a pure game of chance; but a game that took strength, and nerve, a sturdy soul, to play.

Still, the gold was there, locked up in divers storing places in the lap of the earth, awaiting those virile enough to find and take. And out beyond, in the crowded places of the earth, were innumerable gateways to comfort and pleasure which could be opened with gold. It remained only to balance the one against the other. Just as she had often planned according to her opportunities when she was a wage slave in the office of Bush and Company, so now did she plan for the future on a broader scale, now that the North promised to open its treasure vault to them — an attitude which Bill Wagstaff encouraged and abetted in his own whimsical fashion. There was nothing too good for them, he sometimes observed, provided it could be got. But there was one profound difference in their respective temperaments, Hazel sometimes reflected. Bill would shrug his wide shoulders, and forget or forego the unattainable, where she would chafe and fume. She was quite positive of this.

But as the days passed there seemed no question of their complete success. Bill fabricated his rocker, a primitive, boxlike device with a blanket screen and transverse slats below. It was faster than the pan, even rude as it was, and it caught all but the finer particles of gold. Hazel helped operate the rocker, and took her turn at shoveling or filling the box with water while Bill rocked. Each day's end sent her to her bed healthily tired, but happily conscious that she had helped to accomplish something.

A queer twist of luck put the cap-sheaf on their undertaking. Hazel ran a splinter of wood into her hand, thus putting a stop to her activities with shovel and pail. Until the wound lost its soreness she was forced to sit idle. She could watch Bill ply his rocker while she fought flies on the bank. This grew tiresome, particularly since she had the sense to realize that a man who works with sweat streaming down his face and a mind wholly absorbed in the immediate task has no desire to be bothered with inconsequential chatter. So she rambled along the creek one afternoon, armed with hook and line on a pliant willow in search of sport.

The trout were hungry, and struck fiercely at the bait. She soon had plenty for supper and breakfast. Wherefore she abandoned that diversion, and took to prying tentatively in the lee of certain bowlders on the edge of the creek — prospecting on her own initiative, as it were. She had no pan, and only one hand to work with, but she knew gold when she saw it — and, after all, it was but an idle method of killing time.

She noticed behind each rock and in every shallow, sheltered place in the stream a plentiful gathering of tiny red stones. They were of a pale, ruby cast, and mostly flawed; dainty trifles, translucent and full of light when she held them to the sun. She began a search for a larger specimen. It might mount nicely into a stickpin for Bill, she thought; a memento of the Klappan Range.

And in this search she came upon a large, rusty pebble, snuggled on the downstream side of an over-hanging rock right at the water's edge. It attracted her first by its symmetrical form, a perfect oval; then, when she lifted it, by its astonishing weight. She continued her search for the pinkish-red stones,

230

carrying the rusty pebble along. Presently she worked her way back to where Roaring Bill labored prodigiously.

"I feel ashamed to be loafing while you work so hard, Billy-boy," she greeted.

"Give me a kiss and I'll call it square," he proposed cheerfully. "Got to work like a beaver, kid. This hot weather'll put us to the bad before long. There'll be ten feet of water roaring down here one of these days."

"Look at these pretty stones I found," she said. "What are they, Bill?"

"Those?" He looked at her outstretched palm. "Garnets."

"Garnets? They must be valuable, then," she observed. "The creek's full of them."

"Valuable? I should say so," he grinned. "I sent a sample to a Chicago firm once. They replied to the effect that they would take all I could deliver, and pay thirty-six dollars a ton, f. o. b., my nearest railroad station."

"Oh!" she protested. "But they're pretty."

"Yes, if you can find one of any size. What's the other rock?" he inquired casually. "You making a collection of specimens?"

"That's just a funny stone I found," she returned. "It must be iron or something. It's terribly heavy for its size."

"Eh? Let me see it," he said.

She handed it over.

He weighed it in his palm, scrutinized it closely, turning it over and over. Then he took out his knife and scratched the rusty surface vigorously for a few minutes.

"Huh!" he grunted. "Look at your funny stone."

He held it out for her inspection. The blade of his knife had left a dull, yellow scar.

"Oh!" she gasped. "Why — it's gold!"

"It is, woman," he declaimed, with mock solemnity. "Gold — glittering gold!

"Say, where did you find this?" he asked, when Hazel stared at the nugget, dumb in the face of this unexpected stroke of fortune.

"Just around the second bend," she cried. "Oh, Bill, do you suppose there's any more there?"

"Lead me to it with my trusty pan and shovel, and we'll see," Bill smiled.

Forthwith they set out. The overhanging bowlder was a scant ten minute's walk up the creek.

Bill leaned on his shovel, and studied the ground. Then, getting down on his knees at the spot where the marks of Hazel's scratching showed plain enough, he began to paw over the gravel.

Within five minutes his fingers brought to light a second lump, double the size of her find. Close upon that he winnowed a third. Hazel leaned over him, breathless. He sifted the gravel and sand through his fingers slowly, picking out and examining all that might be the precious metal, and as he picked and clawed the rusty, brown nuggets came to light. At last he reached bottom. The bowlder thrust out below in a natural shelf. From this Bill carefully scraped the accumulation of black sand and gravel, gleaning as a result of his labor a baker's dozen of assorted chunks — one giant that must have weighed three pounds. He sat back on his haunches, and looked at his wife, speechless.

"Is that truly *all* gold, Bill?" she whispered incredulously.

"It certainly is — as good gold as ever went into the mint," he assured. "All laid in a nice little nest on this shelf of rock. I've heard of such things up in this country, but I never ran into one before — and I've always taken this pocket theory with a grain of salt. But there you are. That's a real, honest-to-God pocket. And a well-lined one, if you ask me. This rusty-colored outside is oxidized iron — from the black sand, I guess. Still, it might be something else. But I know what the inside is, all right, all right."

"My goodness!" she murmured. "There might be wagonloads of it in this creek."

"There might, but it isn't likely." Bill shook his head. "This is a simon-pure pocket, and it would keep a graduate mineralogist guessing to say how it got here, because it's a different proposition from the wash gold in the creek bed. I've got all that's here, I'm pretty sure. And you might prospect this creek from end to end and never find another nugget bigger than a pea. It's rich placer ground, at that — but this pocket's almost unbelievable. Must be forty pounds of gold there. And you found it. You're the original mascot, little person."

He bestowed a bearlike hug upon her.

"Now what?" she asked. "It hardly seems real to pick up several thousand dollars in half an hour or so like this. What will we do?"

"Do? Why, bless your dear soul," he laughed. "We'll just consider ourselves extra lucky, and keep right on with the game till the high water makes us quit."

Which was a contingency nearer at hand than even Bill, with a firsthand knowledge of the North's vagaries in the way of flood, quite anticipated.

Three days after the finding of the pocket the whole floor of the creek was awash. His rocker went down stream overnight. To the mouth of the cañon where the branch sought junction with the parent stream they could ascend, and no farther. And when Bill saw that he rolled himself a cigarette, and, putting one long arm across his wife's shoulders, said whimsically:

"What d'you say we start home?"

CHAPTER
TWENTY-THREE

The Stress of the Trail

Roaring Bill dumped his second pack on the summit of the Klappan, and looked away to where the valley that opened out of the basin showed its blurred hollow in the distance. But he uttered no useless regrets. With horses they could have ridden south through a rolling country, where every stretch of timber gave on a grass-grown level. Instead they were forced back over the rugged route by which they had crossed the range the summer before. Grub, bedding, furs, and gold totaled two hundred pounds. On his sturdy shoulders Bill could pack half that weight. For his wife the thing was a physical impossibility, even had he permitted her to try. Hence every mile advanced meant that he doubled the distance, relaying from one camp to the next. They cut their bedding to a blanket apiece, and that was Hazel's load — all he would allow her to carry.

"You're no pack mule, little person," he would say. "It don't hurt me. I've done this for years."

But even with abnormal strength and endurance, it was killing work to buck those ragged slopes with a heavy load. Only by terrible, unremitting effort could he advance any appreciable distance. From day-break till noon they would climb and rest alternately. Then, after a meal and a short breathing spell, he would go back alone after the second load. They were footsore, and their bodies ached with weariness that verged on pain when they gained the pass that cut the summit of the Klappan Range.

"Well, we're over the hump," Bill remarked thankfully. "It's a downhill shoot to the Skeena. I don't think it's more than fifty or sixty miles to where we can take to the water."

They made better time on the western slope, but the journey became a matter of sheer endurance. Summer was on them in full blaze. The creeks ran full and strong. Thunderstorms blew up out of a clear sky to deluge them. Food was scanty — flour and salt and tea; with meat and fish got by the way. And the black flies and mosquitoes swarmed about them maddeningly day and night.

So they came at last to the Skeena, and Hazel's heart misgave her when she took note of its swirling reaches, the sinuous eddies — a deep, swift, treacherous stream. But Bill rested overnight, and in the morning sought and felled a sizable cedar, and began to hew. Slowly the thick trunk shaped itself to the form of a boat under the steady swing of his ax. Hazel had seen the type in use among the coast Siwashes, twenty-five feet in length, narrow-beamed, the sides cut to a half inch in thickness, the bottom left heavier to withstand scraping over rock, and to keep it on an even keel. A rude and tricky craft, but one wholly efficient in capable hands.

236

In a week it was finished. They loaded the sack of gold, the bundle of furs, their meager camp outfit amidships, and swung off into the stream.

The Skeena drops fifteen hundred feet in a hundred miles. Wherefore there are rapids, boiling stretches of white water in which many a good canoe has come to grief. Some of these they ran at imminent peril. Over the worst they lined the canoe from the bank. One or two short cañons they portaged, dragging the heavy dugout through the brush by main strength. Once they came to a wall-sided gorge that ran away beyond any attempt at portage, and they abandoned the dugout, to build another at the lower end. But between these natural barriers they clicked off the miles in hot haste, such was the swiftness of the current. And in the second week of July they brought up at the head of Kispiox Cañon. Hazleton lay a few miles below. But the Kispiox stayed them, a sluice box cut through solid stone, in which the waters raged with a deafening roar. No man ventured into that wild gorge. They abandoned the dugout. Bill slung the sack of gold and the bale of furs on his back.

"It's the last lap, Hazel," said he. "We'll leave the rest of it for the first Siwash that happens along."

So they set out bravely to trudge the remaining distance. And as the fortunes of the trail sometimes befall, they raised an Indian camp on the bank of the river at the mouth of the cañon. A ten-dollar bill made them possessors of another canoe, and an hour later the roofs of Hazleton cropped up above the bank.

"Oh, Bill," Hazel called from the bow. "Look! There's the same old steamer tied to the same old bank. We've been gone a year, and yet the world hasn't changed a mite. I wonder if Hazleton has taken a Rip van Winkle sleep all this time?"

"No fear," he smiled. "I can see some new houses — quite a few, in fact. And look — by Jiminy! They're working on the grade. That railroad, remember? See all those teams? Maybe I ought to have taken up old Hackaberry on that town-lot proposition, after all."

"Fiddlesticks!" she retorted, with fine scorn of Hazleton's real-estate possibilities. "You could buy the whole town with this."

She touched the sack with her toe.

"Not quite," Bill returned placidly. "I wouldn't, anyway. We'll get a better run for our money than that. I hope old Hack didn't forget to attend to that ranch business for me."

He drove the canoe alongside a float. A few loungers viewed them with frank curiosity. Bill set out the treasure sack and the bale of furs, and tied the canoe.

"A new hotel, by Jove!" he remarked, when upon gaining the level of the town a new two-story building blazoned with a huge sign its function as a hostelry. "Getting quite metropolitan in this neck of the woods. Say, little person, do you think you can relish a square meal? Planked steak and lobster salad — huh? I wonder if they *could* rustle a salad in this man's town? Say, do you know I'm just beginning to find out how hungry I am for the flesh-pots. What's the matter with a little variety? — as Lin MacLean said. Aren't you, hon?"

She was; frankly so. For long, monotonous months she had been struggling against just such cravings, impossible of realization, and therefore all the more tantalizing. She had been a year in the wilderness, and the wilderness had not only lost its glamour, but had become a thing to flee from. Even the rude motley of Hazleton was a welcome change. Here at least — on a minor scale, to be sure — was that which she craved, and to which she had been accustomed — life, stir, human activity, the very antithesis of the lonely mountain fastnesses. She bestowed a glad pressure on her husband's arm as they walked up the street, Bill carrying the sack of gold perched carelessly on one shoulder.

"Say, their enterprise has gone the length of establishing a branch bank here, I see."

He called her attention to a square-fronted edifice, its new-boarded walls as yet guiltless of paint, except where a row of black letters set forth that it was the Bank of British North America.

"That's a good place to stow this bullion," he remarked. "I want to get it off my hands."

So to the bank they bent their steps. A solemn, horse-faced Englishman weighed the gold, and issued Bill a receipt, expressing a polite regret that lack of facility to determine its fineness prevented him from converting it into cash.

"That means a trip to Vancouver," Bill remarked outside. "Well, we can stand that."

From the bank they went to the hotel, registered, and were shown to a room. For the first time since the summit of the Klappan Range, where her tiny hand glass had suffered disaster, Hazel was permitted a clear view of herself in a mirror.

"I'm a perfect fright!" she mourned.

"Huh!" Bill grunted. "*You're* all right. Look at me."

The trail had dealt hardly with both, in the matter of their personal appearance. Tanned to an abiding brown, they were, and Hazel's one-time smooth face was spotted with fly bites and marked with certain scratches suffered in the brush as they skirted the Kispiox. Her hair had lost its sleek, glossy smoothness of arrangement. Her hands were reddened and rough. But chiefly she was concerned with the sad state of her apparel. She had come a matter of four hundred miles in the clothes on her back — and they bore unequivocal evidence of the journey.

"I'm a perfect fright," she repeated pettishly. "I don't wonder that people lapse into semi-barbarism in the backwoods. One's manners, morals, clothing, and complexion all suffer from too close contact with your beloved North, Bill."

"Thanks!" he returned shortly. "I suppose I'm a perfect fright, too. Long hair, whiskers, grimy, calloused hands, and all the rest of it. A shave and a hair cut, a bath and a new suit of clothes will remedy that. But I'll be the same personality in every essential quality that I was when I sweated over the Klappan with a hundred pounds on my back."

"I hope so," she retorted. "I don't require the shave, thank goodness, but I certainly need a bath — and clothes. I wish I had the grāy suit that's probably getting all moldy and moth-eaten at the Pine River cabin. I wonder if I can get anything fit to wear here?"

"Women live here," Bill returned quietly, "and I suppose the stores supply 'em with duds. Unlimber that bank roll of yours, and do some shopping."

She sat on the edge of the bed, regarding her reflection in the mirror with extreme disfavor. Bill fingered his thick stubble of a beard for a thoughtful minute. Then he sat down beside her.

"Wha's a mollah, hon?" he wheedled. "What makes you such a crosser patch all at once?"

"Oh, I don't know," she answered dolefully. "I'm tired and hungry, and I look a fright — and — oh, just everything."

"Tut, tut!" he remonstrated good-naturedly. "That's just mood again. We're out of the woods, literally and figuratively. If you're hungry, let's go and see what we can make this hotel produce in the way of grub, before we do anything else."

"I wouldn't go into their dining-room looking like this for the world," she said decisively. "I didn't realize how dirty and shabby I was."

"All right; you go shopping, then," he proposed "while I take these furs up to old Hack's place and turn them into money. Then we'll dress, and make this hotel feed us the best they've got. Cheer up. Maybe it was tough on you to slice a year out of your life and leave it in a country where there's nothing but woods and eternal silence — but we've got around twenty thousand dollars to show for it, Hazel. And one can't get something for nothing. There's a price mark on it somewhere, always. We've got all our lives before us, little person, and a better chance for happiness than most folks have. Don't let little things throw you into the blues. Be my good little pal — and see if you can't make one of these stores dig up a white waist and a black skirt, like you had on the first time I saw you."

He kissed her, and went quickly out. And after a long time of sober staring at her image in the glass Hazel shook herself impatiently.

"I'm a silly, selfish, incompetent little beast," she whispered. "Bill ought to thump me, instead of being kind. I can't do anything, and I don't know much, and I'm a scarecrow for looks right now. And I started out to be a real partner."

She wiped an errant tear away, and made her way to a store — a new place sprung up, like the bank and the hotel, with the growing importance of the town. The stock of ready-made clothing drove her to despair. It seemed that what women resided in Hazleton must invariably dress in Mother Hubbard gowns of cheap cotton print with other garments to match. But eventually they found for her undergarments of a sort, a waist and skirt, and a comfortable pair of shoes. Hats, as a milliner would understand the term, there were none. And in default of such she stuck to the gray felt sombrero she had worn into the Klappan and out again — which, in truth, became her very well, when tilted at the proper angle above her heavy black hair. Then she went back to the hotel, and sought a bathroom.

242

Returning from this she found Bill, a Bill all shaved and shorn, unloading himself of sundry packages of new attire.

"Aha, everything is lovely," he greeted enthusiastically. "Old Hack jumped at the pelts, and paid a fat price for the lot. Also the ranch deal has gone through. He's a prince, old Hack. Sent up a man and had it surveyed and classified and the deed waiting for me. And — oh, say, here's a letter for you."

"For me? Oh, yes," as she looked at the hand-writing and postmark. "I wrote to Loraine Marsh when we were going north. Good heavens, look at the date — it's been here since last September!"

"Hackaberry knew where we were," Bill explained. "Sometimes in camps like this they hold mail two or three years for men that have gone into the interior."

She put aside the letter, and dressed while Bill had his bath. Then, with the smoke and grime of a hard trail obliterated, and with decent clothes upon them, they sought the dining-room. There, while they waited to be served, Hazel read Loraine Marsh's letter, and passed it to Bill with a self-conscious little laugh.

"There's an invitation there we might accept," she said casually.

Bill read. There were certain comments upon her marriage, such as the average girl might be expected to address to her chum who has forsaken spinsterhood, a lot of chatty mention of Granville people and Granville happenings, which held no particular interest for Bill since he knew neither one nor the other, and it ended with an apparently sincere hope that Hazel and her

243

husband would visit Granville soon as the Marshes' guests.

He returned the letter as the waitress brought their food.

"Wouldn't it be nice to take a trip home?" Hazel suggested thoughtfully. "I'd love to."

"We are going home," Bill reminded gently.

"Oh, of course," she smiled. "But I mean to Granville. I'd like to go back there with you for a while, just to — just to —"

"To show 'em," he supplied laconically.

"Oh, Bill!" she pouted.

Nevertheless, she could not deny that there was a measure of truth in his brief remark. She did want to "show 'em." Bill's vernacular expressed it exactly. She had compassed success in a manner that Granville — and especially that portion of Granville which she knew and which knew her — could appreciate and understand and envy according to its individual tendencies.

She looked across the table at her husband, and thought to herself with proud satisfaction that she *had* done well. Viewed from any angle whatsoever, Bill Wagstaff stood head and shoulders above all the men she had ever known. Big, physically and mentally, clean-minded and capable — indubitably she had captured a lion, and, though she might have denied stoutly the imputation, she wanted Granville to see her lion and hear him roar.

Whether they realize the fact or not, to the average individual, male or female, reflected glory is better than

244

none at all. And when two people stand in the most intimate relation to each other, the success of one lends a measure of its luster to the other. Those who had been so readily impressed by Andrew Bush's device to singe her social wings with the flame of gossip had long since learned their mistake. She had the word of Loraine Marsh and Jack Barrow that they were genuinely sorry for having been carried away by appearances. And she could nail her colors to the mast if she came home the wife of a man like Bill Wagstaff, who could wrest a fortune from the wilderness in a briefer span of time than it took most men to make current expenses. Hazel was quite too human to refuse a march triumphal if it came her way. She had left Granville in bitterness of spirit, and some of that bitterness required balm.

"Still thinking Granville?" Bill queried, when they had finished an uncommonly silent meal.

Hazel flushed slightly. She was, and momentarily she felt that she should have been thinking of their little nest up by Pine River Pass instead. She knew that Bill was homing to the cabin. She herself regarded it with affection, but of a different degree from his. Her mind was more occupied with another, more palpitating circle of life than was possible at the cabin, much as she appreciated its green and peaceful beauty. The sack of gold lying in the bank had somehow opened up far-flung possibilities. She skipped the interval of affairs which she knew must be attended to, and betook herself and Bill to Granville, thence to the bigger, older cities, where money shouted in the voice of command, where all things were possible to those who had the price.

She had had her fill of the wilderness — for the time being, she put it. It loomed behind her — vast bleak, a desolation of loneliness from which she must get away. She knew now, beyond peradventure, that her heart had brought her back to the man in spite of, rather than because of, his environment. And secure in the knowledge of his love for her and her love for him, she was already beginning to indulge a dream of transplanting him permanently to kindlier surroundings, where he would have wider scope for his natural ability and she less isolation.

But she was beginning to know this husband of hers too well to propose anything of the sort abruptly. Behind his tenderness and patience she had sometimes glimpsed something inflexible, unyielding as the wilderness he loved. So she merely answered:

"In a way, yes."

"Let's go outside where I can smoke a decent cigar on top of this fairly decent meal," he suggested. "Then we'll figure on the next move. I think about twenty-four hours in Hazleton will do me. There's a steamer goes down-river to-morrow."

CHAPTER
TWENTY-FOUR

Neighbors

Four days later they stood on the deck of a grimy little steamer breasting the outgoing tide that surged through the First Narrows. Wooded banks on either hand spread dusky green in the hot August sun. On their left glinted the roofs and white walls of Hollyburn, dear to the suburban heart. Presently they swung around Brockton Point, and Vancouver spread its peninsular clutter before them. Tugs and launches puffed by, about their harbor traffic. A ferry clustered black with people hurried across the inlet. But even above the harbor noises, across the intervening distance they could hear the vibrant hum of the industrial hive.

"Listen to it," said Bill. "Like surf on the beaches. And, like the surf, it's full of treacherous undercurrents, a bad thing to get into unless you can swim strong enough to keep your head above water."

"You're a thoroughgoing pessimist," she smiled.

"No," he shook his head. "I merely know that it's a hard game to buck, under normal conditions. We're of the fortunate few, that's all."

"You're not going to spoil the pleasure that's within your reach by pondering the misfortunes of those who are less lucky, are you?" she inquired curiously.

"Not much," he drawled. "Besides, that isn't my chief objection to town. I simply can't endure the noise and confusion and the manifold stinks, and the universal city attitude — which is to gouge the other fellow before he gouges you. Too much like a dog fight. No, I haven't any mission to remedy social and economic ills. I'm taking the egotistic view that it doesn't concern me, that I'm perfectly justified in enjoying myself in my own way, seeing that I'm in a position to do so. We're going to take our fun as we find it. Just the same," he finished thoughtfully, "I'd as soon be pulling into that ranch of ours on the hurricane deck of a right good horse as approaching Vancouver's water front. This isn't any place to spend money or to see anything. It's a big, noisy, overgrown village, overrun with business exploiters and real-estate sharks. It'll be a city some day. At present it's still in the shambling stage of civic youth."

In so far as Hazel had observed upon her former visit, this, if a trifle sweeping, was in the main correct. So she had no regrets when Bill confined their stay to the time necessary to turn his gold into a bank account, and allow her to buy a trunkful, more or less, of pretty clothes. Then they bore on eastward and halted at Ashcroft. Bill had refused to commit himself positively to a date for the eastern pilgrimage. He wanted to see the cabin again. For that matter she did, too — so that their sojourn there did not carry them over another

248

winter. That loomed ahead like a vague threat. Those weary months in the Klappan Range had filled her with the subtle poison of discontent, for which she felt that new scenes and new faces would prove the only antidote.

"There's a wagon road to Fort George," he told her. "We could go in there by the B. X. steamers, but I'm afraid we couldn't buy an outfit to go on. I guess a pack outfit from the end of the stage line will be about right."

From Ashcroft an auto stage whirled them swiftly into the heart of the Cariboo country — to Quesnelle, where Bill purchased four head of horses in an afternoon, packed, saddled, and hit the trail at daylight in the morning.

It was very pleasant to loaf along a passable road mounted on a light-footed horse, and Hazel enjoyed it if for no more than the striking contrast to that terrible journey in and out of the Klappan. Here were no heartbreaking mountains to scale. The scourge of flies was well-nigh past. They took the road in easy stages, well-provisioned, sleeping in a good bed at nights, camping as the spirit moved when a likely trout stream crossed their trail, venison and grouse all about them for variety of diet and the sport of hunting.

So they fared through the Telegraph Range, crossed the Blackwater, and came to Fort George by way of a ferry over the Fraser.

"This country is getting civilized," Bill observed that evening. "They tell me the G. T. P. has steel laid to a point three hundred miles east of here. This bloomin' road'll be done in another year. They're grading all along the line. I bought that hundred and sixty acres on pure sentiment, but it looks like it may turn out a profitable business transaction. That railroad is going to flood this country with farmers, and settlement means a network of railroads and skyrocketing ascension of land values."

The vanguard of the land hungry had already penetrated to Fort George. Up and down the Nachaco Valley, and bordering upon the Fraser, were the cabins of the preëmptors. The roads were dotted with the teams of the incoming. A sizable town had sprung up around the old trading post.

"They come like bees when the rush starts," Bill remarked.

Leaving Fort George behind, they bore across country toward Pine River. Here and there certain landmarks, graven deep in Hazel's recollection, uprose to claim her attention. And one evening at sunset they rode up to the little cabin, all forlorn in its clearing.

The grass waved to their stirrups, and the pigweed stood rank up to the very door.

Inside, a gray film of dust had accumulated on everything, and the rooms were oppressive with the musty odors that gather in a closed, untenanted house. But apart from that it stood as they had left it thirteen months before. No foot had crossed the threshold. The pile of wood and kindling lay beside the fireplace as Bill had placed it the morning they left.

" 'Be it ever so humble,' " Bill left the line of the old song unfinished, but his tone was full of jubilation.

Between them they threw wide every door and window. The cool evening wind filled the place with sweet, pine-scented air. Then Bill started a blaze roaring in the black-mouthed fireplace — to make it look natural, he said — and went out to hobble his horses for the night.

In the morning they began to unpack their household goods. Rugs and bearskins found each its accustomed place upon the floor. His books went back on the shelves. With magical swiftness the cabin resumed its old-home atmosphere. And that night Bill stretched himself on the grizzly hide before the fire-place, and kept his nose in a book until Hazel, who was in no humor to read, fretted herself into something approaching a temper.

"You're about as sociable as a clam," she broke into his absorption at last.

He looked up in surprise, then chucked the volume carelessly aside, and twisted himself around till his head rested in her lap.

"Vot iss?" he asked cheerfully. "Lonesome? Bored with yourself? Ain't I here?"

"Your body is," she retorted. "But your spirit is communing with those musty old philosophers."

"Oh, be good — go thou and do likewise," he returned impenitently. "I'm tickled to death to be home. And I'm fairly book-starved. It's fierce to be deprived of even a newspaper for twelve months. I'll be a year getting caught up. Surely you don't feel yourself neglected because I happen to have my nose stuck in a book?"

"Of course not!" she denied vigorously. The childish absurdity of her attitude struck her with sudden force. "Still, I'd like you to talk to me *once* in a while."

" 'Of shoes and ships and sealing wax; of cabbages and kings,' " he flung at her mischievously. "I'll make music; that's better than mere words."

He picked up his mandolin and tuned the strings. Like most things which he set out to do, Bill had mastered his instrument, and could coax out of it all the harmony of which it was capable. He seemed to know music better than many who pass for musicians. But he broke off in the midst of a bar.

"Say, we could get a piano in here next spring," he said. "I just recollected it. We'll do it."

Now, this was something that she had many a time audibly wished for. Yet the prospect aroused no enthusiasm.

"That'll be nice," she said — but not as she would have said it a year earlier. Bill's eyes narrowed a trifle, but he still smiled. And suddenly he stepped around behind her chair, put both hands under her chin, and tilted her head backward.

"Ah, you're plumb sick and tired to death of everything, aren't you?" he said soberly. "You've been up here too long. You sure need a change. I'll have to take you out and give you the freedom of the cities, let you dissipate and pink-tea, and rub elbows with the mob for a while. Then you'll be glad to drift back to this woodsy hiding-place of ours. When do you want to start?"

"Why, Bill!" she protested.

But she realized in a flash that Bill could read her better than she could read herself. Few of her emotions could remain long hidden from that keenly observing and mercilessly logical mind. She knew that he guessed where she stood, and by what paths she had gotten there. Trust him to know. And it made her very tender toward him that he was so quick to understand. Most men would have resented.

"I want to stack a few tons of hay," he went on, disregarding her exclamation. "I'll need it in the spring, if not this winter. Soon as that's done we'll hit the high spots. We'll take three or four thousand dollars, and while it lasts we'll be a couple of — of high-class tramps. Huh? Does it sound good?"

She nodded vigorously.

"High-class tramps," she repeated musingly. "That sounds fine."

"Perk up, then," he wheedled.

"Bill-boy," she murmured, "you mustn't take me too seriously."

"I took you for better or for worse," he answered, with a kiss. "I don't want it to turn out worse. I want you to be contented and happy here, where I've planned to make our home. I know you love me quite a lot, little person. Nature fitted us in a good many ways to be mates. But you've gone through a pretty drastic siege of isolation in this rather grim country, and I guess it doesn't seem such an alluring place as it did at first. I don't want you to nurse that feeling until it becomes chronic. Then we would be out of tune, and it would be good-by happiness. But I think I know the cure for your malady."

That was his final word. He deliberately switched the conversation into other channels.

In the morning he began his hay cutting. About eleven o'clock he threw down his scythe and stalked to the house.

"Put on your hat, and let's go investigate a mystery," said he. "I heard a cow bawl in the woods a minute ago. A regular barnyard bellow."

"A cow bawling?" she echoed. "Sure? What would cattle be doing away up here?"

"That's what I want to know!" Bill laughed. "I've never seen a cow north of the Frazer — not this side of the Rockies, anyway."

They saddled their horses, and rode out in the direction from whence had arisen the bovine complaint. The sound was not repeated, and Hazel had begun to chaff Bill about a too-vivid imagination when within a half mile of the clearing he pulled his horse up short in the middle of a little meadow.

"Look!"

The track of a broad-tired wagon had freshly crushed the thick grass. Bill squinted at the trail, then his gaze swept the timber beyond.

"Well!"

"What is it, Bill?" Hazel asked.

"Somebody has been cutting timber over there," he enlightened. "I can see the fresh ax work. Looks like they'd been hauling poles. Let's follow this track a ways."

254

The tiny meadow was fringed on the north by a grove of poplars. Beyond that lay another clear space of level land, perhaps forty acres in extent. They broke through the belt of poplars — and pulled up again. On one side of the meadow stood a cabin, the fresh-peeled log walls glaring yellow in the sun, and lifting an earth-covered roof to the autumn sky. Bill whistled softly.

"I'll be hanged," he uttered, "if there isn't the cow!"

Along the west side of the meadow ran a brown streak of sod, and down one side of this a man guided the handles of a plow drawn by the strangest yokemates Hazel's eyes had seen for many a day.

"For goodness' sake!" she exclaimed.

"That's the true pioneer spirit for you," Bill spoke absently. "He has bucked his way into the heart of a virgin country, and he's breaking sod with a mule and a cow. That's adaptation to environment with a vengeance — and grit."

"There's a woman, too, Bill. And see — she's carrying a baby!" Hazel pointed excitedly. "Oh, Bill!"

"Let's go over." He stirred up his horse. "What did I tell you about folk that hanker for lots of elbow-room? They're coming."

The man halted his strangely assorted team to watch them come. The woman stood a step outside the door, a baby in her arms, another toddler holding fast to her skirt. A thick-bodied, short, square-shouldered man was this newcomer, with a round, pleasant face.

"Hello, neighbor!" Bill greeted.

255

The plowman lifted his old felt hat courteously. His face lit up.

"*Ach!*" said he. "Neighbor. Dot iss a goot vord in diss country vere dere iss no neighbor. But I am glat to meet you. Vill you come do der house und rest a v'ile?"

"Sure!" Bill responded. "But we're neighbors, all right. Did you notice a cabin about half a mile west of here? That's our place — when we're at home."

"So?" The word escaped with the peculiar rising inflection of the Teuton. "I haf saw dot cabin ven ve come here. But I dink it vass abandon. Und I pick dis place mitout hope off a neighbor. Id iss goot lant. Vell, let us to der house go. Id vill rest der mule — und Gretchen, der cow. Hah!"

He rolled a blue eye on his incongruous team, and grinned widely.

"Come," he invited; "mine vife vill be glat."

They found her a matron of thirty-odd; fresh-cheeked, round-faced like her husband, typically German, without his accent of the Fatherland. Hazel at once appropriated the baby. It lay peacefully in her arms, staring wide-eyed, making soft, gurgly sounds.

"The little dear!" Hazel murmured.

"Lauer, our name iss," the man said casually, when they were seated.

"Wagstaff, mine is," Bill completed the informal introduction.

"So?" Lauer responded. "Id hass a German sount, dot name, yes."

"Four or five generations back," Bill answered. "I guess I'm as American as they make 'em."

256

"I am from Bavaria," Lauer told him. "Vill you shmoke? I light mine bibe — mit your vife's permission.

"Yes," he continued, stuffing the bowl of his pipe with a stubby forefinger, "I am from Bavaria. Dere I vass upon a farm brought oop. I serf in der army my dime. Den Ameriga. Dere I marry my vife, who is born in Milwaukee. I vork in der big brreweries. Afder dot I learn to be a carpenter. Now I am a kink, mit a castle all mine own. I am no more a vage slafe."

He laughed at his own conceit, a great, roaring bellow that filled the room.

"You're on the right track," Bill nodded. "It's a pity more people don't take the same notion. What do you think of this country, anyway?"

"It iss goot," Lauer answered briefly, and with unhesitating certainty. "It iss goot. Vor der boor man it iss — it iss salfation. Mit fife huntret tollars und hiss two hants he can himself a home make — und a lifing be sure off."

Beside Hazel Lauer's wife absently caressed the blond head of her four-year-old daughter.

"No, I don't think I'll ever get lonesome," she said.

"I'm too glad to be here. And I've got lots of work and my babies. Of course, it's natural I'd miss a woman friend running in now and then to chat. But a person can't have it all. And I'd do anything to have a roof of our own, and to have it some place where our livin' don't depend on a pay envelope. Oh, a city's dreadful, I think, when your next meal almost depends on your man holdin' his job. I've lived in town ever since I was fifteen. I lost three babies in Milwaukee — hot weather, bad air, bad milk, bad everything, unless you have plenty of money. Many a time I've sat and cried, just from thinkin' how bad I wanted a little place of our own, where there was grass and trees and a piece of ground for a garden. And I knew we'd never be able to buy it. We couldn't get ahead enough."

"Und so," her husband took up the tale, "I hear off diss country, vere lant can be for noddings got. Und so we scrape und pinch und safe nickels und dimes for fife year. Und here ve are. All der vay from Visconsin in der vaigon, yes. Mit two mules. In Ashcroft I buy der cow, so dot ve haf der fresh milk. Und dot iss lucky. For von mule iss die on der road. So I am plow opp der lant und haul my vaigon mit von mule und Gretchen, der cow."

Hazel had a momentary vision of unrelated hardships by the way, and she wondered how the man could laugh and his wife smile over it. She knew the stifling heat of narrow streets in mid-summer, and the hungry longing for cool, green shade. She had seen something of a city's poverty. But she knew also the privations of the trail. Two thousand miles in a wagon! And at the journey's end only a rude cabin of logs — and years of steady toil. Isolation in a huge and lonely land. Yet these folk were happy. She wondered briefly if her own viewpoint were possibly askew. She knew that she could not face such a prospect except in utter rebellion. Not now. The bleak peaks of the Klappan rose up before her mind's eye, the picture of five horses dead in the snow, the wolves that snapped and snarled over their bones. She shuddered. She was still pondering this when she and Bill dismounted at home.

258

CHAPTER
TWENTY-FIVE

The Dollar Chasers

Granville took them to its bosom with a haste and earnestness that made Hazel catch her breath. The Marshes took possession of them upon their arrival, and they were no more than domiciled under the Marsh roof than all her old friends flocked to call. Tactfully none so much as mentioned Andrew Bush, nor the five-thousand-dollar legacy — the disposition of which sum still perplexed that defunct gentleman's worthy executors. And once more in a genial atmosphere Hazel concluded to let sleeping dogs lie. Many a time in the past two years she had looked forward to cutting them all as dead as they had cut her during that unfortunate period. But once among them, and finding them willing, nay, anxious, to forget that they had ever harbored unjust thoughts of her, she took their proffered friendship at its face value. It was quite gratifying to know that many of them envied her. She learned from various sources that Bill's fortune loomed big, had grown by some mysterious process of Granville tattle, until it had reached the charmed six figures of convention.

That in itself was sufficient to establish their prestige. In a society that lived by and for the dollar, and measured most things with its dollar yardstick, that murmured item opened — indeed, forced open — many doors to herself and her husband which would otherwise have remained rigid on their fastenings. It was pleasant to be sought out and made much of, and it pleased her to think that some of her quondam friends were genuinely sorry that they had once stood aloof. They attempted to atone, it would seem. For three weeks they lived in an atmosphere of teas and dinners and theater parties, a giddy little whirl that grew daily more attractive, so far as Hazel was concerned.

There had been changes. Jack Barrow had consoled himself with a bride. Moreover, he was making good, in the popular phrase, at the real-estate game. The Marshes, as she had previously known them, had been tottering on the edge of shabby gentility. But they had come into money. And as Bill slangily put it, they were using their pile to cut a lot of social ice. Kitty Brooks' husband was now the head of the biggest advertising agency in Granville. Hazel was glad of that mild success. Kitty Brooks was the one person for whom she had always kept a warm corner in her heart. Kitty had stood stoutly and unequivocally by her when all the others had viewed her with a dubious eye. Aside from these there were scores of young people who revolved in their same old orbits. Two years will upon occasion make profound changes in some lives, and leave others untouched. But change or no change, she found herself caught up and carried along on a pleasant tide.

She was inordinately proud of Bill, when she compared him with the average Granville male — yet she found herself wishing he would adopt a little more readily the Granville viewpoint. He fell short of it, or went beyond it, she could not be sure which; she had an uneasy feeling sometimes that he looked upon Granville doings and Granville folk with amused tolerance, not unmixed with contempt. But he attracted attention. Whenever he was minded to talk he found ready listeners. And he did not seem to mind being dragged to various functions, matinées, and the like. He fell naturally into that mode of existence, no matter that it was in profound contrast to his previous manner of life, as she knew it. She felt a huge satisfaction in that. Anything but a well-bred man would have repelled her, and she had recognized that quality in Bill Wagstaff even when he had carried her bodily into the wilderness against her explicit desire that memorable time. And he was now exhibiting an unsuspected polish. She used to wonder amusedly if he were possibly the same Roaring Bill whom she had with her eyes seen hammer a man insensible with his fists, who had kept "tough" frontiersmen warily side-stepping him in Cariboo Meadows. Certainly he was a manysided individual.

Once or twice she conjured up a vision of his getting into some business there, and utterly foregoing the North — which for her was already beginning to take on the aspect of a bleak and cheerless region where there was none of the things which daily whetted her appetite for luxury, nothing but hardships innumerable — and gold. The gold had been their reward — a reward well earned, she thought. Still — they had been wonderfully happy there at the Pine River cabin, she remembered.

They came home from a theater party late one night. Bill sat down by their bedroom window, and stared out at the street lights, twin rows of yellow beads stretching away to a vanishing point in the pitch-black of a cloudy night. Hazel kicked off her slippers, and gratefully toasted her silk-stockinged feet at a small coal grate. Fall had come, and there was a sharp nip to the air.

"Well, what do you think of it as far as you've gone?" he asked abruptly.

"Of what?" she asked, jarred out of meditation upon the play they had just witnessed.

"All this." He waved a hand comprehensively. "This giddy swim we've got into."

"I think it's fine," she candidly admitted. "I'm enjoying myself. I like it. Don't you?"

"As a diversion," he observed thoughtfully, "I don't mind it. These people are all very affable and pleasant, and they've rather gone out of their way to entertain us. But, after all, what the dickens does it amount to? They spend their whole life running in useless circles. I should think they'd get sick of it. You will."

"Hardly, Billum," she smiled. "We're merely making up for two years of isolation. I think we must be remarkable people that we didn't fight like cats and dogs. For eighteen months, you know, there wasn't a soul to talk to, and not much to think about except what you could do if you were some place else."

"You're acquiring the atmosphere," he remarked — sardonically, she thought.

"No; just enjoying myself," she replied lightly.

"Well, if you really are," he answered slowly, "we may as well settle here for the winter — and get settled right away. I'm rather weary of being a guest in another man's house, to tell you the truth."

"Why, I'd love to stay here all winter," she said. "But I thought you intended to knock around more or less."

"But don't you see, you don't particularly care to," he pointed out; "and it would spoil the fun of going any place for me if you were not interested. And when it comes to a show-down I'm not aching to be a bird of passage. One city is pretty much like another to me. You seem to have acquired a fairly select circle of friends and acquaintances, and you may as well have your fling right here. We'll take a run over to New York. I want to get some books and things. Then we'll come back here and get a house or a flat. I tell you right now," he laughed not unpleasantly, "I'm going to renig on this society game. You can play it as hard as you like, until spring. I'll be there with bells on when it comes to a dance. And I'll go to a show — when a good play comes along. But I won't mix up with a lot of silly women and equally silly she-men, any more than is absolutely necessary."

"Why, Bill!" she exclaimed, aghast.

"Well, ain't it so?" he defended lazily. "There's Kitty Brooks — she has certainly got intelligence above the

263

average. That Lorimer girl has brains superimposed on her artistic temperament, and she uses 'em to advantage. Practically all the rest that I've met are intellectual nonentities — strong on looks and clothes and amusing themselves, and that lets them out. And they have no excuse, because they've had unlimited advantages. The men divide themselves into two types. One that chases the dollar, talks business, thinks business, knows nothing outside of business, and their own special line of business at that; the other type, like these Arthur fellows, and Dave Allan and T. Fordham Brown, who go in for afternoon teas and such gentlemanly pastimes, and whose most strenuous exercise is a game of billiards. Shucks, there isn't a real man in the lot. Maybe I'll run across some people who don't take a two-by-four view of life if I stay around here long enough, but it hasn't happened to me yet. I hope I'm not an intellectual snob, little person, any more than I'm puffed up over happening to be a little bigger and stronger than the average man, but I must say that the habitual conversation of these people gives me a pain. That platitudinous discussion of the play to-night, for instance."

"That *was* droll." Hazel chuckled at the recollection, and she recalled the weary look that had once or twice flitted over Bill's face during that after-theater supper.

But she herself could see only the humor of it. She was fascinated by the social niceties and the surroundings of the set she had drifted into. The little dinners, the impromptu teas, the light chatter and general atmosphere of luxury more than counterbalanced any other lack. She wanted only to play, and she was prepared to seize avidly on any form of pleasure, no matter if in last analysis it were utterly frivolous. She could smile at the mental vacuity she encountered, and think nothing of it, if with that vacuity went those material factors which made for ease and entertainment. The physical side of her was all alert. Luxury and the mild excitements of a social life that took nothing seriously, those were the things she craved. For a long time she had been totally deprived of them. Nor had such unlimited opportunities ever before been in her grasp.

"Yes, that was droll," she repeated.

Bill snorted.

"Droll? Perhaps," he said. "Blatant ignorance, coupled with a desire to appear the possessor of culture, is sometimes amusing. But as a general thing it simply irritates."

"You're hard to please," she replied. "Can't you enjoy yourself, take things as they come, without being so critical?"

He shrugged his shoulders, and remained silent.

"Well," he said presently, "we'll take that jaunt to New York day after to-morrow."

He was still sitting by the window when Hazel was ready to go to bed. She came back into the room in a trailing silk kimono, and, stealing softly up behind him, put both hands on his shoulders.

"What are you thinking so hard about, Billy-boy?" she whispered.

"I was thinking about Jake Lauer, and wondering how he was making it go," Bill answered. "I was also picturing to myself how some of these worthy citizens would mess things up if they had to follow in his steps. Hang it, I don't know but we'd be better off if we were pegging away for a foothold somewhere, like old Jake."

"If we *had* to do that," she argued, "I suppose we would, and manage to get along. But since we don't have to, why wish for it? Money makes things pleasanter."

"If money meant that we would be compelled to lead the sort of existence most of these people do," he retorted, "I'd take measures to be broke as soon as possible. What the deuce is there to it? The women get up in the morning, spend the forenoon fixing themselves up to take in some innocuous gabblefest after luncheon. Then they get into their war paint for dinner, and after dinner rush madly off to some other festive stunt. Swell rags and a giddy round. If it were just fun, it would be all right. But it's the serious business of life with them. And the men are in the same boat. All of 'em collectively don't amount to a pinch of snuff. This thing that they call business is mostly gambling with what somebody else has sweated to produce. They're a soft-handed, soft-bodied lot of incompetent egotists, if you ask me. Any of 'em would lick your boots in a genteel sort of way if there was money in it; and they'd just as cheerfully chisel their best friend out of his last dollar, if it could be done in a business way. They haven't even the saving grace of physical hardihood."

266

"You're awful!" Hazel commented.

Bill snorted again.

"To-morrow, you advise our hostess that we're traveling," he instructed. "When we come back we'll make headquarters at a hotel until we locate a place of our own — if you are sure you want to winter here."

Her mind was quite made up to spend the winter there, and she frankly said so — provided he had no other choice. They had to winter somewhere. They had set out to spend a few months in pleasant idleness. They could well afford that. And, unless he had other plans definitely formed, was not Granville as good as any place? Was it not better, seeing that they did know some one there? It was big enough to afford practically all the advantages of any city.

"Oh, yes, I suppose so. All right; we'll winter here," Bill acquiesced. "That's settled."

And, as was his habit when he had come to a similar conclusion, he refused to talk further on that subject, but fell to speculating idly on New York. In which he was presently aided and abetted by Hazel, who had never invaded Manhattan, nor, for that matter, any of the big Atlantic cities. She had grown up in Granville, with but brief journeys to near-by points. And Granville could scarcely be classed as a metropolis. It numbered a trifle over three hundred thousand souls. Bill had termed it "provincial." But it meant more to her than any other place in the East, by virtue of old associations and more recent acquaintance. One must have a pivotal point of such a sort, just as one cannot forego the possession of a nationality.

New York, she was constrained to admit, rather overwhelmed her. She traversed Broadway and other world-known arteries, and felt a trifle dubious amid the unceasing crush. Bill piloted her to famous cafés, and to equally famous theaters. She made sundry purchases in magnificent shops. The huge conglomeration of sights and sounds made an unforgettable impression upon her. She sensed keenly the colossal magnitude of it all. But she felt a distinct wave of relief when they were Granville bound once more.

In a week they were settled comfortably in a domicile of their own — five rooms in an up-to-date apartment house. And since the social demands on Mrs. William Wagstaff's time grew apace, a capable maid and a cook were added to the Wagstaff establishment. Thus she was relieved of the onus of housework. Her time was wholly her own, at her own disposal or Bill's, as she elected.

But by imperceptible degrees they came to take diverse roads in the swirl of life which had caught them up. There were so many little woman affairs where a man was superfluous. There were others which Bill flatly refused to attend. "Hen parties," he dubbed them. More and more he remained at home with his books. Invariably he read through the daytime, and unless to take Hazel for a walk or a drive, or some simple pleasure which they could indulge in by themselves, he would not budge. If it were night, and a dance was to the fore, he would dress and go gladly. At such, and upon certain occasions when a certain little group would take supper at some café, he was apparently in his element. But there was always a back fire if Hazel managed to persuade him to attend anything in the nature of a formal affair. He drew the line at what he defined as social tommyrot, and he drew it more and more sharply.

Sometimes Hazel caught herself wondering if they were getting as much out of the holiday as they should have gotten, as they had planned to get when they were struggling through that interminable winter. *She* was. But not Bill. And while she wished that he could get the same satisfaction out of his surroundings and opportunities as she conceived herself to be getting, she often grew impatient with his sardonic, tolerant contempt toward the particular set she mostly consorted with. If she ventured to give a tea, he fled the house as if from the plague. He made acquaintances of his own, men from God only knew where, individuals who occasionally filled the dainty apartment with malodorous tobacco fumes, and who would cheerfully sit up all night discoursing earnestly on any subject under the sun. But so long as Bill found Granville habitable she did not mind.

Above all, as the winter and the winter gayety set in together with equal vigor, she thought with greater reluctance of the ultimate return to that hushed, deep-forested area that surrounded the cabin.

She wished fervently that Bill would take up some business that would keep him in touch with civilization. He had the capital, she considered, and there was no question of his ability. Her faith in his power to encompass whatever he set about was strong. Other men, less gifted, had acquired wealth, power, even a measure of fame, from a less auspicious beginning. Why not he?

It seemed absurd to bury one's self in an uninhabited waste, when life held forth so much to be grasped. Her friends told her so — thus confirming her own judgment. But she could never quite bring herself to put it in so many words to Bill.

CHAPTER
TWENTY-SIX

A Business Proposition

The cycle of weeks brought them to January. They had dropped into something of a routine in their daily lives. Bill's interest and participation in social affairs became negligible. Of Hazel's circle he classed some half dozen people as desirable acquaintances, and saw more or less of them — Kitty Brooks and her husband; Vesta Lorimer, a keen-witted young woman upon whom nature had bestowed a double portion of physical attractiveness and a talent akin to genius for the painting of miniatures; her Brother Paul, who was the silent partner in a brokerage firm; Doctor Hart, a silent, grim-visaged physician, whose vivacious wife was one of Hazel's new intimates. Of that group Bill was always a willing member. The others he met courteously when he was compelled to meet them; otherwise he passed them up entirely.

When he was not absorbed in a book or magazine, he spent his time in some downtown haunt, having acquired membership in a club as a concession to their manner of life. Once he came home with flushed face and overbright eyes, radiating an odor of whisky. Hazel had never seen him drink to excess. She was

271

correspondingly shocked, and took no pains to hide her feelings. But Bill was blandly undisturbed.

"You don't need to look so horrified," he drawled. "I won't beat you up nor wreck the furniture. Inadvertently took a few too many, that's all. Nothing else to do, anyhow. Your friend Brooks' Carlton Club is as barren a place as one of your tea fights. They don't do anything much but sit around and drink Scotch and soda, and talk about the market. I'm drunk, and glad of it. If I were in Cariboo Meadows, now," he confided owlishly, "I'd have some fun with the natives. You can't turn yourself loose here. It's too blame civilized and proper. I had half a notion to lick a Johnnie or two, just for sport, and then I thought probably they'd have me up for assault and battery. Just recollected our social reputation — long may she wave — in time."

"*Your* reputation certainly won't be unblemished if any one saw you come in in that condition," she cried, in angry mortification. "Surely you could find something better to do than to get drunk."

"I'm going straight to bed, little person," he returned. "Scold not, nor fret. William will be himself again ere yet the morrow's sun shall clear the horizon. Let us avoid recrimination. The tongue is, or would seem to be, the most vital weapon of modern society. Therefore let us leave the trenchant blade quiescent in its scabbard. *I'd* rather settle a dispute with my fists, or even a gun. Good night."

He made his unsteady way to their extra bedroom, and he was still there with the door locked when Hazel returned from a card party at the Krones'. It was the first night they had spent apart since their marriage, and Hazel was inclined to be huffed when he looked in before breakfast, dressed, shaved, and smiling, as if he had never had even a bowing acquaintance with John Barleycorn. But Bill refused to take her indignation seriously, and it died for lack of fuel.

A week or so later he became suddenly and unexpectedly active. He left the house as soon as his breakfast was eaten, and he did not come home to luncheon — a circumstance which irritated Hazel, since it was one of those rare days when she herself lunched at home. Late in the afternoon he telephoned briefly that he would dine downtown. And when he did return, at nine or thereabouts in the evening, he clamped a cigar between his teeth, and fell to work covering a sheet of paper with interminable rows of figures.

Hazel had worried over the possibility of his having had another tilt with the Scotch and sodas. He relieved her of that fear, and she restrained her curiosity until boredom seized her. The silence and the scratching of his pen began to grate on her nerves.

"What is all the clerical work about?" she inquired. "Reckoning your assets and liabilities?"

Bill smiled and pushed aside the paper.

"I'm going to promote a mining company," he told her, quite casually. "It has been put up to me as a business proposition — and I've got to the stage where I have to do *something*, or I'll sure have the Willies."

She overlooked the latter statement; it conveyed no special significance at the time. But his first statement

273

opened up possibilities such as of late she had sincerely hoped would come to pass, and she was all interest.

"Promote a mining company?" she repeated. "That sounds extremely businesslike. How — when — where?"

"Now — here in Granville," he replied. "The how is largely Paul Lorimer's idea. You see," he continued, warming up a bit to the subject, "when I was prospecting that creek where we made the clean-up last summer, I ran across a well-defined quartz lead. I packed out a few samples in my pockets, and I happened to show them as well as one or two of the nuggets to some of these fellows at the club a while back. Lorimer took a piece of the quartz and had it assayed. It looms up as something pretty big. So he and Brooks and a couple of other fellows want me to go ahead and organize and locate a group of claims in there. Twenty or thirty thousand dollars capital might make 'em all rich. Of course, the placer end of it will be the big thing while the lode is being developed. It should pay well from the start. Getting the start is easy. As a matter of fact, you could sell any old wildcat that has the magic of gold about it. Men seem to get the fever as soon as they finger the real yellow stuff. These fellows I've talked to are dead anxious to get in."

"But" — her knowledge of business methods suggested a difficulty — "you can't sell stock in a business that has no real foundation — yet. Don't you have to locate those claims first?"

"Wise old head; you have the idea, all right." He smiled. "But this is not a stock-jobbing proposition. I wouldn't be in on it if it were, believe me. It's to be a corporation, where not to exceed six men will own all the stock that's issued. And so far as the claims are concerned, I've got Whitey Lewis located in Fort George, and I've been burning the wires and spending a bundle of real money getting him grub-staked. He has got four men besides himself all ready to hit the trail as soon as I give the word."

"*You* won't have to go?" she put in quickly.

"No," he murmured. "It isn't necessary, at this particular stage of the game. But I wouldn't mind popping a whip over a good string of dogs, just the same."

"B-r-r-r!" she shivered involuntarily. "Four hundred miles across that deep snow, through that steady, flesh-searing cold. I don't envy them the journey."

Bill relapsed into unsmiling silence, sprawling listless in his chair, staring absently at the rug, as if he had lost all interest in the matter.

"If you stay here and manage this end of it," she pursued lightly, "I suppose you'll have an office downtown."

"I suppose so," he returned laconically.

She came over and stood by him, playfully rumpling his brown hair with her fingers.

"I'm glad you've found something to loose that pent-up energy of yours on, Billy-boy," she said. "You'll make a success of it, I know. I don't see why you shouldn't make a success of any kind of business. But I didn't think you'd ever tackle business. You have such peculiar views about business and business practice."

275

"I despise the ordinary business ethic," he returned sharply. "It's a get-something-for-nothing proposition all the way through; it is based on exploiting the other fellow in one form or another. I refuse to exploit my fellows along the accepted lines — or any lines. I don't have to; there are too many other ways of making a living open to me. I don't care to live fat and make some one else foot the bill. But I can exploit the resources of nature. And that is my plan. If we make money it won't be filched by a complex process from the other fellow's pockets; it won't be wealth created by shearing lambs in the market, by sweatshop labor, or adulterated food, or exorbitant rental of filthy tenements. And I have no illusions about the men I'm dealing with. If they undertake to make a get-rich-quick scheme of it I'll knock the whole business in the head. I'm not overly anxious to get into it with them. But it promises action of some sort — and I have to do something till spring."

In the spring! That brief phrase set Hazel to sober thinking. With April or May Bill would spread his wings for the North. There would be no more staying him than the flight of the wild goose to the reedy nesting grounds could be stayed. Well, a summer in the North would not be so bad, she reflected. But she hated to think of the isolation. It grieved her to contemplate exchanging her beautifully furnished apartment for a log cabin in the woods. There would be a dreary relapse into monotony after months of association with clever people, the swift succession of brilliant little functions. It all delighted her; she responded to her present surroundings as naturally as a grain of wheat responds to the germinating influences of warmth and moisture. It did not occur to her that saving Bill Wagstaff's advent into her life she might have been denied all this. Indeed she felt a trifle resentful that he should prefer the forested solitudes to the pleasant social byways of Granville.

Still she had hopes. If he plunged into business associations with Jimmie Brooks and Paul Lorimer and others of that group, there was no telling what might happen. His interests might become permanently identified with Granville. She loved her big, wide-shouldered man, anyway. So she continued to playfully rumple his hair and kept her thoughts to herself.

Bill informed her from time to time as to the progress of his venture. Brooks and Lorimer put him in touch with two others who were ready to chance money on the strength of Bill's statements. The company was duly incorporated, with an authorized capital of one hundred thousand dollars, five thousand dollars' worth of stock being taken out by each on a cash basis — the remaining seventy-five thousand lying in the company treasury, to be held or sold for development purposes as the five saw fit when work began to show what the claims were capable of producing.

Whitey Lewis set out. Bill stuck a map on their living-room wall and pointed off each day's journey with a pin. Hazel sometimes studied the map, and pitied them. So many miles daily in a dreary waste of snow; nights when the frost thrust its keen-pointed lances into their tired bodies; food cooked with numbed fingers; the dismal howling of wolves; white frost and clinging icicles upon their beards as they trudged across trackless areas; and over all that awesome hush which she had learned to dread — breathless, brooding silence. Gold madness or trail madness, or simply adventurous unrest? She could not say. She knew only that a certain type of man found pleasure in such mad undertakings, bucked hard trails and plunged headlong into vast solitudes, and permitted no hardship nor danger to turn him back.

Bill was tinged with that madness for unbeaten trails. But surely when a man mated, and had a home and all that makes home desirable, he should forsake the old ways? Once when she found him studying the map, traversing a route with his forefinger and muttering to himself, she had a quick catch at her heart — as if hers were already poised to go. And she could not follow him. Once she had thought to do that, and gloried in the prospect. But his trail, his wilderness trail, and his trail gait, were not for any woman to follow. It was too big a job for any woman. And she could not let him go alone. He might never come back.

Not so long since she and Kitty Brooks had been discussing a certain couple who had separated. Vesta Lorimer sat by, listening.

"How could they help but fail in mutual flight?" the Lorimer girl had demanded. "An eagle mated to a domestic fowl!"

And, watching Bill stare at the map, his body there but the soul of him tramping the wild woods, she recalled Vesta Lorimer's characterization of that other

278

pair. Surely this man of hers was of the eagle brood. But there, in her mind, the simile ended.

In early March came a telegram from Whitey Lewis saying that he had staked the claims, both placer and lode; that he was bound out by the Telegraph Trail to file at Hazleton. Bill showed her the message — wired from Station Six.

"I wish I could have been in on it — that was some trip," he said — and there was a trace of discontent in his tone. "I don't fancy somebody else pawing my chestnuts out of the coals for me. It was sure a man's job to cross the Klappan in the dead of winter."

The filing completed, there was ample work in the way of getting out and whipsawing timber to keep the five men busy till spring — the five who were on the ground. Lewis sent word that thirty feet of snow lay in the gold-bearing branch. And that was the last they heard from him. He was a performer, Bill said, not a correspondent.

So in Granville the affairs of the Free Gold Mining Company remained at a standstill until the spring floods should peel off the winter blanket of the North. Hazel was fully occupied, and Bill dwelt largely with his books, or sketched and figured on operations at the claims. Their domestic affairs moved with the smoothness of a perfectly balanced machine. To the very uttermost Hazel enjoyed the well-appointed orderliness of it all, the unruffled placidity of an existence where the unexpected, the disagreeable, the uncouth, was wholly eliminated, where all the strange shifts and struggles of her two years beyond the Rockies were altogether absent and impossible. Bill's views he kept largely to himself. And Hazel began to nurse the idea that he was looking upon civilization with a kindlier eye.

Ultimately, spring overspread the eastern provinces. And when the snows of winter successively gave way to muddy streets and then to clean pavements in the city of Granville, a new gilt sign was lettered across the windows of the brokerage office in which Paul Lorimer was housed.

FREE GOLD MINING COMPANY

P. H. Lorimer, Pres.   J. L. Brooks, Sec.-Treas.
William Wagstaff, Manager.

So it ran. Bill was commissioned in the army of business at last.

CHAPTER
TWENTY-SEVEN

A Business Journey

"I have to go to the Klappan," Bill apprised his wife one evening. "Want to come along?"

Hazel hesitated. Her first instinctive feeling was one of reluctance to retrace that nerve-trying trail. But neither did she wish to be separated from him.

"I see you don't," he observed dryly. "Well, I can't say that I blame you. It's a stiff trip. If your wind and muscle are in as poor shape as mine, I guess it would do you up — the effort would be greater than any possible pleasure."

"I'm sorry I can't feel any enthusiasm for such a journey," she remarked candidly. "I could go as far as the coast with you, and meet you there when you come out. How long do you expect to be in there?"

"I don't know exactly," he replied. "I'm not going in from the coast, though. I'm taking the Ashcroft-Fort George Trail. I have to take in a pack train and more men and get work started on a decent scale."

"But you won't have to stay there all summer and oversee the work, will you?" she inquired anxiously.

"I should," he said.

For a second or two he drummed on the table top.

"I should do that. It's what I had in mind when I started this thing," he said wistfully. "I thought we'd go in this spring and rush things through the good weather, and come out ahead of the snow. We could stay a while at the ranch, and break up the winter with a jaunt here or some place."

"But is there any real necessity for you to stay on the ground?" She pursued her own line of thought. "I should think an undertaking of this size would justify hiring an expert to take charge of the actual mining operations. Won't you have this end of it to look after?"

"Lorimer and Brooks are eminently capable of upholding the dignity and importance of that sign they've got smeared across the windows downtown," he observed curtly. "The chief labor of the office they've set up will be to divide the proceeds. The work will be done and the money made in the Klappan Range. You sabe that, don't you?"

"I'm not stupid," she pouted.

"I know you're not, little person," he said quietly. "But you've changed a heap in the last few months. You don't seem to be my pal any more. You've fallen in love with this butterfly life. You appear to like me just as much as ever, but if you could you'd sentence me to this kid-glove existence for the rest of my natural life. Great Cæsar's ghost!" he burst out. "I've laid around like a well-fed poodle for seven months. And look at me — I'm mush! Ten miles with a sixty-pound pack would make my tongue hang out. I'm thick-winded, and twenty pounds overweight — and you talk calmly about my settling down to office work!"

282

His semi-indignation, curiously enough, affected Hazel as being altogether humorous. She had a smile-compelling vision of that straight, lean-limbed, powerful body developing a protuberant waistline and a double chin. That was really funny, so far-fetched did it seem. And she laughed. Bill froze into rigid silence.

"I'm going to-morrow," he said suddenly. "I think, on the whole, it'll be just as well if you don't go. Stay here and enjoy yourself. I'll transfer some more money to your account. I think I'll drop down to the club."

She followed him out into the hall, and, as he wriggled into his coat, she had an impulse to throw her arms around his neck and declare, in all sincerity, that she would go to the Klappan or to the north pole or any place on earth with him, if he wanted her. But by some peculiar feminine reasoning she reflected in the same instant that if Bill were away from her in a few weeks he would be all the more glad to get back. That closed her mouth. She felt too secure in his affection to believe it could be otherwise. And then she would cheerfully capitulate and go back with him to his beloved North, to the Klappan or the ranch or wherever he chose. It was not wise to be too meek or obedient where a husband was concerned. That was another mite of wisdom she had garnered from the wives of her circle.

So she kissed Bill good-by at the station next day with perfect good humor and no parting emotion of any particular keenness. And if he were a trifle sober he showed no sign of resentment, nor uttered any futile wishes that she could accompany him.

"So long," he said from the car steps. "I'll keep in touch — all I can."

Then he was gone.

Somehow, his absence made less difference than Hazel had anticipated. She had secretly expected to be very lonely at first. And she was not. She began to realize that, unconsciously, they had of late so arranged their manner of life that separation was a question of degree rather than kind. It seemed that she could never quite forego the impression that Bill was near at hand. She always thought of him as downtown or in the living-room, with his feet up on the mantel and a cigar in his mouth. Even when in her hand she held a telegram dated at a point five hundred or a thousand miles or double that distance away she did not experience the feeling of complete bodily absence. She always felt as if he were near. Only at night, when there was no long arm to pillow her head, no good-night kiss as she dozed into slumber, she missed him, realized that he was far away. Even when the days marched past, mustering themselves in weekly and monthly platoons and Bill still remained in the Klappan, she experienced no dreary leadenness of soul. Her time passed pleasantly enough.

Early in June came a brief wire from Station Six. Three weeks later the Free Gold Mining Company set up a mild ripple of excitement along Broad Street by exhibiting in their office window a forty-pound heap of coarse gold; raw, yellow gold, just as it had come from the sluice. Every day knots of men stood gazing at the treasure. The Granville papers devoted sundry columns to this remarkably successful enterprise of its local business men. Bill had forwarded the first clean-up.

And close on the heels of this — ten days later, to be exact — he came home.

CHAPTER
TWENTY-EIGHT

The Bomb

"You great bear," Hazel laughed, in the shelter of his encircling arms. "My, it's good to see you again."

She pushed herself back a little and surveyed him admiringly, with a gratified sense of proprietorship. The cheeks of him were tanned to a healthy brown, his eyes clear and shining. The offending flesh had fallen away on the strenuous paths of the Klappan. He radiated boundless vitality, strength, alertness, that perfect coordination of mind and body that is bred of faring resourcefully along rude ways. Few of his type trod the streets of Granville. It was a product solely of the outer places. And for the time being the old, vivid emotion surged strong within her. She thrilled at the touch of his hand, was content to lay her head on his shoulder and forget everything in the joy of his physical nearness. But the maid announced dinner, and her man must be fed. He had missed luncheon on the train, he told her, by reason of an absorbing game of whist.

"Come, then," said she. "You must be starving."

They elected to spend the evening quietly at home, as they used to do. To Hazel it seemed quite like old

286

times. Bill told her of the Klappan country, and their prospects at the mine.

"It's going to be a mighty big thing," he declared.

"I'm so glad," said Hazel.

"We've got a group of ten claims. Whitey Lewis and the original stakers hold an interest in their claims. I, acting as agent for these other fellows in the company, staked five more. I took in eight more men — and, believe me, things were humming when I left. Lewis is a great rustler. He had out lots of timber, and we put in a wing dam three hundred feet long, so she can flood and be darned; they'll keep the sluice working just the same. And that quartz lead will justify a fifty-thousand-dollar mill. So I'm told by an expert I took in to look it over. And, say, I went in by the ranch. Old Jake has a fine garden. He's still pegging away with the mule 'und Gretchen, der cow.' I offered him a chance to make a fat little stake at the mine, but he didn't want to leave the ranch. Great old feller, Jake. Something of a philosopher in his way. Pretty wise old head. He'll make good, all right."

In the morning, Bill ate his breakfast and started downtown.

"That's the dickens of being a business man," he complained to Hazel, in the hallway. "It rides a man, once it gets hold of him. I'd rather get a machine and go joy riding with you than anything else. But I have to go and make a long-winded report; and I suppose those fellows will want to talk gold by the yard. Adios, little person. I'll get out for lunch, business or no business."

287

Eleven-thirty brought him home, preoccupied and frowning. And he carried his frown and his preoccupation to the table.

"Whatever is the matter, Bill?" Hazel anxiously inquired.

"Oh, I've got a nasty hunch that there's a nigger in the woodpile," he replied.

"What woodpile?" she asked.

"I'll tell you more about it to-night," he said bluntly. "I'm going to pry something loose this afternoon or know the reason why."

"Is something the matter about the mine?" she persisted.

"No," he answered grimly. "There's nothing the matter with the mine. It's the mining company."

And that was all he vouchsafed. He finished his luncheon and left the house. He was scarcely out of sight when Jimmie Brooks' runabout drew up at the curb. A half minute later he was ushered into the living-room.

"Bill in?" was his first query.

"No, he left just a few minutes ago," Hazel told him.

Mr. Brooks, a short, heavy-set, neatly dressed gentleman, whose rather weak blue eyes loomed preternaturally large and protuberant behind pince-nez that straddled an insignificant snub nose, took off his glasses and twiddled them in his white, well-kept fingers.

"Ah, too bad!" he murmured. "Thought I'd catch him.

"By the way," he continued, after a pause, "you — ah — well, frankly, I have reason to believe that you have a good deal of influence with your husband in business matters, Mrs. Wagstaff. Kitty says so, and she don't make mistakes very often in sizing up a situation."

"Well, I don't know; perhaps I have." Hazel smiled noncommittally. She wondered what had led Kitty Brooks to that conclusion. "Why?"

"Well — ah — you see," he began rather lamely. "The fact is — I hope you'll regard this as strictly confidential, Mrs. Wagstaff. I wouldn't want Bill to think I, or any of us, was trying to bring pressure on him. But the fact is, Bill's got a mistaken impression about the way we're conducting the financial end of this mining proposition. You understand? Very able man, your husband, but headstrong as the deuce. I'm afraid — to speak frankly — he'll create a lot of unpleasantness. Might disrupt the company, in fact, if he sticks to the position he took this morning. Thought I'd run in and talk it over with him. Fellow's generally in a good humor, you know, when he's lunched comfortably at home."

"I'm quite in the dark," Hazel confessed. "Bill seemed a trifle put out about something. He didn't say what it was about."

"Shall I explain?" Mr. Brooks suggested. "You'd understand — and you might be able to help. I don't as a rule believe in bringing business into the home, but this bothers me. I hate to see a good thing go wrong."

"Explain, by all means," Hazel promptly replied. "If I can help, I'll be glad to."

"Thank you." Mr. Brooks polished his glasses industriously for a second and replaced them with painstaking exactitude. "Now — ah — this is the situation: When the company was formed, five of us, including your husband, took up enough stock to finance the preliminary work of the undertaking. The remaining stock, seventy-five thousand dollars in amount, was left in the treasury, to be held or put on the market as the situation warranted. Bill was quite conservative in his first statements concerning the property, and we all felt inclined to go slow. But when Bill got out there on the ground and the thing began to pay enormously right from the beginning, we — that is, the four of us here, decided we ought to enlarge our scope. With the first clean-up, Bill forwarded facts and figures to show that we had a property far beyond our greatest expectations. And, of course, we saw at once that the thing was ridiculously undercapitalized. By putting the balance of the stock on the market, we could secure funds to work on a much larger scale. Why, this first shipment of gold is equal to an annual dividend of ten percent on four hundred thousand dollars capital. It's immense, for six weeks' work.

"So we held a meeting and authorized the secretary to sell stock. Naturally, your husband wasn't cognizant of this move, for the simple reason that there was no way of reaching him — and his interests were thoroughly protected, anyway. The stock was listed on Change. A good bit was disposed of privately. We now have a large fund in the treasury. It's a cinch. We've got the property, and it's rich enough to pay dividends on a million. The decision of the stockholders is unanimously for enlargement of the capital stock. The quicker we get that property to its maximum output the more we make, you see. There's a fine vein of quartz to develop, expensive machinery to install. It's no more than fair that these outsiders who are clamoring to get aboard should pay their share of the expense of organization and promotion. You understand? You follow me?"

"Certainly," Hazel answered. "But what is the difficulty with Bill?"

Mr. Brooks once more had recourse to polishing his pince-nez.

"Bill is opposed to the whole plan," he said, pursing up his lips with evident disapproval of Bill Wagstaff and all his works. "He seems to feel that we should not have taken this step. He declares that no more stock must be sold; that there must be no enlargement of capital. In fact, that we must peg along in the little one-horse way we started. And that would be a shame. We could make the Free Gold Mining Company the biggest thing on the map, and put ourselves all on Easy Street."

He spread his hands in a gesture of real regret.

"Bill's a fine fellow," he said, "and one of my best friends. But he's a hard man to do business with. He takes a very peculiar view of the matter. I'm afraid he'll queer the company if he stirs up trouble over this. That's why I hope you'll use whatever influence you have, to induce him to withdraw his opposition."

"But," Hazel murmured, in some perplexity, "from what little I know of corporations, I don't see how he can set up any difficulty. If a majority of the stockholders decide to do anything, that settles it, doesn't it? Bill is a minority of one, from what you say. And I don't see what difference his objections make, anyway. How can he stop you from taking any line of action whatever?"

"Oh, not that at all," Brooks hastily assured. "Of course, we can outvote him, and put it through. But we want him with us, don't you see? We've a high opinion of his ability. He's the sort of man who gets results; practical, you know; knows mining to a T. Only he shies at our financial method. And if he began any foolish litigation, or silly rumors got started about trouble among the company officers, it's bound to hurt the stock. It's all right, I assure you. We're not foisting a wildcat on the market. We've got the goods. Bill admits that. It's the regular method, not only legitimate, but good finance. Every dollar's worth of stock sold has the value behind it. Distributes the risk a little more, that's all, and gives the company a fund to operate successfully.

"If Bill mentions it, you might suggest that he look into the matter a little more fully before he takes any definite action," Brooks concluded, rising. "I must get down to the office. It's his own interests I'm thinking of, as much as my own. Of course, he couldn't block a reorganization — but we want to satisfy him in every particular, and, at the same time, carry out these plans. It's a big thing for all of us. A big thing, I assure you."

He rolled away in his car, and Hazel watched him from the window, a trifle puzzled. She recalled Bill's remark at luncheon. In the light of Brooks' explanation, she could see nothing wrong. On the other hand, she knew Bill Wagstaff was not prone to jump at rash conclusions. It was largely his habit to give others the benefit of the doubt. If he objected to certain manipulations of the Free Gold Mining Company, his objection was likely to be based on substantial grounds. But then, as Brooks had observed, or, rather, inferred, Bill was not exactly an expert on finance, and this new deal savored of pure finance — a term which she had heard Bill scoff at more than once. At any rate, she hoped nothing disagreeable would come of it.

So she put the whole matter out of her mind. She had an engagement with a dressmaker, and an invitation to afternoon tea following on that. She dressed, and went whole-heartedly about her own affairs.

Dinner time was drawing close when she returned home. She sat down by a window that overlooked the street to watch for Bill. As a general thing he was promptness personified, and since he was but twenty-four hours returned from a three months' absence, she felt that he would not linger — and Granville's business normally ceased at five o'clock.

Six passed. The half-hour chime struck on the mantel clock. Hazel grew impatient, petulant, aggrieved. Dinner would be served in twenty minutes. Still there was no sign of him. And for lack of other occupation she went into the hall and got the evening paper, which the carrier had just delivered.

A staring headline on the front page stiffened her to scandalized attention. Straight across the tops of two columns it ran, a facetious caption:

WILLIAM WAGSTAFF IS A BEAR

Under that the subhead:

Husky Mining Man Tumbles Prices and Brokers, Whips Four men in Broad Street Office. Slugs Another on Change. His Mighty Fists Subdue Society's Finest. Finally Lands in Jail.

The body of the article Hazel read in what a sob sister would describe as a state of mingled emotions.

William Wagstaff is a mining gentleman from the northern wilds of British Columbia. He is a big man, a natural-born fighter. To prove this he inflicted a black eye and a split lip on Paul Lorimer, a broken nose and sundry bruises on James L. Brooks. Also Allen T. Bray and Edward Gurney Parkinson suffered certain contusions in the mêlée. The fracas occurred in the office of the Free Gold Mining Company, 1546 Broad Street, at three-thirty this afternoon. While hammering the brokers a police officer arrived on the scene and Wagstaff was duly escorted to the city bastile. Prior to the general encounter in the Broad Street office Wagstaff walked into the Stock Exchange, and made statements about the Free Gold Mining

Company which set all the brokers by the ears. Lorimer was on the floor, and received his discolored optic there.

Lorimer is a partner in the brokerage firm of Bray, Parkinson & Co., and is president of the Free Gold Mining Company. Brooks is manager of the Acme Advertisers, and secretary of Free Gold. Bray and Parkinson are stockholders, and Wagstaff is a stockholder and also manager of the Free Gold properties in B. C. All are well known about town.

A reporter was present when Wagstaff walked on the floor of the Stock Exchange. He strode up to the post where Lorimer was transacting business.

"I serve notice on you right now," he said loudly and angrily, "that if you sell another dollar's worth of Free Gold stock, I'll put you out of business."

Lorimer appeared to lose his temper. Some word was passed which further incensed Wagstaff. He smote the broker and the broker smote the floor. Wagstaff's punch would do credit to a champion pugilist, from the execution it wrought. He immediately left the Stock Exchange, and not long afterward Broad Street was electrified by sounds of combat in the Free Gold office. It is conceded that Wagstaff had the situation and his three opponents well in hand when the cop arrived.

None of the men concerned would discuss the matter. From the remarks dropped by Wagstaff, however, it appears that the policy of marketing

Free Gold stock was inaugurated without his knowledge or consent.

Be that as it may, all sorts of rumors are in circulation, and Free Gold stock, which has been sold during the past week as high as a dollar forty, found few takers at par when Change closed. There has been a considerable speculative movement in the stock, and the speculators are beginning to wonder if there is a screw loose in the company affairs.

Wagstaff's case will come up to-morrow forenoon. A charge of disturbing the peace was placed against him. He gave a cash bond and was at once released. When the hearing comes some of the parties to the affair may perchance divulge what lay at the bottom of the row.

Any fine within the power of the court to impose is a mere bagatelle, compared to the distinction of scientifically manhandling four of society's finest in one afternoon. As one bystander remarked in the classic phraseology of the street:

"Wagstaff's a bear!"

The brokers concerned might consider this to have a double meaning.

Hazel dropped the paper, mortified and wrathful. The city jail seemed the very Pit itself to her. And the lurid publicity, the lifted eyebrows of her friends, maddened her in prospect. Plain street brawling, such as one might expect from a cabman or a taxi mahout, not from a man like her husband. She involuntarily assigned the blame to him. Not for the cause — the cause was of no importance whatever to her — but for the act itself. Their best friends! She could hardly realize it. Jimmie Brooks, jovial Jimmie, with a broken nose and sundry bruises! And Paul Lorimer, distinguished Paul, who had the courtly bearing which was the despair of his fellows, and the manner of a dozen generations of culture wherewith to charm the women of his acquaintance. He with a black eye and a split lip! So the paper stated. It was vulgar. Brutal! The act of a cave man.

She was on the verge of tears.

And just at that moment the door opened, and in walked Bill.

CHAPTER
TWENTY-NINE

The Note Discordant

Bill had divested himself of the scowl. He smiled as a man who has solved some knotty problem to his entire satisfaction. Moreover, he bore no mark of conflict, none of the conventional scars of a rough-and-tumble fight. His clothing was in perfect order, his tie and collar properly arranged, as a gentleman's tie and collar should be. For a moment Hazel found herself believing the *Herald* story a pure canard. But as he walked across the room her searching gaze discovered that the knuckles of both his hands were bruised and bloody, the skin broken. She picked up the paper.

"Is this true?" she asked tremulously, pointing to the offending headlines.

Bill frowned.

"Substantially correct," he answered coolly.

"Bill, how could you?" she cried. "It's simply disgraceful. Brawling in public like any saloon loafer, and getting in jail and all. Haven't you any consideration for me — any pride?"

His eyes narrowed with an angry glint.

"Yes," he said deliberately. "I have. Pride in my word as a man. A sort of pride that won't allow any bunch of

298

lily-fingered crooks to make me a party to any dirty deal. I don't propose to get the worst of it in that way. I won't allow myself to be tarred with their stick."

"But they're not trying to give you the worst of it," she burst out. Visions of utter humiliation arose to confront and madden her. "You've insulted and abused our best friends — to say nothing of giving us all the benefit of newspaper scandal. We'll be notorious!"

"Best friends? God save the mark!" he snorted contemptuously. "Our best friends, as you please to call them, are crooks, thieves, and liars. They're rotten. They stink with their moral rottenness. And they have the gall to call it good business."

"Just because their business methods don't agree with your peculiar ideas is no reason why you should call names," she flared. "Mr. Brooks called just after you left at noon. *He* told me something about this, and assured me that you would find yourself mistaken if you'd only take pains to think it over. I don't believe such men as they are would stoop to anything crooked. Even if the opportunity offered, they have too much at stake in this community. They couldn't afford to be crooked."

"So Brooks came around to talk it over with you, eh?" Bill sneered. "Told you it was all on the square, did he? Explained it all very plausibly, I suppose. Probably suggested that you try smoothing me down, too. It would be like 'em."

"He did explain about this stock-selling business," Hazel replied defensively. "And I can't see why you find it necessary to make a fuss. I don't see where the cheating and crookedness comes in. Everybody who buys stock gets their money's worth, don't they? But I don't care anything about your old mining deal. It's this fighting and quarreling with people who are not used to that sort of brute action — and the horrid things they'll say and think about us."

"About you, you mean — as the wife of such a boor — that's what's rubbing you raw," Bill flung out passionately. "You're acquiring the class psychology good and fast. Did you ever think of anybody but yourself? Have I ever betrayed symptoms of idiocy? Do you think it natural or even likely for me to raise the devil in a business affair like this out of sheer malice? Don't I generally have a logical basis for any position I take? Yet you don't wait or ask for any explanation from me. You stand instinctively with the crowd that has swept you off your feet in the last six months. You take another man's word that it's all right and I'm all wrong, without waiting to hear my side of it. And the petty-larceny incident of my knocking down two or three men and being under arrest as much as thirty minutes looms up before you as the utter depths of disgrace. Disgrace to you! It's all you — you! How do you suppose it strikes me to have my wife take sides against me on snap judgment like that? It shows a heap of faith and trust and loyalty, doesn't it? Oh, it makes me real proud and glad of my mate. It does. By thunder, if Granville had ever treated me as it tried to treat you one time, according to your own account, I'd wipe my feet on them at every opportunity."

"If you'd explain," Hazel began hesitatingly. She was thoroughly startled at the smoldering wrath that flared out in this speech of his. She bitterly resented being talked to in that fashion. It was unjust. Particularly that last fling. And she was not taking sides. She refused to admit that — even though she had a disturbing consciousness that her attitude could scarcely be construed otherwise.

"I'll explain nothing," Bill flashed stormily. "Not at this stage of the game. I'm through explaining. I'm going to act. I refuse to be raked over the coals like a naughty child, and then asked to tell why I did it. I'm right, and when I know I'm right I'll go the limit. I'm going to take the kinks out of this Free Gold deal inside of forty-eight hours. Then I'm through with Granville. Hereafter I intend to fight shy of a breed of dogs who lose every sense of square dealing when there is a bunch of money in sight. I shall be ready to leave here within a week. And I want you to be ready, too."

"I won't," she cried, on the verge of hysterics. "I won't go back to that cursed silence and loneliness. You made this trouble here, not I. I won't go back to Pine River, or the Klappan. I won't, I tell you!"

Bill stared at her moodily for a second.

"Just as you please," he said quietly.

He walked into the spare bedroom. Hazel heard the door close gently behind him, heard the soft click of a well-oiled lock. Then she slumped, gasping, in the wide-armed chair by the window, and the hot tears came in a blinding flood.

CHAPTER
THIRTY

The Aftermath

They exchanged only bare civilities at the breakfast table, and Bill at once went downtown. When he was gone, Hazel fidgeted uneasily about the rooms. She had only a vague idea of legal processes, having never seen the inside of a courtroom. She wondered what penalty would be inflicted on Bill, whether he would be fined or sent to prison. Surely it was a dreadful thing to better men like Brooks and Lorimer and Parkinson. They might even make it appear that Bill had tried to murder them. Her imagination magnified and distorted the incident out of all proportion.

And brooding over these things, she decided to go and talk it over with Kitty Brooks. Kitty would not blame her for these horrid man troubles.

But she was mistaken there. Kitty was all up in arms. She was doubly injured. Her husband had suffered insult and brutal injury. Moreover, he was threatened with financial loss. Perhaps that threatened wound in the pocketbook loomed larger than the physical hurt. At any rate, she vented some of her spleen on Hazel.

"Your husband started this mining thing," she declared heatedly. "Jimmie says that if he persists in trying to turn things upside down it will mean a loss of thousands. And we haven't any money to lose — I'm sure Jimmie has worked hard for what he's got. I'm simply sick over it. It's bad enough to have one's husband brought home looking as if he'd been slugged by footpads, and to have the papers go on about it so. But to have a big loss inflicted on us just when we were really beginning to get ahead, is too much. I wish you'd never introduced your miner to us."

That speech, of course, obliterated friendship on the spot, as far as Hazel was concerned. Even though she was quite prepared to have Bill blamed for the trouble, did in fact so blame him herself, she could not stomach Kitty's language nor attitude. But the humiliation of the interview she chalked up against Bill. She went home with a red spot glowing on either cheekbone. A rather incoherent telephone conversation with Mrs. Allen T. Bray, in which that worthy matron declared her husband prostrated from his injuries, and in the same breath intimated that Mr. Wagstaff would be compelled to make ample reparation for his ruffianly act, did not tend to soothe her.

Bill failed to appear at luncheon. During the afternoon an uncommon number of her acquaintances dropped in. In the tactful manner of their kind they buzzed with the one absorbing topic. Some were vastly amused. Some were sympathetic. One and all they were consumed with curiosity for detailed inside information on the Free Gold squabble. One note rang consistently in their gossipy song: The Free Gold Company was going to lose a pot of money in some manner, as a consequence of the affair. Mr. Wagstaff had put some surprising sort of spoke in the company's wheel. They had that from their husbands who trafficked on Broad Street. By what power he had accomplished this remained a mystery to the ladies. Singly and collectively they drove Hazel to the verge of distraction. When the house was at last clear of them she could have wept. Through no fault of her own she had given Granville another choice morsel to roll under its gossipy tongue.

So that when six o'clock brought Bill home, she was coldly disapproving of him and his affairs in their entirety, and at no pains to hide her feelings. He followed her into the living-room when the uncomfortable meal — uncomfortable by reason of the surcharged atmosphere — was at an end.

"Let's get down to bed rock, Hazel," he said gently. "Doesn't it seem rather foolish to let a bundle of outside troubles set up so much friction between us two? I don't want to stir anything up; I don't want to quarrel. But I can't stand this coldness and reproach from you. It's unjust, for one thing. And it's so unwise — if we value our happiness as a thing worth making some effort to save."

"I don't care to discuss it at all," she flared up "I've heard nothing else all day but this miserable mining business and your ruffianly method of settling a dispute. I'd rather not talk about it."

"But we must talk about it," he persisted patiently. "I've got to show you how the thing stands, so that you can see for yourself where your misunderstanding comes in. You can't get to the bottom of anything without more or less talk."

"Talk to yourself, then," she retorted ungraciously. And with that she ran out of the room.

But she had forgotten or underestimated the catlike quickness of her man. He caught her in the doorway and the grip of his fingers on her arm brought a cry of pain.

"Forgive me. I didn't mean to hurt," he said contritely. "Be a good girl, Hazel, and let's get our feet on earth again. Sit down and *put* your arm around my neck and be my pal, like you used to be. We've got no business nursing these hard feelings. It's folly. I haven't committed any crime. I've only stood for a square deal. Come on; bury the hatchet, little person."

"Let me go," she sobbed, struggling to be free.. "I h-hate you!"

"Please, little person. I can't eat humble pie more than once or twice."

"Let me go," she panted. "I don't want you to touch me."

"Listen to me," he said sternly. "I've stood about all of your nonsense I'm able to stand. I've had to fight a pack of business wolves to keep them from picking my carcass, and, what's more important to me, to keep them from handing a raw deal to five men who wallowed through snow and frost and all kinds of hardship to make these sharks a fortune. I've got down to their level and fought them with their own weapons and the thing is settled. I said last night I'd be through here inside a week. I'm through now — through here. I have business in the Klappan; to complete this thing I've set my hand to. Then I'm going to the ranch and try to get the bad taste out of my mouth. I'm going to-morrow. I've no desire or intention to coerce you. You're my wife, and your place is with me, if you care anything about me. And I want you. You know that, don't you? I wouldn't be begging you like this if I didn't. *I* haven't changed, nor had my eyes dazzled by any false gods. But it's up to you. I don't bluff. I'm going, and if I have to go without you I won't come back. Think it over, and just ask yourself honestly if it's worth while."

He drew her up close to him and kissed her on one anger-flushed cheek, and then, as he had done the night before, walked straight away to the bedroom and closed the door behind him.

Hazel slept little that night. A horrid weight seemed to rest suffocatingly upon her. More than once she had an impulse to creep in there where Bill lay and forget it all in the sweep of that strong arm. But she choked back the impulse angrily. She would not forgive him. He had made her suffer. For his high-handedness she would make him suffer in kind. At least, she would not crawl to him begging forgiveness.

When sunrise laid a yellow beam, all full of dancing motes, across her bed, she heard Bill stir, heard him moving about the apartment with restless steps. After a time she also heard the unmistakable sound of a trunk lid thrown back, and the movements of him as he gathered his clothes - so she surmised. But she did not rise till the maid rapped on her door with the eight o'clock salutation:

"Breakfast, ma'am."

They made a pretense of eating. Hazel sought a chair in the living-room. A book lay open in her lap. But the print ran into blurred lines. She could not follow the sense of the words. An incessant turmoil of thought harassed her. Bill passed through the room once or twice. Determinedly she ignored him. The final snap of the lock on his trunk came to her at last, the bumping sounds of its passage to the hall. Then a burly expressman shouldered it into his wagon and drove away.

A few minutes after that Bill came in and took a seat facing her.

"What are you going to do, Hazel?" he asked soberly.

"Nothing," she curtly replied.

"Are you going to sit down and fold your hands and let our air castles come tumbling about our ears, without making the least effort to prevent?" he continued gently. "Seems to me that's not like you at all. I never thought you were a quitter."

"I'm not a quitter," she flung back resentfully. "I refuse to be browbeaten, that's all. There appears to be only one choice — to follow you like a lamb. And I'm not lamblike. I'd say that you are the quitter. You have stirred up all this trouble here between us. Now you're running away from it. That's how it looks to me. Go on! I can get along."

"I dare say you can," he commented wearily. "Most of us can muddle along somehow, no matter what happens. But it seems a pity, little person. We had all the chance in the world. You've developed an abnormal streak lately. If you'd just break away and come back with me. You don't know what good medicine those old woods are. Won't you try it a while?"

"I am not by nature fitted to lead the hermit existence," she returned sarcastically.

And even while her lips were uttering these various unworthy little bitternesses she inwardly wondered at her own words. It was not what she would have said, not at all what she was half minded to say. But a devil of perverseness spurred her. She was full of protest against everything.

"I wish we'd had a baby," Bill murmured softly. "You'd be different. You'd have something to live for besides this frothy, neurotic existence that has poisoned you against the good, clean, healthy way of life. I wish we'd had a kiddie. We'd have a fighting chance for happiness now; something to keep us sane, something outside of our own ego to influence us."

"Thank God there isn't one!" she muttered.

"Ah, well," Bill sighed, "I guess there is no use. I guess we can't get together on anything. There doesn't seem to be any give-and-take between us any longer."

He rose and walked to the door. With his hand on the knob, he turned.

"I have fixed things at the bank for you," he said abruptly.

Then he walked out, without waiting for an answer.

She heard the soft whir of the elevator. A minute later she saw him on the sidewalk. He had an overcoat on his arm, a suit case in his hand. She saw him lift a finger to halt a passing car.

It seemed incredible that he should go like that. Surely he would come back at noon or at dinner time. She had always felt that under his gentleness there was iron. But deep in her heart she had never believed him so implacable of purpose where she was concerned.

She waited wearily, stirring with nervous restlessness from room to room.

Luncheon passed. The afternoon dragged by to a close. Dusk fell. And when the night wrapped Granville in its velvet mantle, and the street lights blinked away in shining rows, she cowered, sobbing, in the big chair by the window.

He was gone.

Gone, without even saying good-by!

CHAPTER
THIRTY-ONE

A Letter from Bill

All through the long night she lay awake, struggling with the incredible fact that Bill had left her; trying to absolve herself from blame; flaring up in anger at his unyielding attitude, even while she was sorely conscious that she herself had been stubbornly unyielding. If he had truly loved her, she reiterated, he would never have made it an issue between them. But that was like a man — to insist on his own desires being made paramount; to blunder on headlong, no matter what antagonisms he aroused. And he was completely in the wrong, she reasserted.

She recapitulated it all. Through the winter he had consistently withdrawn into his shell. For her friends and for most of her pleasures he had at best exhibited only tolerance. And he had ended by outraging both them and her, and on top of that demanded that she turn her back at twenty-four hours' notice, on Granville and all its associations and follow him into a wilderness that she dreaded. She had full right to her resentment. As his partner in the chancy enterprise of marriage were not her feelings and desires entitled to equal consideration? He had assumed the rôle of dictator. And she had revolted. That was all. She was justified.

Eventually she slept. At ten o'clock, heavy-eyed, suffering an intolerable headache, she rose and dressed.

Beside her plate lay a thick letter addressed in Bill's handwriting. She drank her coffee and went back to the bedroom before she opened the envelope. By the postmark she saw that it had been mailed on a train.

DEAR GIRL: I have caught my breath, so to speak, but I doubt if ever a more forlorn cuss listened to the interminable clicking of car wheels. I am tempted at each station to turn back and try again. It seems so unreal, this parting in hot anger, so miserably unnecessary. But when I stop to sum it up again, I see no use in another appeal. I could come back — yes. Only the certain knowledge that giving in like that would send us spinning once more in a vicious circle prevents me. I didn't believe it possible that we could get so far apart. Nor that a succession of little things could cut so weighty a figure in our lives. And perhaps you are very sore and resentful at me this morning for being so precipitate.

I couldn't help it, Hazel. It seemed the only way. It seems so yet to me. There was nothing more to keep me in Granville — everything to make me hurry away. If I had weakened and temporized with you it would only mean the deferring of just what has happened. When you declared yourself flatly and repeatedly it seemed hopeless to argue further. I am a poor pleader, perhaps; and I do not believe in compulsion between

311

us. Whatever you do you must do of your own volition, without pressure from me. We couldn't be happy otherwise. If I compelled you to follow me against your desire we should only drag misery in our train.

I couldn't even say good-by. I didn't want it to be good-by. I didn't know if I could stick to my determination to go unless I went as I did. And my reason told me that if there must be a break it would better come now than after long-drawn-out bickerings and bitterness. If we are so diametrically opposed where we thought we stood together we have made a mistake that no amount of adjusting, nothing but separate roads, will rectify. Myself I refuse to believe that we have made such a mistake. I don't think that honestly and deliberately you prefer an exotic, useless, purposeless, parasitic existence to the normal, whole-some life we happily planned. But you are obsessed, intoxicated — I can't put it any better — and nothing but a shock will sober you. If I'm wrong, if love and Bill's companionship can't lure you away from these other things — why, I suppose you will consider it an ended chapter. In that case you will not suffer. The situation as it stands will be a relief to you. If, on the other hand, it's merely a stubborn streak, that won't let you admit that you've carried your proud little head on an overstiff neck, do you think it's worth the price? I don't.

I'm not scolding, little person. I'm sick and sore at the pass we've come to. No damn-fool pride can close my eyes to the fact or keep me from admitting freely that I love you just as much and want you as longingly as I did the day I put you aboard the *Stanley D.* at Bella Coola. I thought you were stepping gladly out of my life then. And I let you go freely and without anything but a dumb protest against fate, because it was your wish. I can step out of your life again — if it is your wish. But I can't imprison myself in your cities. I can't pretend, even for your sake, to play the game they call business. I'm neither an idler nor can I become a legalized buccaneer. I have nothing but contempt for those who are. Mind you, this is not so sweeping a statement as it sounds. No one has a keener appreciation of what civilization means than I. Out of it has arisen culture and knowledge, much of what should make the world a better place for us all. But somehow this doesn't apply to the mass, and particularly not to the circles we invaded in Granville. With here and there a solitary exception that class is hopeless in its smug self-satisfaction — its narrowness of outlook, and unblushing exploitation of the less fortunate, repels me.

And to dabble my hands in their muck, to settle down and live my life according to their bourgeois standards, to have grossness of soft flesh replace able sinews, to submerge mentality in favor of a specious craftiness of mind which passes in the "city" for brains — well, I'm on the road. And, oh, girl, girl, I wish you were with me.

I must explain this mining deal — that phase of it which sent me on the rampage in Granville. I should have done so before, should have insisted on making it clear to you. But a fellow doesn't always do the proper thing at the proper time. All too frequently we are dominated by our emotions rather than by our judgment. It was so with me. The other side had been presented to you rather cleverly at the right time. And your ready acceptance of it angered me beyond bounds. You were prejudiced. It stirred me to a perfect fury to think you couldn't be absolutely loyal to your pal. When you took that position I simply couldn't attempt explanations. Do you think I'd ever have taken the other fellow's side against you, right or wrong?

Anyway, here it is: You got the essentials, up to a certain point, from Brooks. But he didn't tell it all — his kind never does, not by a long shot. They, the four of them, it seems, held a meeting as soon as I shipped out that gold and put through that stock-selling scheme. That was legitimate. I couldn't restrain them from that, being a hopeless minority of one. Their chief object, however, was to let two or three friends in on the ground floor of a good thing; also, they wanted each a good bundle of that stock while it was cheap — figuring that with the prospects I had opened up it would sell high. So they had it on the market, and in addition had everything framed up to reorganize with a capitalization of two hundred and fifty thousand dollars. This all cut and dried before I got there. Now, as it originally stood, the five of us would each have made a small fortune on these Klappan claims. They're good. But with a quarter of a million in outstanding stock — well, it would be all right for the fellow with a big block. But you can see where I would get off with a five-thousand-dollar interest. To be sure, a certain proportion of the money derived from the sale of this

314

stock should be mine. But it goes into the treasury, and they had it arranged to keep it in the treasury, as a fund for operations, with them doing the operating. They had already indicated their bent by voting an annual stipend of ten thousand and six thousand dollars to Lorimer and Brooks as president and secretary respectively. Me, they proposed to quiet with a manager's wage of a mere five thousand a year — after I got on the ground and began to get my back up.

Free Gold would have been a splendid Stock Exchange possibility. They had it all doped out how they could make sundry clean-ups irrespective of the mine's actual product. That was the first thing that made me dubious. They were stock-market gamblers, manipulators pure and simple. But I might have let it go at that, seeing it was their game and not one that I or anybody I cared about would get fleeced at. I didn't approve of it, you understand. It was their game.

But they capped the climax with what I must cold-bloodedly characterize as the baldest attempt at a dirty fraud I ever encountered. And they had the gall to try and make me a party to it. To make this clear you must understand that I, on behalf of the company and acting as the company's agent, grubstaked Whitey Lewis and four others to go in and stake those claims. I was empowered to arrange with these five men that if the claims made a decent showing each should receive five thousand dollars in stock for assigning their claims to the company, and should have employment at top wages while the claims were operated.

They surely earned it. You know what the North is in the dead of winter. They bucked their way through a hell of frost and snow and staked the claims. If ever men were entitled to what was due them, they were. And not one of them stuttered over his bargain, even though they were taking out weekly as much gold as they were to get for their full share. They'd given their word, and they were white men. They took me for a white man also. They took my word that they would get what was coming to them, and gave me in the company's name clear title to every claim. I put those titles on record in Hazleton, and came home.

Lorimer and Brooks deliberately proposed to withhold that stock, to defraud these men, to steal — oh, I can't find words strong enough. They wanted to let the matter stand; wanted me to let it be adjusted later; anything to serve as an excuse for delay. Brooks said to me, with a grin: "The property's in the company's name — let the roughnecks sweat a while. They've got no come-back, anyhow."

That was when I smashed him. Do you blame me? I'd taken over those fellows' claims in good faith. Could I go back there and face those men and say: "Boys, the company's got your claims, and they won't pay for them." Do you think for a minute I'd let a bunch of lily-fingered crooks put anything like that over on simple, square-dealing fellows who were too honest to protect their own interests from sharp practice? A quartet of soft-bodied mongrels who sat in upholstered office chairs while these others wallowed through six feet of snow for three weeks, living on bacon and beans, to grab a pot of gold for them! It makes my fist double up when I think about it.

And I wouldn't be put off or placated by a chance to fatten my own bank roll. I didn't care if I broke the Free Gold Mining Company and myself likewise. A dollar doesn't terrify nor yet fascinate me — I hope it never will. And while, perhaps, it was not what they would call good form for me to lose my temper and go at them with my fists, I was fighting mad when I thoroughly sensed their dirty project. Anyway, it helped bring them to time. When you take a man of that type and cuff him around with your two hands he's apt to listen serious to what you say. And they listened when I told them in dead earnest next day that Whitey Lewis and his partners must have what was due them, or I'd wreck the bunch of them if it took ten years and every dollar I had to do it. And I could have put them on the tramp, too — they'd already dipped their fingers in where they couldn't stand litigation. I'm sure of that — or they would never have come through; which they did.

But I'm sorry I ever got mixed up with them. I'm going to sell my stock and advise Lewis and the others to do the same while we can get full value for it. Lorimer and that bunch will manipulate the outfit to death, no matter how the mine produces. They'll have a quarter of a million to work on pretty soon, and they'll work it hard. They're shysters — but it's after all only a practical demonstration of the ethics of the type — "Do everybody you can — if you can do 'em so there's no come-back."

317

That's all of that. I don't care two whoops about the money. There is still gold in the Klappan Range and other corners of the North, whenever I need it. But it nauseated me. I can't stand that cutthroat game. And Granville, like most other cities of its kind, lives by and for that sort of thing. The pressure of modern life makes it inevitable. Anyway, a town is no place for me. I can stomach it about so long, and no longer. It's too cramped, too girded about with petty-larceny conventions. If once you slip and get down, every one walks on you. Everything's restricted, priced, tinkered with. There is no real freedom of body or spirit. I wouldn't trade a comfy log cabin in the woods with a big fireplace and a shelf of books for the finest home on Maple Drive — not if I had to stay there and stifle in the dust and smoke and smells. That would be a sordid and impoverished existence. I cannot live by the dog-eat-dog code that seems to prevail wherever folk get jammed together in an unwieldy social mass.

I have said the like to you before. By nature and training I'm unfitted to live in these crowded places. I love you, little person, I don't think you realize how much, but I can't make you happy by making myself utterly miserable. That would only produce the inevitable reaction. But I still think you are essentially enough like me to meet me on common ground. You loved me and you found contentment and joy at our little cabin once. Don't you think it might be waiting there again?

If you really care, if I and the old North still mean anything to you, a few days or weeks, or even month of separation won't matter. An affection that can't survive six months is too fragile to go through life on. I don't ask you to jump the next train and follow me. I don't ask you to wire me, "Come back, Bill." Though I would come quick enough if you called me. I merely want you to think it over soberly and let your heart decide. You know where I stand, don't you, Hazel, dear? I haven't changed — not a bit — I'm the same old Bill. But I'd rather hit the trail alone than with an unwilling partner. Don't flounder about in any quicksand of duty. There is no "I ought to" between us.

So it is up to you once more, little person. If my way is not to be your way I will abide by your decision without whining. And whenever you want to reach me, a message to Felix Courvoiseur, Fort George will eventually find me. I'll fix it that way.

I don't know what I'll do after I make that Klappan trip. I'm too restless to make plans. What's the use of planning when there's nobody but myself to plan for?

So long, little person. I like you a heap, for all your cantankerous ways. BILL.

She laid aside the letter, with a lump in her throat. For a brief instant she was minded to telegraph the word that would bring him hurrying back. But — some of the truths he had set down in cold black and white cut her deep. Of a surety she had drawn her weapon on the wrong side in the mining trouble. Over hasty? — yes. And shamefully disloyal. Perhaps there was something in it, after all; that is to say, it might be they had made a mistake. She saw plainly enough that unless she could

319

get back some of the old enthusiasm for that wilderness life, unless the fascination of magnificent distances, of silent, breathless forests, of contented, quiet days on trail and stream, could lay fast hold of her again, they would only defer the day of reckoning, as Bill had said.

And she was not prepared to go that far. She still harbored a smoldering grudge against him for his volcanic outburst in Granville, and too precipitate departure. He had given her no time to think, to make a choice. The flesh-pots still seemed wholly desirable — or, rather, she shrank from the alternative. When she visualized the North it uprose always in its most threatening presentment, indescribably lonely, the playground of ruthless, elemental forces, terrifying in its vast emptinesses. It appalled her in retrospect, loomed unutterably desolate in contrast to her present surroundings.

No, she would not attempt to call him back. She doubted if he would come. And she would not go — not yet. She must have time to think.

One thing pricked her sorely. She could not reconcile the roguery of Brooks and Lorimer with the men as she knew them. Not that she doubted Bill's word. But there must be a mistake somewhere. Ruthless competition in business she knew and understood. Only the fit survived — just as in her husband's chosen field only the peculiarly fit could hope to survive. But she rather resented the idea that pleasant, well-bred people could be guilty of coarse, forthright fraud. Surely not!

Altogether, as the first impression of Bill's letter grew less vivid to her she considered her grievances more.

And she was minded to act as she had set out to do —
to live her life as seemed best to her, rather than pocket
her pride and rejoin Bill. The feminine instinct to
compel the man to capitulate asserted itself more and
more strongly.

Wherefore, she dressed carefully and prepared to
meet a luncheon engagement which she recalled as
being down for that day. No matter that her head ached
woefully. Thought maddened her. She required
distraction, craved change. The chatter over the
teacups, the cheerful nonsense of that pleasure-seeking
crowd might be a tonic. Anything was better than to sit
at home and brood.

CHAPTER
THIRTY-TWO

The Spur

A month passed.

During that thirty-day period she received a brief note from Bill. Just a few lines to say:

> Hit the ranch yesterday, little person. Looks good to me. Have had Lauer do some work on it this summer. Went fishing last night about sundown. Trout were rising fine. Nailed a two-pounder. He jumped a foot clear of the water after my fly, and gave me a hot time for about ten minutes. Woke up this morning at daylight and found a buck deer with two lady friends standing in the middle of the clearing. I loafed a fews days in Fort George, sort of thinking I might hear from you. Am sending this out by Jake. Will start for the Klappan about day after to-morrow.

She had not answered his first letter. She had tried to. But somehow when she tried to set pen to paper the right words would not come. She lacked his facility of expression. There was so much she wanted to say, so little she seemed able to say. As the days passed she felt less sure of her ground, less sure that she had not sacrificed something precious to a vagary of self, an obsession of her own ego.

Many things took on a different complexion now that she stood alone. No concrete evidence of change stood forth preëminent. It was largely subjective, atmospheric, intangible impressions.

Always with a heart sinking she came back to the empty apartment, knowing that it would be empty. During Bill's transient absence of the spring she had missed him scarcely at all. She could not say that now.

And slowly but surely she began to view all her activities of her circle with a critical eye. She was brought to this partly in self-defense. Certain of her friends had become tentative enemies. Kitty Brooks and the Bray womenfolk, who were a numerous and influential tribe, not only turned silent faces when they met, but they made war on her in the peculiar fashion of women. A word here, a suggestive phrase there, a shrug of the shoulders. It all bore fruit. Other friends conveyed the avid gossip. Hazel smiled and ignored it. But in her own rooms she raged unavailingly.

Her husband had left her. There was a man in the case. They had lost everything. The first count was sufficiently maddening because it was a half truth. And any of it was irritating — even if few believed — since it made a choice morsel to digest in gossipy corners, and brought sundry curious stares on Hazel at certain times. Also Mr. Wagstaff had caused the stockholders of Free Gold a heavy loss — which was only offset by the fact that the Free Gold properties were producing richly. None of this was even openly flung at her. She gathered it piecemeal. And it galled her. She could not openly defend either Bill or herself against the shadowy scandalmongers.

Slowly it dawned upon her, with a bitterness born of her former experience with Granville, that she had lost something of the standing that certain circles had accorded her as the wife of a successful mining man. It made her ponder. Was Bill so far wrong, after all, in his estimate of them? It was a disheartening conclusion. She had come of a family that stood well in Granville; she had grown up there; if life-time friends blew hot and cold like that, was the game worth playing?

In so far as she could she gave the lie to some of the petty gossip. Whereas at first she had looked dubiously on spending Bill's money to maintain the standard of living they had set up, she now welcomed that deposit of five thousand dollars as a means to demonstrate that even in his absence he stood behind her financially — which she began to perceive counted more than anything else. So long as she could dress in the best, while she could ride where others walked, so long as she betrayed no limitation of resources, the doors stood wide. Not what you are, but what you've got — she remembered Bill saying that was their holiest creed.

It repelled her. And sometimes she was tempted to sit down and pour it all out in a letter to him. But she could not quite bring herself to the point. Always behind Bill loomed the vast and dreary Northland, and she shrank from that.

On top of this, she began to suffer a queer upset of her physical condition. All her life she had been splendidly healthy; her body a perfect-working machine, afflicted with no weaknesses. Now odd spasmodic pains recurred without rhyme or reason in her head, her back, her limbs, striking her with sudden poignancy, disappearing as suddenly.

She was stretched on the lounge one afternoon wrestling nervously with a particularly acute attack, when Vesta Lorimer was ushered in.

"You're almost a stranger," Hazel remarked, after the first greetings. "Your outing must have been pleasant, to hold you so long."

"It would have held me longer," Vesta returned, "if I didn't have to be in touch with my market. I could live quite happily on my island eight months in the year. But one can't get people to come several hundred miles to a sitting. And I feel inclined to acquire a living income while my vogue lasts."

"You're rather a wilderness lover, aren't you?" Hazel commented. "I don't think you'd love it as dearly if you were buried alive in it."

"That would all depend on the circumstances," Vesta replied. "One escapes many disheartening things in a country that is still comparatively primitive. The continual grind of keeping one's end up in town gets terribly wearisome. I'm always glad to go to the woods, and sorry when I have to leave. But I suppose it's largely in one's point of view."

They chatted of sundry matters for a few minutes.

"By the way, is there any truth in the statement that this Free Gold row has created trouble between you and your husband?" Vesta asked abruptly. "I dare say it's quite an impertinent question, and you'd be well within your rights to tell me it's none of my business. But I should like to confound some of these petty tattlers. I haven't been home forty-eight hours; yet I've heard tongues wagging. I hope there's nothing in it. I warned Mr. Wagstaff against Paul."

"Warned him? Why?" Hazel neglected the question entirely. The bluntness of it took her by surprise. Frank speech was not a characteristic of Vesta Lorimer's set.

The girl shrugged her shoulders.

"He is my brother, but that doesn't veil my eyes," she said coolly. "Paul is too crooked to lie straight in bed. I'm glad Mr. Wagstaff brought the lot of them up with a round turn — which he seems to have done. If he had used a club instead of his fists it would have been only their deserts. I suppose the fuss quite upset you?"

"It did," Hazel admitted grudgingly. "It did more than upset me."

"I thought as much," Vesta said slowly. "It made you inflict an undeserved hurt on a man who should have had better treatment at your hands; not only because he loves you, but because he is one of the few men who deserve the best that you or any woman can give."

Hazel straightened up angrily.

"Where do you get your astonishing information, pray?" she asked hotly. "And where do you get your authority to say such things to me?"

Vesta tucked back a vagrant strand of her tawny hair. Her blue eyes snapped, and a red spot glowed on each smooth, fair cheek.

"I don't get it; I'm taking it," she flung back. "I have eyes and ears, and I have used them for months. Since you inquire, I happened to be going over the Lake Division on the same train that carried your husband back to the North. You can't knife a man without him bearing the marks of it; and I learned in part why he was going back alone. The rest I guessed, by putting two and two together. You're a silly, selfish, shortsighted little fool, if my opinion is worth having."

"You've said quite enough," Hazel cried. "If you have any more insults, please get rid of them elsewhere. I think you are —"

"Oh, I don't care what you think of me," the girl interrupted recklessly. "If I did I wouldn't be here. I'd hide behind the conventional rules of the game and let you blunder along. But I can't. I'm not gifted with your blind egotism. Whatever you are, that Bill of yours loves you, and if you care anything for him, you should be with him. I would, if I were lucky enough to stand in your shoes. I'd go with him down into hell itself gladly if he wanted me to!"

"Oh!" Hazel gasped. "Are you clean mad?"

"Shocked to death, aren't you?" Vesta fleered. "You can't understand, can you? I love him — yes. I'm not ashamed to own it. I'm no sentimental prude to throw up my hands in horror at a perfectly natural emotion. But he is not for me. I dare say I couldn't give him an added heartbeat if I tried. And I have a little too much pride — strange as it may seem to you — to try, so long as he is chained hand and foot to your chariot. But you're making him suffer. And I care enough to want him to live all his days happily. He is a *man*, and there are so few of them, *real* men. If you can make him happy I'd compel you to do so, if I had the power. You couldn't understand that kind of a love. Oh, I could choke you for your stupid disloyalty. I could do almost anything that would spur you to action. I can't rid myself of the hopeless, reckless mood he was in. There are so few of his kind, the patient, strong, loyal, square-dealing men, with a woman's tenderness and a lion's courage. Any woman should be proud and glad to be his mate, to mother his children. And you —"

She threw out her hands with a sudden, despairing gesture. The blue eyes grew misty, and she hid her face in her palms. Before that passionate outburst Hazel sat dumbly amazed, staring, uncertain. In a second Vesta lifted her head defiantly.

"I had no notion of breaking out like this when I came up," she said quietly. "I was going to be very adroit. I intended to give you a friendly boost along the right road, if I could. But it has all been bubbling inside me for a long time. You perhaps think it very unwomanly — but I don't care much what you think. My little heartache is incidental, one of the things life deals us whether we will or not. But if you care in the least for your husband, for God's sake make some effort, some sacrifice of your own petty little desires, to make his road a little pleasanter, a little less gray than it must be now. You'll be well repaid — if you are the kind that must always be paid in full. Don't be a stiff-necked idiot. That's all I wanted to say. Good-by!"

She was at the door when she finished. The click of the closing catch stirred Hazel to speech and action.

"Vesta, Vesta!" she cried, and ran out into the corridor.

But Vesta Lorimer neither heeded nor halted. And Hazel went back to her room, quivering. Sometimes the truth is bitter and stirs to wrath. And mingled with other emotions was a dull pang of jealousy — the first she had ever known. For Vesta Lorimer was beautiful beyond most women; and she had but given ample evidence of the bigness of her soul. With shamed tears creeping to her eyes, Hazel wondered if *she* could love even Bill so intensely that she would drive another woman to his arms that he might win happiness.

But one thing stood out clear above that painful meeting. She was done fighting against the blankness that seemed to surround her since Bill went away. Slowly but steadily it had been forced upon her that much which she deemed desirable, even necessary, was of little weight in the balance with him. Day and night she longed for him, for his cheery voice, the whimsical good humor of him, his kiss and his smile. Indubitably Vesta Lorimer was right to term her a stiff-necked, selfish fool. But if all folk were saturated with the essence of wisdom — well, there was but one thing to be done. Silly pride had to go by the board. If to face gayly a land she dreaded were the price of easing his heartache — and her own — that price she would pay, and pay with a grace but lately learned.

329

She lay down on the lounge again. The old pains were back. And as she endured, a sudden startling thought flashed across her mind. A possibility? — yes. She hurried to dress, wondering why it had not before occurred to her, and, phoning up a taxi, rolled downtown to the office of Doctor Hart. An hour or so later she returned. A picture of her man stood on the mantel. She took it down and stared at it with a tremulous smile.

"Oh, Billy-boy, Billy-boy, I wish you knew," she whispered. "But I was coming, anyway, Bill!"

That evening, stirring about her preparations for the journey, she paused, and wondered why, for the first time since Bill left, she felt so utterly at peace.

CHAPTER
THIRTY-THREE

Home Again

Twelve months works many a change on a changing frontier. Hazel found this so. When she came to plan her route she found the G. T. P. bridging the last gap in a transcontinental system, its trains westbound already within striking distance of Fort George. She could board a sleeping car at Granville and detrain within a hundred miles of the ancient trading post — with a fast river boat to carry her the remaining distance.

Fort George loomed up a jumbled area of houses and tents, log buildings, frame structures yellow in their newness, strangers to paint as yet. On every hand others stood in varying stages of erection. Folks hurried about the sturdy beginning of a future greatness. And as she left the boat and followed a new-laid walk of planks toward a hotel, Jake Lauer stepped out of a store, squarely into her path.

His round face lit up with a smile of recognition And Hazel, fresh from the long and lonesome journey, was equally glad to set eyes on a familiar, a genuinely friendly face.

"I am pleased to welgome you back to Gott's country, Mrs. Vagstaff," he said. "Und let me carry dot suid case alretty."

They walked two blocks to the King's Hotel, where Lauer's family was housed. He was in for supplies, he told her, and, of course, his wife and children accompanied him.

"Not dat Gredda iss afraid. She iss so goot a man as I on der ranch ven I am gone," he explained. "But for dem it iss a change. Und I bring by der town a vaigonloat off bodadoes. By cosh, dem bodadoes iss sell high."

It flashed into Hazel's mind that here was a Heavensent opportunity to reach the cabin without facing that hundred miles in the company of chance-hired strangers. But she did not broach the subject at once. Instead, she asked eagerly of Bill. Lauer told her that Bill had tarried a few days at the cabin, and then struck out alone for the mines. And he had not said when he would be back.

Mrs. Lauer, unchanged from a year earlier, welcomed her with pleased friendliness. And Jake left the two of them and the chubby kiddies in the King's office while he betook himself about his business. Hazel haled his wife and the children to her room as soon as one was assigned to her. And there, almost before she knew it, she was murmuring brokenly her story into an ear that listened with sympathy and understanding. Only a woman can grasp some of a woman's needs. Gretta Lauer patted Hazel's shoulder with a motherly hand, and bade her cheer up.

"Home's the place for you, dear," she said smilingly. "You just come right along with us. Your man will come quick enough when he gets word. And we'll take good care of you in the meantime. La, I'm all excited over it. It's the finest thing could happen for you both. Take it from me, dearie. I know. We've had our troubles, Jake and I. And, seeing I'm only six months short of being a graduate nurse, you needn't fear. Well, well!"

"I'll need to have food hauled in," Hazel reflected. "And some things I brought with me. I wish Bill were here. I'm afraid I'll be a lot of bother. Won't you be heavily loaded, as it is?"

She recalled swiftly the odd, makeshift team that Lauer depended on — the mule, lop-eared and solemn, "und Gretchen, der cow." She had cash and drafts for over three thousand dollars on her person. She wondered if it would offend the sturdy independence of these simple, kindly neighbors, if she offered to supply a four-horse team and wagon for their mutual use? But she had been forestalled there, she learned in the next breath.

"Oh, bother nothing," Mrs. Lauer declared. "Why, we'd be ashamed if we couldn't help a little. And far's the load goes, you ought to see the four beautiful horses your husband let Jake have. You don't know how much Jake appreciates it, nor what a fine man he thinks your husband is. We needed horses so bad, and didn't have the money to buy. So Mr. Wagstaff didn't say a thing but got the team for us, and Jake's paying for them in clearing and plowing and making improvements on your land. Honest, they could pull twice the load *we'll* have. There's a good wagon road most of the way now. Quite a lot of settlers, too, as much as fifty or sixty miles out. And we've got the finest garden you ever saw. Vegetables enough to feed four families all winter. Oh, your old cities! I never want to live in one again. Never a day have the kiddies been sick. Suppose it is a bit out of the world? You're all the more pleased when somebody does happen along. Folks is so different in a new country like this. There's plenty for everybody — and everybody helps, like neighbors ought to."

Lauer came up after a time, and Hazel found herself unequivocally in their hands. With the matter of transporting herself and supplies thus solved, she set out to find Felix Courvoiseur — who would know how to get word to Bill. He might come back to the cabin in a month or so; he might not come back at all unless he heard from her. She was smitten with a great fear that he might give her up as lost to him, and plunge deeper into the wilderness in some mood of recklessness. And she wanted him, longed for him, if only so that she could make amends.

She easily found Courvoiseur, a tall, spare Frenchman, past middle age. Yes, he could deliver a message to Bill Wagstaff; that is, he could send a man. Bill Wagstaff was in the Klappan Range.

"But if he should have left there?" Hazel suggested uneasily.

" 'E weel leave weeth W'itey Lewees word of w'ere 'e go," Courvoiseur reassured her. "An' my man, w'ich ees my bruzzer-law, w'ich I can mos' fully trus', 'e weel follow 'eem. So Beel 'e ees arrange. 'E ees say mos'

334

parteecular if madame ees come or weesh for forward message, geet heem to me queeck. *Oui*. Long tam Beel ees know me. I am for depend always."

Courvoiseur kept a trader's stock of goods in a weather-beaten old log house which sprawled a hundred feet back from the street. Thirty years, he told her, he had kept that store in Fort George. She guessed that Bill had selected him because he was a fixture. She sat down at his counter and wrote her message. Just a few terse lines. And when she had delivered it to Courvoiseur she went back to the hotel. There was nothing now to do but wait. And with the message under way she found herself impatient to reach the cabin, to spend the waiting days where she had first found happiness. She could set her house in order against her man's coming. And if the days dragged, and the great, lone land seemed to close in and press inexorably upon her, she would have to be patient, very patient.

Jake was held up, waiting for supplies. Fort George suffered a sugar famine. Two days later, the belated freight arrived. He loaded his wagon, a ton of goods for himself, a like weight of Hazel's supplies and belongings. A goodly load, but he drove out of Fort George with four strapping bays arching their powerful necks, and champing on the bit.

"Four days ve vill make it by der ranch," Jake chuckled. "Mit der mule und Gretchen, der cow, von veek it take me, mit half der loat."

Four altogether pleasant and satisfying days they were to Hazel. The worst of the fly pests were vanished for the season. A crisp touch of frost sharpened the night winds. Indian summer hung its mellow haze over the land. The clean, pungent air that sifted through the forests seemed doubly sweet after the vitiated atmosphere of town. Fresh from a gridiron of dusty streets and stone pavements, and but stepped, as one might say, from days of imprisonment in the narrow confines of a railway coach, she drank the winey air in hungry gulps, and joyed in the soft yielding of the turf beneath her feet, the fern and pea-vine carpet of the forest floor.

It was her pleasure at night to sleep as she and Bill had slept, with her face bared to the stars. She would draw her bed a little aside from the camp fire and from the low seclusion of a thicket lie watching the nimble flames at their merry dance, smiling lazily at the grotesque shadows cast by Jake and his frau as they moved about the blaze. And she would wake in the morning clear-headed, alert, grateful for the pleasant woodland smells arising wholesomely from the fecund bosom of the earth.

Lauer pulled up before his own cabin at mid-afternoon of the fourth day, unloaded his own stuff, and drove to his neighbor's with the rest.

"I'll walk back after a little," Hazel told him, when he had piled her goods in one corner of the kitchen.

The rattle of the wagon died away. She was alone — at home. Her eyes filled as she roved restlessly from kitchen to living-room and on into the bedroom at the end. Bill had unpacked. The rugs were down, the books stowed in familiar disarray upon their shelves, the bedding spread in semi-disorder where he had last slept and gone away without troubling to smooth it out in housewifely fashion.

She came back to the living-room and seated herself in the big chair. She had expected to be lonely, very lonely. But she was not. Perhaps that would come later. For the present it seemed as if she had reached the end of something, as if she were very tired, and had gratefully come to a welcome resting place. She turned her gaze out the open door where the forest fell away in vast undulations to a range of snow-capped mountains purple in the autumn haze, and a verse that Bill had once quoted came back to her:

> "Oh, to feel the Wind grow strong
>   Where the Trail leaps down.
> I could never learn the way
>   And wisdom of the Town."

She blinked. The town — it seemed to have grown remote, a fantasy in which she had played a puppet part. But she was home again. If only the gladness of it endured strong enough to carry her through whatever black days might come to her there alone.

She would gladly have cooked her supper in the kitchen fireplace, and laid down to sleep under her own roof. It seemed the natural thing to do. But she had not expected to find the cabin livably arranged, and she had promised the Lauers to spend the night with them. So presently she closed the door and walked away through the woods.

CHAPTER
THIRTY-FOUR

After Many Days

September and October trooped past, and as they marched the willow thickets and poplar groves grew yellow and brown, and carpeted the floor of the woods with fallen leaves. Shrub and tree bared gaunt limbs to every autumn wind. Only the spruce and pine stood forth in their year-round habiliments of green. The days shortened steadily. The nights grew long, and bitter with frost. Snow fell, blanketing softly the dead leaves. Old Winter cracked his whip masterfully over all the North.

Day by day, between tasks, and often while she worked, Hazel's eyes would linger on the edges of the clearing. Often at night she would lift herself on elbow at some unexpected sound, her heart leaping wild with expectation. And always she would lie down again, and sometimes press her clenched hand to her lips to keep back the despairing cry. Always she adjured herself to be patient, to wait doggedly as Bill would have waited, to make due allowance for immensity of distance for the manifold delays which might overtake a messenger faring across those silent miles or a man hurrying to his home. Many things might hold him back. But he would come. It was inconceivable that he might not come.

Meantime, with only a dim consciousness of the fact, she underwent a marvelous schooling in adaptation, self-restraint. She had work of a sort, tasks such as every housewife finds self-imposed in her own home. She was seldom lonely. She marveled at that. It was unique in her experience. All her old dread of the profound silence, the pathless forests which infolded like a prison wall, distances which seemed impossible of span, had vanished. In its place had fallen over her an abiding sense of peace, of security. The lusty storm winds whistling about the cabin sang a restful lullaby. When the wolves lifted their weird, melancholy plaint to the cold, star-jeweled skies, she listened without the old shudder. These things, which were wont to oppress her, to send her imagination reeling along morbid ways, seemed but a natural aspect of life, of which she herself was a part.

Often, sitting before her glowing fireplace, watching a flame kindled with her own hands with wood she herself had carried from the pile outside, she pondered this. It defied her powers of self-analysis. She could only accept it as a fact, and be glad. Granville and all that Granville stood for had withdrawn to a more or less remote background. She could look out over the frost-spangled forests and feel that she lacked nothing — nothing save her mate. There was no impression of transient abiding; no chafing to be elsewhere, to do otherwise. It *was* home, she reflected; perhaps that was why.

339

A simple routine served to fill her days. She kept her house shining, she cooked her food, carried in her fuel. Except on days of forthright storm she put on her snowshoes, and with a little rifle in the crook of her arm prowled at random through the woods — partly because it gave her pleasure to range sturdily afield, partly for the physical brace of exertion in the crisp air. Otherwise she curled comfortably before the fireplace, and sewed, or read something out of Bill's catholic assortment of books.

It was given her, also, to learn the true meaning of neighborliness, that kindliness of spirit which is stifled by stress in the crowded places, and stimulated by like stress amid surroundings where life is noncomplex, direct, where cause and effect tread on each other's heels. Every day, if she failed to drop into their cabin, came one of her neighbors to see if all were well with her. Quite as a matter of course Jake kept steadily replenished for her a great pile of firewood. Or they would come, babies and all, bundled in furs of Jake's trapping, jingling up of an evening behind the frisky bays. And while the bays munched hay in Roaring Bill Wagstaff's stable, they would cluster about the open hearth, popping corn for the children, talking, always with cheerful optimism.

Behind Lauer's mild blue eyes lurked a mind that burrowed incessantly to the roots of things. He had lived and worked and read, and, pondering it all, he had summed up a few of the verities.

"Life, it iss giffen us, und ve must off it make der best ve can," he said once to Hazel, fondling a few books he had borrowed to read at home. "Life iss goot, yust der liffing off life, if only ve go not astray afder der voolish dings — und if der self-breservation struggle vears us not out so dot ve gannot enjoy being alife. So many iss struggle und slave under terrible conditions. Und it iss largely because off ignorance. Ve know not vot ve can do — und ve shrink vrom der unknown. Here iss acres by der dousand vree to der man vot can off it make use — und dousands vot liffs und dies und neffer hass a home. Here iss goot, glean air — und in der shmoke und shmells und dirty streets iss a ravage of tuberculosis. Der balance iss not true. Und in der own vay der rich iss full off drouble — drunk mit eggcitement, veary mit bleasures. *Ach*, der voods und mountains und streams, blenty off food, und a kindly neighbor — iss not dot enough? Only der abnormal vants more as dot. Und I dink der drouble iss largely dot der modern, high-bressure cifilization makes for der abnormal, vedder a man iss a millionaire or vorks in der brewery, contentment iss a state off der mind — und if der mind vorks mit logic it vill content find in der simple dings."

It sounded like a pronouncement of Bill's. But Lauer did not often grow serious. Mostly he was jovially cheerful, and his wife likewise. The North had emancipated them, and they were loyal to the source of their deliverance. And Hazel understood, because she herself had found the wild land a benefactor, kindly in its silence, restful in its forested peace, a cure for sickness of soul. Twice now it had rescued her from herself.

November and December went their appointed way — and still no word of Bill. If now and then her pillow was wet she struggled mightily against depression. She was not lonely in the dire significance of the word — but she longed passionately for him. And she held fast to her faith that he would come.

The last of the old year she went little abroad, ventured seldom beyond the clearing. And on New Year's Eve Jake Lauer's wife came to the cabin to stay.

Hazel sat up, wide awake, on the instant. There was not the slightest sound. She had been deep in sleep. Nevertheless she felt, rather than knew, that some one was in the living-room. Perhaps the sound of the door opening had filtered through her slumber. She hesitated an instant, not through fear, because in the months of living alone fear had utterly forsaken her; but hope had leaped so often, only to fall sickeningly, that she was half persuaded it must be a dream. Still the impression strengthened. She slipped out of bed. The door of the bedroom stood slightly ajar.

Bill stood before the fireplace, his shaggy fur cap pushed far back on his head, his gauntlets swinging from the cord about his neck. She had left a great bed of coals on the hearth, and the glow shone redly on his frost-scabbed face. But the marks of bitter trail bucking, the marks of frostbite, the stubby beard, the tiny icicles that still clustered on his eyebrows; while these traces of hardship tugged at her heart they were forgotten when she saw the expression that overshadowed his face. Wonder and unbelief and longing were all mirrored there. She took a shy step forward to see what riveted his gaze. And despite the choking sensation in her throat she smiled — for she had taken off her little, beaded house moccasins and left them lying on the bearskin before the fire, and he was staring down at them like a man fresh-wakened from a dream, unbelieving and bewildered.

With that she opened the door and ran to him. He started, as if she had been a ghost. Then he opened his arms and drew her close to him.

"Bill, Bill, what made you so long?" she whispered. "I guess it served me right, but it seemed a never-ending time."

"What made me so long?" he echoed, bending his rough cheek down against the warm smoothness of hers. "Lord, *I* didn't know you wanted me. I ain't no telepathist, hon. You never yeeped one little word since I left. How long you been here?"

"Since last September." She smiled up at him. "Didn't Courvoiseur's man deliver a message from me to the mine? Didn't you come in answer to my note?"

"Great Cæsar's ghost — since September — alone! You poor little girl!" he murmured. "No, if you sent word to me through Courvoiseur I never got it. Maybe something happened his man. I left the Klappan with the first snow. Went poking aimlessly over around the Finlay River with a couple of trappers. Couldn't settle down. Never heard a word from you. I'd given you up. I just blew in this way by sheer accident. Girl, girl, you don't know how good it is to see you again, to have this warm body of yours cuddled up to me again. And you came right here and planted yours self to wait till I turned up?"

"Sure!" She laughed happily. "But I sent you word, even if you never got it. Oh, well, it doesn't matter. Nothing matters now. You're here, and I'm here, and — Oh, Billy-boy, I was an awful pig-headed idiot. Do you think you can take another chance with me?"

"Say" — he held her off at arm's length admiringly — "do you want to know how strong I am for taking a chance with you? Well, I was on my way out to flag the next train East, just to see — just to see if you still cared two pins; to see if you still thought your game was better than mine."

"Well, you don't have to take any eastbound train to find that out," she cried gayly. "I'm here to tell you I care a lot more than any number of pins. Oh, I've learned a lot in the last six months, Bill. I had to hurt myself, and you, too. I had to get a jolt to jar me out of my self-centered little orbit. I got it, and it did me good. And it's funny. I came back here because I thought I ought to, because it was our home, but rather dreading it. And I've been quite contented and happy — only hungry, oh, so dreadfully hungry, for you."

Bill kissed her.

"I didn't make any mistake in you, after all," he said. "You're a real partner. You're the right stuff. I love you more than ever. If you made a mistake you paid for it, like a dead-game sport. What's a few months? We've all our life before us, and it's plain sailing now we've got our bearings again."

344

"Amen!" she whispered. "I — but, say, man of mine, you've been on the trail, and I know what the trail is. You must be hungry. I've got all kinds of goodies cooked in the kitchen. Take off your clothes, and I'll get you something to eat."

"I'll go you," he said. "I am hungry. Made a long mush to get here for the night. I got six huskies running loose outside, so if you hear 'em scuffing around you'll know it's not the wolves. Say, it was some welcome surprise to find a fire when I came in. Thought first somebody traveling through had put up. Then I saw those slippers lying there. That was sure making me take notice when you stepped out."

He chuckled at the recollection. Hazel lit the lamp, and stirred up the fire, plying it with wood. Then she slipped a heavy bath-robe over her nightgown and went into the chilly kitchen, emerging therefrom presently with a tray of food and a kettle of water to make coffee. This she set on the fire. Wherever she moved Bill's eyes followed her with a gleam of joy, tinctured with smiling incredulousness. When the kettle was safely bestowed on the coals, he drew her on his knee. There for a minute she perched in rich content. Then she rose.

"Come very quietly with me, Bill," she whispered, with a fine air of mystery. "I want to show you something."

"Sure! What is it?" he asked.

"Come and see," she smiled, and took up the lamp. Bill followed obediently.

Close up beside her bed stood a small, square crib. Hazel set the lamp on a table, and turning to the bundle of blankets which filled this new piece of furniture, drew back one corner, revealing a round, puckered-up infant face.

"For the love of Mike!" Bill muttered. "Is it — is it —"

"It's our son," she whispered proudly. "Born the tenth of January — three weeks ago to-day. Don't, don't — you great bear — you'll wake him."

For Bill was bending down to peer at the tiny morsel of humanity, with a strange, abashed smile on his face, his big, clumsy fingers touching the soft, pink cheeks. And when he stood up he drew a long breath, and laid one arm across her shoulders.

"Us two and the kid," he said whimsically. "It should be the hardest combination in the world to bust. Are you happy, little person?"

She nodded, clinging to him, wordlessly happy. And presently she covered the baby's face, and they went back to sit before the great fireplace, where the kettle bubbled cheerfully and the crackling blaze sent forth its challenge to the bevy of frost sprites that held high revel outside.

And, after a time, the blaze died to a heap of glowing embers, and the forerunning wind of a northeast storm soughed and whistled about a house deep wrapped in contented slumber, a house no longer divided against itself.

DATE DUE

JUL 16 2012		
FEB 1 4 2013		
FEB 2 6 2016		
MAY 1 2 2018		